# The

# East End

# Healer

**The Battle Between Good and Bad**

**The Cycle of Conflict Between Love and Evil**

"I am aware that I am responsible for my action…
That is my responsibility….!"

"I am aware other people are responsible for their action…
That is their responsibility….!"

Revenge - An emotional state…

Release - To let go…

Relinquish - To give up ownership…

**Forgiveness**
**Means**
**Our**
**Pain**
**Is**
**Not**
**The**
**Final**
**Word**
**On**
**The**
**Matter**

On the tempestuous rocky road to
recovery…
From the deepest, darkest, dense abyss
Emotionally wrecked... Mentally
fragmented… Physically depleted…
Geoffrey and Joanie… Fred and Chloe…
Tommy and Martha…
Individually and as a unit, were left as
vessels without a purpose…
A flicker of light beckoned, then a bright
light shone through the darkness
Shining, illuminating…. leading them…
Hope, belief, courage, forgiveness, growth
and unconditional love…

-

The faceless evil shadows… lurking
menacingly in the darkened corners…
Who are they….?
Shining their own interpretation of light….
They cannot allow this to happen…
This must be stopped, for their own
preservation…
Their darkness must consume…
A dividing line in the space of time, two
sides of a coin…
Will love prevail… or will evil devour
all…?

I am the only son in a family of four; born to a working-class family. We were poor in financial terms but we inherited a rich and interesting history from our ancestors.

Family gathered and the stories of the past thrilled me as a child. There were real life stories of raw emotion and events born out of actual experiences and learning.

I have been on a lifetime journey; personal experience led me to a spiritual pathway and I actively pursue this as an integral part of my very being.

# Chapter 1

## * A Recap of Our Previous Story, The Gift of Love *

"Fred love, answer the phone my hands are wet..."
"Hello Miller residence, can I help you...?"

"You can if that's Fred Miller..."

Fred froze then looked at Chloe; she caught his stair and expression....

"Tommy, Tommy Jackson... is that you...?"

Chloe scuttled up to be beside her husband, looking intently into each other's eyes as she approached him... they cradled the phone between them... listening... hearing every word....

"Yes, it is..."
"How? ... How have you obtained our number..."
"The Wig has his uses, he has contacts..."
"Geoffrey...Geoffrey is with you?"
"Yes... as well as Joan and Martha..."

"Why, what can we do for you" Fred regained his stature, military training inbuilt.

"We have been talking and we all decided it's your round..."

Tears welled into Chloe and Fred's eyes....

"Fred is Chloe with you... its Geoffrey..."

"Yes, she is..."

"Jolly good, that's the way it should be, now old chap, no beating around the bush, we are aware of your circumstances... and we are all in the same boat... and we are still grieving as we know you are..."

"Yes..."

"Something quite profound has happened to all of us, and we wish to carry out our children's wishes.... and share with you and Chloe...

"And that is...?"

"None of us will ever understand the events in life, that change our lives forever, but to try to forgive, for forgiving is a virtue, and this is what our children have asked us to do...."

"Wow Geoffrey that's deep" ... questioned Fred.... "Asked you to do...?"

"And so are your pockets..." Tommy injected...

Fred and Chloe grinned...

"Yes dear chap... it is and it takes some getting your head around it..." emphasised Geoffrey...
"And we have..." stated Tommy

"Fred is Chloe listening in? its Martha and Joan..."

"Yes, she is... Hello Martha... Joan... its Chloe, what's this all about...? we are mystified...?"

"Mystified.... Yes, as were we... our children are trying to help us... to teach us"

"Help us...! Teach us?"

"Yes...!"

"What exactly...?"

"Forgiveness and Unconditional Love...."

"Ok... I can accept that... We want to accept that.... please explain"

"We feel that we need to grieve, to grieve together, to help each other... as the true friends we were... we are"

"If we can that would be brilliant...."

"We can, we can help each other... and then learn to help others..."

"The ripple affect my Dears..." Geoffrey said profoundly

"The pebble in the pond..." Tommy stated earnestly

"Chloe, Fred... its Joan... it's very simple; if we the adults of today do not learn, then the children of today, will become the adults of tomorrow... we must learn..."

"Yes... when can we meet and start..."

"Now... right now, if you open the door, we are sitting in the car outside…" said Martha

"And could do with a wassa...." Tommy shouted

"You never did sell your house..."

"No, you did not, strange that..."
"No offers..."
"No takers..."

"No..."
"No interest at all...."
"Some viewers..."
"Lots of viewers..."
"No bids...,
"No takers..."

"Perhaps that's the way it was meant to be...."
"Perhaps you were never meant to sell it..."

"Strange that... we never thought about it in that way......"
"Perhaps we weren't..."

"Perhaps it's time to move back home..."
"Yes... Move back home..."
"Yes... We think you should move back home..."
"Yes... Where you belong..."


Fred and Chloe smiled... their eyes welled up and tears rolled down their checks...

Martha, Joanie, Geoffrey and Tommy smiled back... mirroring their friend's actions...

And nodded knowingly...........

"Yes, it's time we did..."

| | | |
|---|---|---|
| Tommy Jackson | } | |
| | | }      Young Tommy Jackson |
| Martha Jackson | } | |
| | | |
| Geoffrey Childs | } | |
| | | }      Louise Childs |
| Joan Childs | } | |
| | | |
| Fred Miller | } | |
| | | }      Sophie Miller |
| Chloe Miller | } | |

# Chapter 2

## * The East End Healer *

"Drive slowly Fred, I want to take it all in, returning home."
"Ok love, I'll pull up outside our house."

They sat there in silence.

"Déjà vu Fred…"
"Yes Chloe, it feels that way, Deja vu"
"Are you nervous Fred, coming back, after what happened?"

"Yes of course luv, but they approached us about coming home, they found us"
"And if their sentiment is real"
"Well we know what we have heard"

"They say what they have heard"

"Our children want us to help others"

"It's the least we can do"

"Do you think there is any ulterior motive Fred?"

"I don't think so Chloe, we have heard our daughter's words…"

"Yes, let's go in"
"I thought we would have a reception party"

"Did you inform them when we were coming back?"

"Yes, Martha and Joan have phoned on occasion, quite regularly in fact and I mentioned we had put everything into place and was returning today. Have you heard from Tommy and Geoffrey?

"Same darling, yea"

"I'm sure we mentioned it the last time we all met up"

"Let's go in"

Fred put the key into the lock and turned it…
He opened the door, allowing Chloe to go in first…
Nothing had changed from when they left in the midst of darkness…
It was clean and tidy; they had hired a cleaner to come in so it was presentable for viewers…

Strangely, it was Chloe and Fred who returned to their abandoned home.

"I'll put the kettle on Chloe"
"Ok Fred, I'll open some windows"

They sat in the lounge, in silence
"Fred, can you…
"Yes Chloe, I can"

"She knows we are here, it's her favourite perfume…"

"Fred, I want to go up to Sophies room…
"Of course, Chloe…"

Moisture formed in Chloe's eyes; tears began to cascade down her face…

Fred took Chloe into his arms and held her lovingly…

"Are you sure luv, you want to go up to Sophies room…?"
"Yes…"

They climbed the stairs and stood fast outside Chloe's room.

Fred opened the door, and beckoned Chloe to enter, she hesitated.
"Give me your hand Chloe"
And Fred led the way…

The room looked exactly as it was on the day of the wedding…

Tears began to roll down Fred's cheeks

They held each other … close … tightly … supporting each other…

*"Please help them… please help us…"*

They both shivered…and slightly parted
"Did you hear that; did you hear those words…"

Fred blinked his eyes and swallowed hard…

"Yes Chloe, I did and her perfume is wafting, swirling around the room…"
"I can feel her presence Fred"
"So, can I"
"Is she dancing around us…?"

"What is happening Fred? What does she want us to do…?"

"*Learn to love again, unconditional love*"

"We don't understand what it is you want Sophie…"

"What do you want us to do…?"

"*Move on, forgive and share with others…*"

Chloe and Fred stood like statues, staring at each other, then around the room…

# Chapter 3

"Did you see the car pull up Tommy…"
"Yes, Martha my lovely…"

"Do you think we should go over or give them some space…?"
"I think we should give them some space, then either ring or pop over… or both…"

"Make them feel welcome…"
"Welcome home…"

"How do you think they will adjust…?"
"In time Martha…"

"We all need to help each other…"
"It's what our kids want…"

"I know love, but it's still gonna be difficult…"
"Very…"

"I think it's the right thing to do… and I'm not gonna lie, there are times when…." Tommy clenched his fists so tight; his knuckles went white…

"Come here Jackson and hold me…"

Tommy embraced Martha and cradled her in his arms…

"Tom, I know how you feel, no I don't I'll rephrase that, I know how I feel… and there are times, like you when I'm overwhelmed with anger…"

"You know what you have heard Tommy say…"
"I know what I have heard tommy say…"

"We have heard him together…"

"I know Martha and I have every intention of honouring my, our son…
   But I haven't become a saint or a buddha… I still have human emotions…"

"We can do it Tom, for Tommy, and we can and will support each other"

They sat at the kitchen table, having a wassa…

Then there was a creaking from upstairs…

"Is that coming from Tommy's room…"

"It sounded like it was on the stairs… going up…"

"Have you been sitting here Tommy Jackson, listening to us…?"

"He has probably gone to his room, disappointed in my angry outburst…"
"Our emotional grieving, it comes in many ways and it has to be released…"

"I think I'll pop upstairs Martha my lovely… "
"Ok my hunk… do you wanna be alone…"

"mmmmm… Tommy winked at her... what you thinking…?"

"Animal, mongrel…"

They both laughed

"I'm gonna sit in Tom's room for a while... I get a lot of solace"

"Solace, don't you know, you've been spending too much time with the wig..."

"Yea, it's comforting up there, come and join me..."

They both sniffed up...

"The little sod, he's here ..." Martha smiled...
"It's his aftershave..."

"Come on, let's go and sit in his room, for a while..."

They sat holding hands, Tommy's room was still the same as the day of his wedding...

"He is here Martha; I can feel him..."

"I know Tom, I feel like I can touch him..."

"His smell, his aftershave, his persona..."

"I love you son; we love you son..." they said in unison

They were both crying uncontrollably

*"Love you mum"*
*"Love you dad"*

*"Please forgive her..."*

*"Please forgive them..."*

*"Unconditional love..."*

*"Help others…"*

"How Tommy, How…?"

"How do we do that Tom…?"

# Chapter 4

"Geoffrey dearest they are here"
"Ok Joanie, they did say they would be arriving today"

"The car has pulled up; they are just sitting in the car…"
"Ok we don't need a running commentary…"

"It's not a running commentary, I'm giving precision evidence your honour"
"Counsel, Precision evidence"

"Yes Judge…"
"My dearest beautiful wife, I don't have my wig on…"

"In that case, then, I'm gossiping…"
"A curtain snooper…"

"I resent that remark…"
"I concur…"

"They have gone in…. "
"Ok Guilty as found…"

They both looked at each other…

"We will have to be careful Geoffrey…"
"Yes Joan, I am aware of that…"

"We don't want to create uneasy feeling, by our drama repartee…" Joan smiled
"No Dearest, but we don't want to be walking on egg shells!" Geoffrey said firmly

"We have done the right thing, taken the right course of action, haven't we?" asked Joan

"It was a unanimous decision"

"To reunite?"

"Well yes, and the main evidence was given by our children... was it not?" stated Geoffrey

"Yes, undeniably" ...

"You have heard Louise..." asked Joan

"I have heard Louise's words; I can't deny it..." stated Geoffrey

"The meetings we have had so far have been convivial... yes?" Joan queried

"The conversations have been on a level, of an understanding, but not deep and heart wrenching" added Geoffrey

"The Elephant in the room...!" quipped Joan

"The massive big Elephant...!" Jested Geoffrey

"Can we eradicate the Elephant....?"

"We need too...!"

"Yes, especially if we intend to do our children justice, we will, must, need to overcome our own anger..." mused Joan

"This I fear my dearest Joan, will be the hardest task of all... but with prudence we will persevere and endeavour to overcome our natural human emotions..." Geoffrey spoke very philosophical

"You mean revenge, anger, retaliation, to inflict pain... on those that presided over those who inflicted it...?" Retorted Joan

"If the adults of today do not learn, the children of today, will become the adults of tomorrow…"
"So, we always blame the parents or role models for their adolescents' actions" quantified Joan

"Our off springs pick up the emotions of their role models, Parent, Grandparents etc, then at an age, they start to copy their traits…."
"So, they are programmed from birth, conception… what chance do the little mites stand…?" proclaimed Joan

"There is a thing called free will, Joan, people know right from wrong, by the cultural behaviour we live in, don't always blame someone else…!" stated Geoffrey
"So, they have the chance, ability to change, turn their lives around…" enquired Joan

"But of course, my Dearest Joanie, if they want to and with the right help… Geoffrey paused, looked around the room, then continued "Einstein once said *We cannot solve our problems, with the same level of thinking that created them…*"

"*Then help them, help each other, help others*"
"*Forgive her…*"
"*Forgive them…*"
"*Unconditional love…*"
"*Forgive…*"

"Listen…. My God, Louise, Geoffrey, Louise is here, can you hear her words…?"
"Yes Joan, I can hear our beloved daughter…

"She is close… I can smell her fragrance…'
"I can feel her essence…"

They scurried up the stairs into Louise's room…

It had never changed since the day of her wedding…

"I can feel her very presence…. To touch her… to hold her once again" Joan started to sob…
"I also my love, her touch… come here Joanie…" Geoffrey clasped Joan into his arms…. And tears streamed down his face…

*"Help them…." She whispered in their ears*

"How…?"
"How darling…?"

# Chapter 5

"Come in, come in, please make yourselves comfortable...." Fred and Chloe opened the front door... beckoning them into the living room...

"Are you sure we are not intruding?" Asked Tommy...
"We can always come back tomorrow" said Joan
"You know, when you have had time to settle in..." echoed Martha...

"No now is good..." said Fred
"Come come...! let's go in" exclaimed Geoffrey

"Tea, coffee, something stronger?" asked Chloe...

"Coffee would be fine... yes coffee, coffee, coffee"
"So, coffee all round"

They sat in the living room, sipping their coffees... the silence was deafening
It started to feel uncomfortable

Simultaneously Joan and Martha said, "Chloe have you had time to unpack?"

The Elephant was in the room

Fred in his unflinching manner opened the door, "I know we have had a few meetings and spoke companionably and we are grateful that you made contact with us..."
"Very thankful" interceded Chloe
"Yes, very pleased, and we have been surprised you could find it in your hearts to open your arms to us again, after what happened..."

"Where do we go from here?" Implored Chloe

They all sat in silence for what seemed a decade…

"Candidly expressed, candid my dearest Fredrick…" counted Geoffrey… paused took a breath and continued "Indeed, to the point… the point in question"

"Well, there's no messing Fred, is there? The Elephants out of the room…" quantified Tommy

"There is no point in messing Tom, we all need to know why we are here" stated Fred

"Yes, why are we here? I mean that in the kindest manner" stated Martha

"And what we can do?" said Joan…

"So, lots of questions…who knows the answers?" said Tommy

"It is difficult, it is difficult for all of you, as it's difficult for Fred and myself" stated Chloe

"Well, we have all accepted and expressed that we have heard from our children" summoned Geoffrey "and that in itself, is something I don't personally believe, I would have ever voluntary admitted"

"I second that emotion…" said Tommy earnestly
"Me neither" chocked Martha holding back the tears
"I never believed" sobbed Joan

"Never thought about it" added Chloe
"To be honest, beyond my belief pattern" lamented Fred

"Our Children are asking us to help each other and help others…" Martha stated openly

"I guess we have to be able to understand and talk honestly about our feelings" Fred shared
"Can we do this without falling out?" pleaded Chloe

"Only if we are honest" expressed Joan
"And understand emotions are going to run high" voiced Geoffrey

"At times I should imagine very high" Tommy stated single-mindedly
"You have something you want to say Tom, get off your chest" Fred said unwaveringly

"Before we get into cross examination, does anybody have an idea of how we can find out exactly what is going on with our kids, how are we hearing the voices?" stated Geoffrey

Martha looked at Tommy and everyone picked up the vibe….

"Tommy" nodded Martha

They all looked at Tommy…

"I endorsed the wig. I didn't think I'd ever admit I believed in it… perhaps it frightens me, the unknown… But… my mum, god bless her was very much into the movement…"

"Movement?" interrupted Fred

"Yea" continued Tommy "the Spiritual Movement, life after life… she had people come around the house and she would give them messages…".

"I've heard of this" said Chloe "mediumship"

"That's it, she also went to Spiritual Church…" added Martha

"So, you saying you have this ability Tommy" asked Joan

"I'm not saying that, but I am hearing Tommy's voice, we are all hearing the voices individually"

"Perhaps the children will talk to us as a collective?" mused Geoffrey
"Should we ask them?" deliberated Chloe

"Or seek professional advice" reflected Martha

"I think before we go down that road and I'm not saying I don't agree on both points; I think we need to discuss how we feel and there must be many questions to ask…" declared Fred

"You mean like a debriefing Fred…?" Asked Geoffrey
"After one of your military sorties" jibed Tommy

"It wasn't a military sortie Tommy, what happened on the occasion" defended Fred
"The occasion…" snapped Tommy
"The occasion Fred was our son's wedding day" stated Martha bluntly

"Also, our daughter's wedding day" glared Joan

"Tempers are getting frayed already", said Chloe sombrely

"I think we need to bring some order to this discussion and calm down, in saying that, I might add, Fred, it was also my daughter who was murdered on *the Occasion...*" Geoffrey bit his bottom lip... "and my wrath is rising. So, if we are going to discuss how we can move forward and help, honour our children, as they have so asked, then it may help if the correct or a least thoughtful terminology in language may be appropriate..." presided Geoffrey

"That includes you and Chloe's daughter Fred" Joan supplemented

Silence reigned

"Point taken" Chloe nodded
"Ok" said Fred "I was trying to be diplomatic in my words, it's not easy for us to say murdered, our daughter murdered your children, our friends on their wedding day... believe me, not easy at all" and Fred swallowed hard and put his fist to his mouth, biting his knuckle, holding back the tears

Chloe welled up, and took Fred in her arms.... "I know it's devastating for all of you, I can't imagine how you feel toward our daughter, and possibly us, so believe me when I say this isn't no fucking picnic for us... it's a nightmare"

Again silence....

"I believe this could get somewhat tetchy" uttered Joan...
"Have we really thought this out?" She continued
"There is already an atmosphere" expressed Martha

28

"To the point of hostility" she stated

"Well, we didn't need Sherlock and Watson to know that was gonna be the likely outcome." said Tommy

"It was always going to be difficult" voiced Geoffrey

"Putting it mildly" Tommy added

"I believe it's time to adjourn, and to take stock of our dilemma, is it achievable, great consideration must be taken" … concluded Geoffrey
The six were now standing with their heads down, looking pensive

*"Please…"*

*"Please for us…"*

*"Please forgive…"*

Geoffrey, Joan, Fred, Chloe, Martha and Tommy looked up, startled…


"Louise…"
"Sophie…"
"Tommy…"

They sang out in unison…

"Are you here…?" Demanded Tommy

"What do you want us to do…" sobbed Martha

"Children please…" pleaded Fred

"Tell us what you want, this is driving me mad…" sobbed Chloe

"Please instruct us" implored Geoffrey

"Direct us, we can hear you… instructed Joan…

"I need a drink…" exploded Chloe "anyone care to join me…?"

And she started to walk toward the cabinet

"Not now…!" commanded Fred…  "Leave the booze alone"

Everyone stared at Fred, then turned their attention to Chloe…who had stopped in her tracks, all a bit shocked.

"Perhaps we should reconvene tomorrow, are we all free?" stated and asked Geoffrey

"Yea good idea" Tommy nodded his head; he walked toward Fred and held his hand out…
 Fred clasped his hand and they shook… no words needed

The tense atmospherics softened…

"See you tomorrow…"
"We can do this…"
"Whatever this is…"

*"Unconditional love… forgive"* echoed around the room

# Chapter 6

"Tommy what did you make of it? the situation I mean" asked Martha as she poured Tommy and herself a wassa, without tea or coffee, straight scotch....
"Definitely strained darling, definitely..."

"I know what we hear, and I think it helped when you told them about your mum... they know we have our feet on the ground and we aren't off with the fairies..."

"When people are grieving babe, they say many things and are lost, so maybe believing in the fairies helps them ... I know I've seen hard men in the East End and further afield, crumble when they have lost someone they love"

"Growing up with your mum Tom, did you see or hear things..."
"Our house was always weird... comings and goings... everyone seemed to turn to mum...
I used to play in the garden and I'd be chatting away to my imaginary friends... cowboys and Indians, strangely I always wanted to be the red Indian..."

"Really... a Red Indian... I'm pleased you wasn't a cowboy..." she giggled....
"What did your mum say, you sitting in the garden talking to yourself...?"

"Piss taker" he laughed "she said they were my spirit friends"

"What about your other mates when you were growing up, did, they have spirit friends?
Did you tell them?"

"Are you extracting the urine out of me…"
"I know it's serious my Hunk, I just need some levity…"

"Two questions for one, buy one get one free, "No, they
didn't, or they never mention it and neither did I… they
would definitely have extracted the urine out of me…"

"But now you hear Louise's voice and so do I" she
looked at Tommy adoringly…
"Do you think we are all going to be able to talk about
what happened, without anger, resentment, revenge in our
hearts…?"

I'm not kidding babe, for me it's gonna be hard, I fight
every day to keep my temper under wraps… I want
revenge, I want to hurt…. I want to rip someone's head
off with a claw hammer and shit inside them. But who do
we hurt, Fred who taught her how to shoot or Chloe who
encouraged her and taught her archery… both can be a
killing tool?"

"Tommy, I feel the same… I'm exploding inside… I
want someone to pay for my baby's murder…"

"Are you asking me to sort something out"
"What?"

"You heard me Martha, I can make a phone call, or go
back down the town"

Silence, Tommy took a mouthful of his scotch….
As did Martha, they looked intently at each other

"Tom NO" … "We left that behind us…."

"You said you wanted revenge…!"

"I know… But no that would make us as bad as Sophie" … "we are better than that, we brought our son up to be better than that…"

"Our Tommy is dead, because she blew his fucking head off…" Tommy yelled angrily
"I know that, I know that… don't you think I fucking hurt" Martha grabbed Tommy and he held her tight… "Sorry luv…"

"So, she gets away with it, they get away with it…".
"They as you put it, are Chloe and Fred, who have been great friends of ours since we moved here, they didn't do it"

"I know, I know…" Tommy pushed his hands through his hair

"So, I go back to my earlier comment… You hear Tommy's voice, and so do I, which in itself is strange, cos I never had any dealings in spooky stuff…" said Martha and she shivered

"So, is it in our imagination, does it suit us to hear Tommy's voice, to help us cope with our grief?" questioned Tommy

"Tom, do you believe that? So, we hear Tommy's voice to help get over grief… what about what he says, help them, help us… unconditional love, forgive them… really and there's both of us who want to commit severe damage to… anyone who gets in our way… so would we really be imagining those kind words?"

"We do hear them Luv, don't we?
"Yep…"

"By the way, what did you make of Fred's reaction when Chloe said she needed a drink? "
"By his reaction, I'd say he's heard that too many times…"

"You think Chloe might have taken to the booze, to cope?"
"Possibly, it was a bit harsh, I mean we got home and you poured us both a large scotch, have we got a drink problem…?"

"He barked at her…!"
"And no, we haven't, we drink sociably…" … "we don't need it, we don't rely on it to get us through..."

"Martha, we don't know she does…."
"True, seemed strange then, the way he reacted… somewhat aggressive"

"So, if she has got a booze problem, and she is using it to cover up her grief, who's to say if she's on it every day…and Fred don't like it"
"Lots of people do… he is probably worried she might become addicted, Alcoholic"

"I think it's time for bed my luvva …"
"I second that emotion,
*Night mum…*
*Night dad…*

They cuddled up

"Night son…"

# Chapter 7

"Geoffrey how do you think that meeting went....?"
inquired Joan
"I have my reservations dear..." Geoffrey answered

"Reservations in trying to achieve what our children
want; whatever it is they want us to do?" Joan quizzed
"Reservations all round dearest..." Geoffrey smiled
"How do you mean darling?" Joan probed
"Let's break it down, firstly; we are quite grounded
people with our feet firmly on the floor, we have never
delved into the realms of the spiritual world. We live
within the world of logic, clarity and focus."
Geoffrey looked at Joan with his hands out...
"I concur" Joan agreed
"Yet we both hear our Louise's voice speaking, do we
hear it or do we imagine it in our minds?"

Geoffrey paused once again...

"We both hear it; we comment straight away. If you and I
both heard it in our minds at the same time, how could
we be imagining Louise's exact words..." Joan paused
for a moment... "only if it's planted into our minds at the
same time..." explained Chloe
"Exactly my dearest, my understanding from researching
is that it is possible, my understanding is that you, we,
whoever, can.... Also see spirit... Geoffrey raised his
eyebrows

"Invaluable, but we both know we hear Louise's
voice..." stated Chloe
"Concurred and upon that we are agreed..." Geoffrey
nodded

"Secondly: The state of anger that has already been portrayed after one open candid exchange is frightening... hostile..." Geoffrey continued
"Yes, hardly a massive surprise to anyone's frame of thinking" expressed Joan
"Without doubt considering what took place..." Geoffrey frowned deeply, his face creased

"Did memories come back to you Geoffrey of the events of their wedding day...?" Joan asked
"Yes, like a video show... vivid, clear, reliving those macabre events..." Geoffrey's face screwed up
"Is that when you admitted your anger?" Joan queried
"Are you cross examining me Joanie..." Geoffrey looked at her
"No, my love, just letting you know I love you and I see, I feel, your pain..."

"Sorry" Geoffrey sobbed "You are in as much pain as me my love, as we all... we all, must be going through..."

"No loss can be compared, to another, who has lost, that's their loss... their individual pain, grief, we can only be there for them, a supporting word, a comforting arm...." Joan wept unreservedly
Geoffrey and Joan comforted each other tightly...

"And do you know what infuriates me Joanie...?" Geoffrey asked her
"Pray tell?"

"When some Smart-Alec, who I'm sure means well and as a good heart, says; come on now pull yourself together, it's time to get over it, move on with your life now, that's what they would want you to do... grrrrr" Geoffrey growled

"I'm sure they mean well"

"Yes, I know they do" Geoffrey smiled then his face grimaced again "but it's not their grief, their loss, their bereavement, it's my pain, our pain…. our time to mourn"

"And we are love, in our own way, in our own time, individually and together…" sobbed Joan

They hugged firmly….

"Do you think we can be open and honest about our feelings, without it all getting rather nasty?" Joan questioned

"On today's evidence of words and actions, to be honest I don't know…" Geoffrey paused… "perhaps the more dialogue we have, communication may become easier…"

"I know you picked up on Fred's reaction when Chloe said she needed a drink" Joan noted

Geoffrey raised his eyebrows "evidential"

"Do you think there is an alcohol issue ….?"

"One cannot and should not judge without conclusive evidence…" quantified Geoffrey

"You're being evasive, I'm asking for your opinion on what you witnessed…?" Joan probed

"On what I observed, I'd say, with not being a professional Dr…" Geoffrey mused…. "Fred's reaction indicated that Chloe was not adverse or shy in turning to the bottle"

Objection, a Point of order Judge, yes, or no? Joanie queried

"I surrender" Geoffrey put his hands up… "yes I would say so"

"What do you think the children want us to achieve…?"
Joan enquired
"To help others, people, parents who are in the same
situation as us" Geoffrey was calm
"How…?"
"$64-million-dollar question Joanie…."

*"Love…"*
*"Forgiveness…"*
*"Unconditional…"*

The words surrounded them…

# Chapter 8

"We all accept, that emotions and tempers were somewhat frayed last night, we must be able to express our feelings freely, with diplomacy, giving some thought to the delicacy of what we are discussing…" opened Geoffrey

All six had reconvened at Geoffrey and Joan's house

"Well put Judge, what happens when emotion and tempers get hot again…" asked Tommy
"And no doubt they will" endorsed Fred
"Animosity already" countered Joan
"Can we please keep it civil?" Pleaded Chloe
"Just being honest" said Tommy
"Cards on the table…" countered Fred

"Before we put our cards on the table" Martha interjected
"I want to ask a question to each and every one of you, including myself…". She looked at all of them individually

Everyone nodded in approval

"What do you think our children want us to do…?"
Martha paused and then continued…
"Fred …. Please?"
"They want us to help others, they want us to come to terms with what happened and find a way to help others…." Fred answered
"Chloe …. Please?"
"It's what Fred said, to forgive, to help others, in some way finding a peace for ourselves…" Chloe answered
"Joan …. Please?" Martha quizzed

"My feelings are for us to, move on… please don't shoot me…." She realised what she had said

The room went silent…

"Somewhat inappropriate…" growled Tommy

Martha threw him a look….

"Yes, I'm sorry, wrong wording, not diplomatic or delicate… my apologies… but as I was saying, to move on with our lives, they want us to create something to help people in our situation…" Joan answered

"Geoffrey …. Please?"
"Mmmm" Geoffrey cleared his throat "I endorse what Joan has signified, to bring some kind of value to their lives, as short as they were, a meaning, a legacy"

"Tommy …. Please?" Martha looked at her husband
"They keep saying forgive, how do we forgive? They keep saying move on, how? They keep saying unconditional love… to whom?" Tommy paused "I want my son back; I want him to have his life back…. We help others and that will give us our peace of mind…. Really"
"What do you think our Tommy would want us to do…?" asked Martha
Tommy took a deep breath …. "To forgive" he croaked "to move on, to help others… that's the kind of man we gave life to". Tears rolled down his cheeks…

"And you Martha ….?" Asked Joan

"You have all said the same thing, and I can resonate with your sentiments… as hard as it will be, it comes to mind they want us to engineer something…. To help others, to give us focus, so their lives where not in vain…." Martha wiped her eyes

"So, moving on" Geoffrey paused, "walking on egg shells, being frightened to use a phrase, careful of what we say, in case it's not politically correct. I'm sorry my friends but we have got to be able to speak with freedom in our words, can we agree to this…?"

"In moderation…. We must keep it within the boundaries of civilised communication…". Added Joan looking at her husband

"Moderation, everything in moderation, including moderation…" Tommy said with a grin…
"That I agree on" added Fred….
"Positivity" … Martha said with a smile

"Yea but, honesty is the best policy, speak as you find…" Tommy marked
"Back to the elephant in the room" observed Joan
"So, does anybody have any ideas, in which direction we could go…" asked Chloe
"A trust of some kind…" said Joan…
"Some kind of association…" said Fred
"A group" added Martha

"Tommy any ideas…? asked Geoffrey….
"All of what you have said…" Tommy bit his bottom lip "but don't you think we are running before we can walk… I mean, I don't know about anyone else, but I've got questions, that I need answers to…" his voice slightly raised
"Yes, point taken" nodded Geoffrey…

"Why don't you three fellows go down the pub" suggested Martha

"Good idea, maybe you need some space to chat, like blokes do…" agreed Joan

"Yes, and we girls can have a glass of wine or two…" Chloe pipped in

Fred looked at Chloe, they all glanced at Chloe…then at Fred

"Not too much Chloe" Fred stated to his wife his head bowed

# Chapter 9

The three of them sat in the pub garden with a pint on the table…

They sat there quite pensive, unlike the past, pre-wedding, when the one-liners would flow…

"Ok chaps if we are going to deal with this situation and move on and help other people, this is what our children are indicating for us to do. Then first, I'm not a counsellor, but from my years on the bench, presiding over many court cases, I know we have to seek the truth and be honest, candid" opened Geoffrey "this will help us move on… in helping ourselves understand what, and why…."

"I agree" said Fred…."

"Me to" said Tommy "so I'm happy to start…. Fred why did Sophie do it, why did she kill her two best friends, on their wedding day?"

"I do not know…!" snapped Fred

"Fredrick dear chap, was there any inclination on the day or to the build-up, any strange behaviour…?" Inquired Geoffrey

"No…!" pleaded Fred "none…."

"Fred mate, there must have been something, you don't turn up at a wedding as the bridesmaid, and blow you're two best friends away…" Tommy had tears in his eyes

"I know Sophie was upset that Louise and Tommy had fallen in love, because she loved Tommy and wanted to be with him, marry him…" Fred paused… wiping tears from his eyes…"she always saw herself and Tommy together. She also loved Louise like a sister…."

"Strange way of showing it Fred…." quipped Tommy…

Fred looked at Tommy stony eyed

"Thomas please…" Geoffrey pleaded "You witnessed nothing Fred…?"

"NO…! don't you think I would have stopped her…" Fred continued…
"I was in the forces, that's no secret, I was in special services, you know that. I got shot on active duty, that's how I met Chloe, she was a nurse…you know that." Fred paused….
"I was undercover, I had to learn to lie, to deceive, to fit in, to act out who I was portraying. To be aware, always on my toes, looking over my shoulder, who are you? We were trained to do this. We were also trained to recognise if someone had infiltrated our cover. If they were aware of who we were, cat and mouse, life and death. We had to suss them out, one step in front. We were taught psychology, subliminal investigation, to identify if, was, were, maybe, the slightest inclination that someone was lying, deceiving, acting, a danger to life…our life…" Fred had tears rolling down his face….
"I never saw it coming… I failed and I live with that every day…"

All three sat in silence…

Then it was broken…

"Then for the mother of all Gods, what turned her mind to kill them, she lost both of them…. there is no sanity in this…" Tommy had his head in his hands

"None" said Geoffrey gravely "none at all, jealousy is an emotion; fiercely protective, afraid, suspicious, or resentful of rivalry in love or affection, envious of a person or persons advantage", he paused "no sanity Tom"

"Jealousy…!" Exclaimed Tommy…. "Jealousy, Geoffrey, is that all you can fucking say… jealousy. You do remember the date, you do remember the day, your daughter's wedding day, my son's wedding day. You do remember the fucking gruesome events of that day…. You do, don't you…?"

Fred sat in silence waiting for Geoffrey's outburst…

"How dare you, how dare you insinuate, question me…! Infer that I have no reminiscence of that day, the macabre proceedings of that day. I revisit it quite too often Thomas" Geoffrey leaned forward, with a menacing look on his face, he then turned to look at Fred, then at the two of them "Don't concern yourself about that. If I had the chance again, do you think I would have placed my darling daughter in that peril. We would never have moved here"

"So, what you saying, my Tommy wasn't good enough for Louise, we are not upper class…" squared up Tommy

"I'm not saying that at all" Geoffrey never backed down "I'm saying I, we, Joan and I were over the moon that our gorgeous daughter was marrying young Tommy" he paused "but if I had, had an inkling of what would have happened, we would never, have put her in such a perilous position, ever"

"I'm sure if we had the chance again, none of us would have been here" added Fred

"But that's all you can say Geoffrey, Jealousy is the root cause of Sophie, murdering our two kids" again exclaimed Tommy

"What do you want me to say, I despise her, I loathe her, I resent the breath that she breathed, yes, I fucking do…" Geoffrey clenched his fists "Now are you happy, happy that I have resorted to my lowest form of communication, emotion, feelings, and expressed them…"

"Yes, I am, because now I know we are on the same wave length…." confirmed Tommy nodding his head, then continued….

 "I know you're an educated man Geoffrey and I've learnt over the years you cover up, hide, protect, whatever, but you don't show your emotions…!" he continued "You bottle them up, well I don't, I show them, I express them, I say it as it is." He paused "Warts and all, that's me, take it or leave it…"

"I can't help it, that's how I was brought up… men don't show their emotions, that men don't cry, that's a weakness…" Geoffrey's eyes moistened and a tear rolled down his cheek.

"Stiff upper lip Geoff … Judge I respect you; I like you; I always have… a strength in right and wrong, morals, principles, honour…. but sometimes mate, you have got to break out of that shell. Be the person you are truly meant to be…. be true to yourself. Forget the crap men don't cry, it's a weakness, no it is not….!" Tommy paused and his eyes welled up…. "Strong men cry, tough men cry…real men cry…" he sighed; a tear fell...

"And that is something I've always liked and respected in you Tommy, your honesty, forthwith, a quality I admire and lack." positioned Geoffrey

"Not at all, you, all people, just do it in a different way Judge, we all have ways of expressing ourselves, that's what makes us unique. Sadly, you just bury your emotions and refuse to share them…" said Tommy

There was silence
Then Fred clapped his hands "What a sermon, pat yourselves on the back boy's, sounded like a self-appreciation club… I guessed I missed out… wasn't part of the trio"

"Don't be sarcastic Fred, not really appropriate is it, sarcasm is the lowest form of wit" stated Geoffrey

"I'm not being sarcastic …. gentlemen, just listening with interest, how embroiled you are, comrades"

"Or jealous Fred…." jibed Tommy

"No not jealous Tommy, I always believed we all blended and were close friends, appears now you were more of a twosome"

"Is that how Sophie felt Fred" crossed Tommy

Fred looked them both in the face… "I have no idea, as I said earlier, I saw no change, I had no inkling of Sophie's feelings or of her intentions "

"I must say Fred it's a fair question" added Geoffrey… "It is a known fact, from conception the foetus, child, picks up their role models, emotions and traits"

"Are you a jealous person Fred… do you get the hump if you're left out?" quizzed Tommy

"So, you're both saying I turned my child into a killer"

"Not as far as being a killer…." stated Geoffrey

"No, I'm not a jealous person, being in the forces, in what I did, where I went, you become self-sufficient, learn to look after yourself, in saying that, in our training, you rely and protect your comrades, friends"

"Is Chloe a jealous person?" Asked Geoffrey....

"No, what is this a fucking kangaroo court?" snapped Fred

# Chapter 10

"So, ladies, the boys have gone to the pub, for a drink and a chat, shall we have a drink…"
Chloe said so innocently as soon as the door closed behind them

"I don't think there will be much chatting, chit chat or boozing, come to think of it…" remarked Martha

"No" said Joan "I think it will be very daunting, if last night's exhibition was a taster of things to come…"
"I hope not" said Martha… "not if we want to do what the kids want… whatever that is…"

"Yes, whatever that is…" added Joan

"We may as well have one drink…" Chloe repeated

"Actually, that's a good idea, I'll put the kettle on… coffee ladies…" Martha took it upon herself even though they were in Joan's kitchen….

"I believe we all need to sit and have a talk, to clear the air" proposed Joan

"I think we need to be open and honest in what we need to discuss, without losing it…" Martha said earnestly

"Tempers you mean… losing it… tempers you mean" said Chloe timidly

"No Chloe not tempers, but we must be able to discuss what happened openly…". Countered Martha

"I'm sure we possibly may get somewhat emotional Cloe as it's a very raw subject that we are broaching" added Joan

Chloe looked at Joan and Martha "We were all so close, us as friends and our children…" she paused *"The Three Musketeers"* she shook her head

There was silence

"Chloe, we, I, am not going to hide the fact that I am very angry and bitter towards Sophie and given the circumstances, I would have to be a Saint, or the Dalai Lama, not to be. I'm resentful, I'm angry, I'm boiling up inside and if she was here, I'd want to…"

"I know…!" Chloe stopped Martha in her tracks, "I know exactly what you would want to do… to my daughter"

"I have to concur with Martha Chloe, my blood boils at the mention of her name and the memories of that ghoulish day, their wedding day. I am afraid I cannot hide my desire for retribution…" choked Joan.

"I know what you want to do" Chloe looked at Martha, "Rip her head off or something just as brutal" she paused "and you want retribution Joan. Well, you both cannot get your wishes and achieve that, towards Sophie, she is dead… remember she died in that asylum" tears flowered down Chloe's cheeks causing her mascara to blacken her eyes, she continued "So if its revenge, vengeance" she looked at Martha, "or retribution" she looked at Joan "that you are seeking, then you will have to put up with Fred and I… is it Fred and I you wish to punish?"

"No, that is not our goal" exclaimed Joan

"No Chloe, revenge was never in our minds when we contacted you and Fred" seconded Martha
"Then why did you go out of your way to find us and make contact with us" asked Chloe

"The voices that we hear." said Martha

"The voices that you and Fred hear" furthered Joan

"So, tell me, did you know Sophie died, in that place, high security hospital they called it… it was a mental asylum" she paused "high security mental asylum for mentally depraved psychopathic killers" burst Chloe

"Yes, we heard, Geoffrey heard through the whispers in corridors at the high court… he was advised of Sophie's demise" said Joan ruefully

"And Geoffrey informed you, Martha and Tommy?" questioned Chloe
"Yes… he did, we had a right to know" defended Martha

"A right, yes of course you did" countered Chloe… "Did you raise a glass or two to Sophies demise, celebration dinner, pop a bottle of champers… the bitch is dead…"

"No, we did not…!" denied Martha strongly

"Absolutely not…!" opposed Joan sturdily

Chloe smiled, total change of persona "So why did you make contact with us?" she asked meekly

"The voices we hear dear" Joan said caringly
"The voices of the children that we all hear Chloe" Martha said soothingly

51

"The voices" Chloe nodded "yes the voices we hear from the dead children" she paused "perhaps we all need to be in that mental asylum"

There was an eerie silence

"Shall we have a drink…?" chirped up Chloe
"No dear, we need to speak without alcohol" confirmed Joan

"It going to be tough" Martha glanced at Joan, then at Chloe "Tough Chloe without alcohol confusing and charging up emotions"

"Yes, we need to keep a clear mind, logical, clarity and to be focused" said Chloe calmly

Martha and Joan glimpsed at each other puzzlingly
"So, what shall we talk about, who wants to start…?" said Chloe

"I think it's quite obvious what we want to talk about'" snapped Martha frustratingly

"What happened on Tommy and Louise's wedding day…?" questioned Joan

"What Sophie did…? she murdered them Chloe" pushed Martha

"Yes, I know, I don't need to be reminded, it lives with me every living moment" declared Chloe

"We all live with it, Chloe, every living second, that vision will never erase from my mind, from any of our minds…. I would presume to say…" Blasted Martha

"But we need to know Chloe…? why in heavens name did she shoot them on their wedding day…? at the alter…!" pressured Joan

"Why did she kill them at all, any day, they were the best of friends…? As far as we know, do you know different…?" Martha stated

"This is what we need to know, why, why why…" Snapped Chloe

"What…!" declared Martha…
"What …?" Joan looked puzzled…

"Why? We don't know the answer to the million-pound question, why…? Fred and I have examined, questioned, puzzled it over in our minds and discussed it, to the enth degree, that it doesn't make sense, until we are exhausted. We can make no conclusion, we have not got a dame clue… why she, our daughter Sophie murdered Louise and Tommy…what more do you want me to say…."

"She, sorry Sophie, never expressed any feelings of discontent toward Tommy and Louise" probed Joan

"Come on Chloe, you must have noticed something in her mood, change of personality…" grilled Martha

"No… she was their bridesmaid, if she was upset, she would not have agreed to be their bridesmaid"

"Did you see her get angry…?" quizzed Joan

"No…!" exclaimed Chloe

"Was she, sorry Sophie, resentful, towards Louise and Tommy being together, in love…?" pursued Joan

"Joan, I'm not in the witness box and you are not at work, Queens Council..." retorted Chloe

"Was Sophie resentful..." snapped Martha menacingly

"No...")! Chloe paused "not once she came to terms with Tommy and Louise being, falling in love, when they were on their holiday, and their plans, after they came back from the holiday"

"Do you think what happened on the holiday, twisted her mind...?" interrogated Martha

# Chapter 11

The same three pints sat on the table, untouched

"No, it's not a kangaroo court" defended Geoffrey "and by the way, it's not a duo show, it was the three of us who had a bond, kinship"

There was a pause

"Was?" asked Fred

"Is Fred, is the three of us, notwithstanding that, these are valid questions to ask Fred, very valid to give us the understanding, of what made Sophie act in the way she did... surely you can see that" replied Geoffrey

"Yes of course I can see it, you obviously despise her, clearly apparent from what has been said... and I cannot defend that. I would be the same if the positions had been reversed, but she is still my daughter. I cannot protect her; I cannot defend her actions I'm ashamed, but Sophie is still my daughter..."

"So, you're not a jealous person Fred and neither is Chloe, so that knocks your theory out of the window Geoffrey...." Said Tommy

"Mmmm possibly" murmured Geoffrey

"I know what happened, Sophie woke up one morning, happened to be on the day of their wedding, ho yea she just happened to be the bridesmaid, and decided, aww today I think I'll murder my two best friends. One of them I'm in love with, the other I love like a sister, I'll blow their heads off... that should be fun...! is that what happened" snarled Tommy

"What like some psychopath, I think I'll go kill some people today?" retorted Fred

"Cap fits" counted Tommy

Fred threw Tommy a look of indignation

"It can happen Fred, there are many instances when for no apparent reason, an individual decides to go and kill, dismember innocent bystanders..." said Geoffrey ruefully

"Not in my head it doesn't or may I say, in Chloe's head...." Fred said defensively

The three gentlemen eyed each other up....

"Say now, you're proposing that we bred a killer...! Gave birth to a psychopath, is that the next accusation..."

"They are not accusations Fred they are indications of what might be, why indeed..." Said Geoffrey

"Not accusations Fred, more logical thinking..." Paused Tommy, "How many people have you killed for Queen and Country, you got up in the morning or maybe an evening sortie, top marksman with a gun, rifle, killing machine, any thoughts before or second thoughts after or just a day's work... perhaps it's in her veins, her DNA"
"Enough Tommy" Fred shouted... "Enough, what I did was for my Queen and Country to keep people like you safe, and I'd do it again. Big tough guys with knives and guns, plastic gangsters, would they fight for their country. Would they fight for those that can't, for freedom, for

democracy? Would you Tom. I'm proud of what I did…. I'm not proud of what my daughter did…"
There was a noticed hush in the beer garden

"And what about Chloe, another top marks woman at archery…. Great team, the two of you… is it some form of mentality, to draw you two together and then we have Sophie, all let's go kill someone… it's a wedding day…" Tommy said sardonically

"That's it, I've had enough of your fucking digs… my daughter is one issue, and as much as I love her, I'm ashamed of her actions. Chloe that's a different level *my friend.* You can dig me out, I can defend myself against you, any time any place. But my wife, you shut your mouth and leave her alone…. She is struggling to cope and survive. She does not need the likes of you questioning her honour."

Again, there was silence

"I might add my Chloe was also in the services, as a nurse, she helped save lives, they lost lives. Mutilated lives, disabled humans…
Working in extreme difficult circumstances, in the most inhumane situations, macabre brutality. And she coped, could you two? However, since the horrific act by our daughter, to your beautiful children, she has not coped…" he paused "she is fragile and take this any way you want, leave her alone…"

"Don't start with the threats Fred, don't give off warning signs, like your gonna put it on us… that don't wash with me Pal, not my cuppa tea, I don't do threats…." Tommy paused… "Now let's get a few items sorted out. No one is digging you out Fred, you're the only one we can ask, have verbal's with and get any details from. As

Sophie never said a word, went all Mutton and Jeff on us at the Court hearing and zipped her mouth up then, oh so conveniently…. died…."

Fred glared at Tommy… with indignation in his eyes

"It's ok Fred, it's ok" Geoffrey said in a very low tone trying to take the heat out of the situation… "let's all calm down, all we are trying to do is ascertain as to why Sophie did what she did…".

"Answers Fred, we need answers, don't you want to know why Sophie acted like she did, why she did this anus act" added Tommy

There was silence and the tension subsided…

"Yes of course, you need some answers, we need some answers, we all need answers. Too many questions. And there's some thoughts I've had, mulled over in my mind and I've got some queries that I need to ask…. That need clearing up…" Fred stated calmly

"Fred… by the way, mate, no one is digging out Chloe, that's not where we're coming from… we don't do that where I come from, as for the Judge, I don't think that's his walk of life. In saying that, if you haven't got any answers, maybe Chloe has… we can leave you to ask her…
I think we all have an idea Chloe's got a problem Fred, we haven't become that insensitive"
Tommy said caringly

"What questions Fred…?" queried Geoffrey

# Chapter 12

"What happened on the holiday, was agreed not to be spoken of again, Sophie didn't want Fred and myself to know" protected Chloe

"It hardly matters now, does it, Sophie is dead, as is Louise and Tommy..." stated Martha

"I didn't mean what happened at the BBQ, I meant Louise and Tommy falling in love, but that may have some bearing... now you have mentioned it... enough to twist anyone's mind..." Joan said pondering on her own thoughts

"What about the voices we all hear" asked Chloe...

"We do hear them, but define what you mean Joan, please" requested Martha

"You mean we are not mad...?" pleaded Chloe
"No, No Chloe we are not mad... our children are in spirit and they are communicating with us, for a reason to be made apparent, soon I hope" Martha looked to the heavens

"I have a theory" announced Joan "what happened at the BBQ, we need to say no more, albeit, Louise and Tommy, more Tommy, came to Sophie's rescue, when she was found in a very perilous situation. Her knight in shining armour, came to her rescue, saved her honour... and then fell in love and planned to marry another, coincidentally, to be her best friend... she could not cope with that, mentally or emotionally"

"She loved Tommy, she was in love with Tommy, Sophie always thought they would marry, she loved Louise as a sister…" Chloe sobbed

"Rejection, resentment, anger, hurt, humiliation, pride" mused Martha

"Jealousy in a nutshell…" concluded Joan coldly

Martha exploded "she murdered, brutally blew my sons head off, killed him on his wedding day, down to being fucking Jealous"

"Please Martha, please" Chloe held her hands out, palms down… sheepishly she continued "I don't know what to say, I don't know if what happened on the holiday effected Sophie, I didn't say jealousy, I don't know…."

"You don't know a lot, non-committal, you didn't see any changes in her, she didn't say anything that may have made you think, that's not normal…woops my daughters a fruit loop, psychopath…. you're a nurse for god's sake… it's what your trained to do. And you didn't notice any abnormal actions in her behaviour"

"Of course, it's jealousy" stormed Joan "she was jealous that my Louise and Tommy fell in love and Sophie, because she couldn't have what she wanted…." Joan paused… "After all she is used to winning, trophy after trophy, guns and archery… accolade of being picked for England. She lost…!" Joan's normal calm demeanour, was growing into an angry rage "she lost and when it's been drummed into you, you're a winner, losing is not acceptable, coming second doesn't count, no one remembers a loser. Win at all cost, she could not have that… she lost" Joan had lost her professional conduct and an emotional grieving mum had let rip

"Bitter and twisted, she murdered my daughter, viciously slew my beautiful girl, she blew her brains out..." Joan had lost all control, tear flowing down her face

"I'm not a psychiatric nurse, I was a field nurse, hospital nurse, rehabilitation nurse... big difference you know..." defended Chloe
"So, tell me is Fred a jealous person?" enquired Joan...

"No, he is not, far from it..." answered Chloe firmly

"Are you a jealous person Chloe...?" prodded Martha

"No definitely not...!" she exclaimed "and I resent your implications...!"

"You resent my implications...!" snarled Martha "fuck resenting my implication...! your daughter brutally murdered my son and I want answers...."

"We want answers Chloe" said Joan sternly

"Neither of us are jealous people, that's not in our makeup, does that satisfy your inquisition...!" responded Chloe firmly

There was sustained silence, adding to the already intense tension

"Is the interrogation over, can we have a drink now...?" enquired Chloe

"Fred is a trained killer, he trained in the services, special services, we all know that, he's killed...!" Joan's outburst was totally out of character...

"My Fred served in the forces, defending this country, he did what he had to do…!" defended Chloe indignantly

"You were in the forces Chloe, true, trained as a nurse, but I bet even nurses are trained to kill in military training" probed Martha

"You two are a right pair of charmers" snarled Chloe "you have properly snared Fred and I, excellent con job. Come home all is forgiven; we have a job to do…for our kids. I suppose Fred's being given the thumb screws… mind he's man enough to take on them two…"

"Come on Chloe, you and Fred where in the forces, you're trained to kill, you, maybe not you, but Fred has probably killed…" blasted Martha

"Is this where Sophie got it from, is it hereditary…." proposed Joan

"I thought we were friends, what a pair of bitches…" Chloe glared at both of them, not blinking an eyelid

Silence prevailed… then the tension diminished

"We are friends, Chloe, I'm sorry for being so malicious" said Joan softly, placing her hand over her mouth, she shook her head. She then continued "emotions, anger and temper have got the better of me…" a tear fell from each eye

"Sorry Chloe, for attacking you so violently, my desire for answers, has taken away all my reasonable thinking. We are friends Chloe; I apologise for my behaviour" said Martha tenderly

"Sophie must have had a reason, reasons for killing Tommy and Louise" queried Joan softly, calmly, aware of how hostile the bombardment of Chloe had become

"Reasons, yes Fred and I have discussed this, what reason would she have to kill her two best friends. One she loved unconditionally and thought, hoped she would marry. The other she loved like a sister.
What reasons could Sophie have had. What turned her so against them, to kill them… we have asked this, many times…." Chloe paused then continued…
"What happened to turn her so viciously against them. These are questions we have…."

# Chapter 13

Fred sat back in his chair; his hands flat on the table

"What questions Fred, what is it you need to know mate....?" Echoed Tommy

"You got in touch with Chloe and me, come home you say, we have a job to do for our kids, you say… we are friends, you say…" Fred paused, composed himself and continued… "And we do…. Like lambs to the slaughter… you have bombarded me, accusations, insinuations, intimidation, cross examination… not just to me… but also" Fred mused… "insults to my wife… and those two in doors, had better not be interrogating my Chloe…."

Geoffrey and Tommy sat in silence and considered their words and actions…

"Emotions have run high Fred, I accept that and in return my only defence is, I, we, all need answers…" lamented Geoffrey wiping tears from his eyes

"Fred mate it's nothing personal as the Judge says… emotions, anger, tempers explode, sorry if I got a bit strong…" Tommy paused "what is it you want to talk about…?"

"Yes Fred, what questions my friend…?" Geoffrey queried

"Ok, fair enough… but you might not like what I've got to say… Chloe and I have pondered these thoughts for some time… they have festered… and now I can share them with you… my friends…"

Geoffrey and Tommy glanced at each other and then back at Fred puzzled, intrigued

"What turned my daughter into a deranged, psychotic, psychopathic cold-blooded murderer, devoid of any human emotion" Fred was cold stony faced

Tommy and Geoffrey both sat up right and a cold shiver went through both of them…

Fred raised his eye brows and continued…
"Why?... you want to know…. Let me tell you both… I want to know, what happened…? mmm what happened between my gentle caring loving sweet, innocent Sophie and Louise and Tommy….
What happened on that holiday…? mmm"

"What are you insinuating…?" demanded Geoffrey…

"What's your point Fred what you getting at… what you trying to say about my Tommy…?".

"Well, they go away best of friends… come back from holiday, Louise and Tommy are all loved up and some cock and bull story about two mongrels trying to rape my daughter and Tommy saves her, with Louise looking on as a witness" Fred was in full flow… "and we can't talk about it, Sophie don't want us to know… that's fucking convenient… it's all hush hush"

"Wait a god dam minute" Geoffrey was flustered...
"I am not having this crap… Tommy said angrily

"Na, it's not fucking nice is it…" Fred never flinched "but let's carry on… so, it's all hush hush what happened behind the building... at the BBQ site, only Louise's and

Tommy's account. What really happened behind there? who tried it on with who…mmmm? or, there they are, away in Portugal, in a villa, three of them, two girls and a man."

"Stop this I am not having this…" Tommy growled...

"All in separate bedrooms, what did he fancy sampling a bit of both … then decide who to keep…" continued Fred

"You're saying your daughter slept with Tommy and he dumped her… what are you saying about your own daughter" questioned Geoffrey

"Sophie would have succumbed to Tommy, she adored him" Fred's face remained stony

"You accusing my dead son of taking advantage of a girl…?" defended Tommy

"No, not accusations, more like indications of what might be" Fred replied

"This is insane…." Prompted Geoffrey
"That's an apt description…. Something made my girl insane" countered Fred

"This is madness... it's not on…" Tommy roared

"Why because it's Tommy and Louise, the innocent parties, my girl was innocent until she came back from that holiday…" Fred paused…
"Who's to say Tommy didn't sleep with my Sophie and Louise didn't like that, she wanted him, so she made herself available…. And he then dumped my Sophie… perhaps Louise was more forthcoming, experienced…"

"No" remonstrated Geoffrey

"Why not, why should Louise get off so lightly…" Fred paused……. then continued
"Who's to say… Tommy tried it on with my Sophie, and she declined his advances, saving herself and Louise found out and thought I'll move in and give him what he wants, because I want him"

"You stop this now or else I'll…."

"Or else what, don't threaten me Tommy…. ever" Fred cut Tommy off

"This is all conjecture, no evidence" declared Geoffrey

"Maybe so, but we all want answers, for every answer there is a question and I've got many…"
Fred continued… "they were all very close, perhaps Louise tried it on with my Sophie…. And Sophie repelled her… in her disappointment Louise turned her passion toward Tommy… now that would turn some one's head…"

"Where are you getting all this from…" asked Geoffrey

"Who knows, maybe there's voices in my head… maybe I'm being asked to question…". Fred continued to express his thoughts…

"Maybe those two mongrels did rape her, maybe Sophie and Tommy had fallen in love and made plans, and then Tommy couldn't cope with the fact Sophie had been raped…" he paused wiping tears from his eyes… "and turned his attentions to Louise for comfort and then they fell in love leaving Sophie distraught abandoned, lonely, dirty, unwanted…"

"If Tommy had fallen in love with Sophie… he would have supported her" guarded Tommy

"How do you know… could you stay with Martha… god forbid… if she got raped by two scum…?" quizzed Fred

"Yes of course!" Tommy resented the question

"How do you know… if it hasn't happened… no one knows until it happens?" Fred bowed his head… emotionally exhausted… then continued….
"How do we know how we will act, if something so powerful changes our mind set… our normal way of thinking… something triggers it…"

There was deadly silence… that seemed to last forever….

"I don't know why Sophie killed Louise and Tommy... I honestly don't know…" Fred paused… shaking his head… "I'm not saying any of the things I've insinuated happened. I don't know and neither do you, any of us… they sound crazy and implausible. All I know is my Sophie never had a bad bone in her body… she could fire a gun with supreme accuracy, a master at archery, we taught her, but I never witnessed her hurt any living thing... she was a passive..."

# Chapter 14

"What questions Chloe…?" queried Joan calmly

"Chloe, please feel free to express yourself, ask anything…?" said Martha

"Would you say that *"The Three Musketeers"* where inseparable, the best of friends?"

"Yes…"
"Yes…"

"Our Sophie, and you knew her well, over the years you would spend time with her. You would have seen her actions; you would have seen her grow…

"Yes, we did" replied Joan
"Of course, the kids were always together…" Martha added

"Sleepovers yes…" continued Chloe

"Yes"
"Yes"

"You would have shared her growth, from a kid when we first moved here…" Chloe paused "we all moved in at the same time, so from a kid to a woman…?"

"Yes"
"Yes"

"Did you ever have to chastise her, when you looked after her…?" Chloe continued in her pursuit…

"No"
"Never"

"Did you ever witness her being disrespectful…?"

"No"
"No, where are you going with this…? quizzed Joan

"Give me time…" quipped Chloe "who took a breath and continued….
"Was she ever spiteful or nasty…?"

"No"
"Chloe…?" Martha held her hands out

"Time…" she paused…
"Was she selfish…?"

"No"
"No"

Joan and Martha resigned themselves to answering…

"Was she hostile in any way…?"
"No…"
"Never…"

"Would you say she was a giving child….?"
"Yes…"
"Yep…"

"Kind, considerate, friendly…."

"Yer, all of those…"
"Yes, she was…"

"Soft, gentle…?"

Joan and Martha both smiled….
Yes…"
"She was that…"

"Did you ever witness Sophie being hostile…?"

"Never…"
"No…."

"Did Sophie ever hurt or harm Louise and Tommy…?"

"NO…!"
"NO…!"

Both Joan and Martha had started to well up….

Then they both came crashing down…

"Only when she killed them…!" Chloe paused…
"Murdered them on their wedding day…!"

Both the ladies where startled by this statement…quite
taken back, shocked….

"Chloe that's spiteful…" retorted Joan
"How callous…" Martha had a stern look on her face

"No, not spiteful, not callous, just truthful…" she
paused… "I have asked you many things relating to
Sophie as the person you knew… in witnessing her, in
growing up and all you answered was good and
positive…"

"And your point…?" asked Joan

"My point…?"

"Yes, what you arriving at…?" pushed Martha

"My point… what I'm arriving at is simple…". Sophie swallowed hard, then took a deep breath…
"What happened…? What changed her whole pattern of beliefs and actions…? What made her do it…?
What happened on that holiday…? What turned my sweet child into a homicidal psychopath…?" Chloe concluded

You could hear a pin drop….

"We know about the two scum who tried to molest Sophie…" stated Martha

"Do we…?" nodded Chloe

"Well yes Louise and Tommy told us in confidence because Sophie didn't want you and Fred to know…." Added Joan

"We also know Louise and Tommy came back madly in love and planned to marry…" Chloe specified

"Yes, they did…!" Martha said firmly
"And what's the dilemma with that" Joan quired

"I'm just wondering, actually Fred and I are just wondering…" Chloe paused and a wry smile appeared on her face "did something more take place, some goings on that have been conveniently swept under the table…?"

"What…?" Martha was startled
"What is it that you are inferring…?" quizzed Joan

"Did something more sinister go on…."

"I think you better spill the beans on what you trying to say…" Martha was irritable

"I think you should state your case, if there is one, with being more candid…." Proposed Joan

"That won't be a problem, quite simple did Tommy try it on with Sophie, when she was drunk, assuming she was drunk and near unconscious, at the BBQ and she rebuked his advances…. He persisted and she screamed. He panicked and ran away… found Louise and made some cock and bull story up, that she went missing."

"That's my son you are accusing…" Martha cut in

"They then did indeed hear Sophies cry of help, they did indeed find her in a state of near unconsciousness and despair. Shock horror confusion clouded her mind, the man that she loved had tried it on and not taken no for an answer…"

"Stop this…!" Martha screamed...
"In this state of mind, abused betrayed, she blocked it out of her conscious mind… she did not want to believe it. She could not bear to acknowledge this had happened…. Not Tommy…" Chloe continued

Martha and Joan where shell shocked

"Realising the state Sophie was in and she did not point the finger at Tommy… they knew that we would be fuming if it came out that they had lost Sophie and she had been attacked". Chloe paused… "So, they pinned the blame on these supposed two drunks… and to put themselves out of blames way, they made up this story of how they found her and Tommy saved her, the great hero and Louise the reliable witness..."

"Are you mad...?" said Joan
"This beggar's belief..." fumed Martha crying in rage

"Oh, I've not finished..." Chloe started up again... "in the state of mind Sophie was in, confused, lost, bewildered, it was easy for them to convinced her of the fairy tale they concocted, the two drunks who had been making lewd, vulgar remarks and suggestions and that Sophie had stupidly wandered off to the toilet on her own. Followed by the drunks who attacked her... and it was they, Louise and Tommy who rescued her... and she believed it... on a conscious level, but subconsciously, sublimely it was their..."

"If this is at all true...? which I cannot believe for one minute, this is why she murdered them...?" Grilled Joan

"Possibly, as it started to unravel in her mind, as time passed it became all apparent, they made up this story, then to cover themselves, decided to tell everyone they fell in love and was going to get married... maybe they did fall in love.... but Sophie would have felt betrayed, used, worthless, garbage, discarded on their honeymoon journey, rubbing salt into the wound asking her to be their bridesmaid...!" Chloe concluded

"If this load of bullshit has any merit, this is why she brutally killed them...." growled Martha

"Possibly on the grounds of diminished responsibility, she cracked, provocation..." Chloe replied

"I cannot possibly believe this, there is no foundation to your fabrication, of the distortion to the truth, that was portrayed to us by Louise and Tommy… it's all lies… lies… I cannot accept this…"   Joan announced shaking her head

"You are bang out of order, bang out of order Chloe, to even suggest this shit… its fucking embarrassing, your embarrassing, it's a load of crap that you have invented…to slander our children's good names…. It is a catalogue of lies…" Martha raged

"Lies, fabrication distortion… yea right… really…" Chloe's face was like granite... she paused … she placed a finger to her mouth and pondered… a smile then appeared on her face and she said… "Ok let's make it simple… Sophie and Tommy were always closer… whilst away they were mutually attracted to one another and romance started to blossom between them…."

"What…?" Raged Martha
"Where does this come from…?" questioned Joan

"Quite obviously my Sophie held onto her dignity, her virginity, her chastity. This in turn frustrated Tommy whose testosterone was raging. Louise who was obviously jealous of their romantic liaison saw this and took advantage to snare him and made herself available…and like a rampant youth he succumbed to her charms…" Chloe smiled at both of them…

"This has gone beyond the realms of probability… anything to deflect from the truth… you are making up anything to deflect from the truth Chloe, to lessen the burden of your responsibility, is it guilt, grief" stated Joan

"There is no dammed possibility… of these vile lies… Chloe how could you...?" Martha looked at Chloe in revulsion

"Well, they came home all loved up and the wedding was planned rather eagerly" paused Chloe... "was she pregnant...?"

"You should be ashamed of yourself, slandering two young innocent beings who were madly in love... And your daughter slayed them through jealousy..." Joan quantified firmly

"Louise was not pregnant, the wedding was not eagerly planned, don't you remember the planning, all of us going out shopping, celebrating... happy... until their wedding day..." Martha sobbed in rage, in frustration, in grief....

# Chapter 15

"Passive, yea right, she just blows peoples head's off, so passive…!" Tommy quipped

Fred looked Tommy in the eyes "Do you want to make this work, or is it all bullshit…?"

"Sorry my dear Fredrick, I must concur with Thomas… that is not a passive action…" sided Geoffrey…

There was silence…

"I said she was passive…! as I've repeatedly stated, I don't know what changed her…. I don't know why she did it…" Fred paused "and I doubt we ever will, we can make all kinds of suppositions… but we will never know…"

"I believe you are correct Fred…" concurred Geoffrey "I don't suppose we ever will…" agreed Tommy

"Can we as a collective accept that… and try to achieve whatever it is, our kids want…?" Fred asked

"Bury the hatchet you mean, and focus on what the kids want…" Tommy clasped his chin in his hand and brushed it… "we can give it a go"

"I believe we must…" Geoffrey nodded in agreement…. "Give it a go"

"Somehow find peace between us…?" Fred asked

"I think we need a drink…" and the three of them downed their pint…

# Chapter 16

"Just saying… could be…" Chloe quipped….

Martha and Joan looked at her puzzled, confused, angry…

"For Fucks sake…. Just saying…! Just saying…! Do you realise what you're saying…?" screamed Martha "Could be…! do you realise how condescending your words are, over something so serious…" remonstrated Joan

"I'm just saying, it could be, that way, how I explained it… all the different scenarios, it could have happened that way…!" Chloe stood her ground

"You cannot say those kind of things Chloe, you have no grounds to make such audacious outrageous accusations… slurring the good character of those kids…none of us know what happened…!" Martha was crying.

"The flippancy of your condemnation, of the reputation of our two innocent children, is utter disgraceful…!" Joan paused and regained her composure "You have no validity of these indictments…. You do not know what happened …!" declared Joan

"Apart from one thing that's for certain, Sophie murdered them… in cold blood…!" Martha had stopped crying and looked at Chloe cold eyed

"And the other thing that's certain, our children are gone…" Sobbed Joan

There was silence… then…

"One thing I know, we know, Fred and I… we don't know why Sophie killed Louise and Tommy… the one thing we do know…" Chloe paused… "Is, we can't bring our children back…! and we live with that fact. Every second… of every day… We live not knowing…." Chloe was disconsolate, sobbing…

There was a total hush…

"Chloe with everything that's been said, you're right, we will never know…" Martha conceded

"For every show of anger, resentment, emotions, accusations, insinuation… we will never know…!" concluded Joan

# Chapter 17

"Let's have another one… offered Fred

Tommy smiled "You're offering to buy another drink… this is not the officers mess ya know… one pound a pint…"

"I know…" Fred smiled "and the judge can get the next one" pointing at Geoffrey

"Be my pleasure…" Geoffrey paused and held his palm upward, to gain their attention…. "May I say" he deliberated for a moment….
"I reason, that some, most people in our situation... who have lost and are grieving. Not taking away from any loss, but certainly losing a child. Turn to a drink and other substances to mask their feelings... to cope! but that isn't the answer… we need a better solution" Geoffrey wept openly as the words flowed

"No, they, we, need help to cope, with the bereavement and the grieving…" stated Fred

"And they're my friends... maybe the answer and our quest…" Tommy looked at them intermittently

# Chapter 18

"Can we make peace…?" Chloe asked quietly
"A peace pact, for harmony and achievement...?"
Motioned Joan
In whatever way we will gain it, smoke the peace pipe…
a truce… for the kids…" declared Martha

A moment of solitude


 "Can we have a drink now? I really need one….! to help
me cope with this… to get by… please" Chloe said
mournfully

"I think we deserve one, but not to help us cope Chloe…
that's just masking the pain" Martha said sombrely

"Yes, Chloe we can have a drink, but drink or any other
substance, is not the answer. Drink or drugs won't help us
in our bereavement and grieving. It's not a crutch to prop
us up… or to help us cope.
It's help we need; specialised help" Joan spoke firmly but
calmly

"Specialised help, how do you mean…?" Inquired Chloe

"Counselling I suppose, somewhere to go, someone to
talk to…people with the same problems… to share..."
said Martha thoughtful

"There ladies, may be the answer, our divine destiny, to
help others in our situation …". Joan resolved.

# Chapter 19

"Alright Tom, how did it go luv?" inquired Martha
"To start with a little bit tender…"

"Right… and then? prodded Martha…
Tommy nodded his head… "Then, it could have turned
into World War 3…"

"Ouch…" Martha responded

"Ouch! with some of the things Fred stuck on us, it was
like having nails stuck in my eyes…"
"I see…" Martha nodded

"It was ruthless at times, he may as well have stuck a
knife in my heart, some of the things he claimed…"

"And then…?" Martha reasoned
"To be honest with ya babe, it could have kicked off, I
don't know how I never lost it..." growled Tommy

"I'm pleased ya didn't…!" Martha emphasised
"Yea, but he at times got a bit cocky…I'll tell ya…!"

"Don't turn it into male ego, who's the guvna…"

"Martha you would probably have swung for him, with
some of the accusations he made toward Tommy…"

"mmm.." Martha knew her husband well enough to let
him get it off his chest…

"Vile, slandering his character, basically saying Tommy,
had both of them at one point, then worse than that, he

tried to rape Sophie…" Tommy paused, took a mouthful of scotch and wiped the tears from his eyes.

"He then covered it up, then convinced her it was the two drunks… and that he and Louis had concocted an alibi for each other and that led them to fall in love…"

"Sounds familiar…" Martha stated

Martha poured Tommy a large scotch… Martha poured herself a large scotch …

"He's a candidate for a pair of concrete boots, propping up a flyover… saying my sons a nonce…!" Tommy was fuming

"You might make that two pair of concrete boots…" Martha took a large swig… "that's a concrete pillar each… buy one… get one free…" Martha's voice was calm … yet chilling

Tommy looked at his wife… "I love you; I would do anything for you, say the word… but sometimes you frighten me…!"

"Like wise…" Martha said softly nodding her head

"So… What's the strength of your story….?" Tommy poured them both a large top up

"Similar by the sounds of it to yours… Martha paused, and took a swig…. "Tommy Louise, Louise Tommy whatever way they play it, it's all down to them… poor Sophie, she suffered so, in their mixed-up fucking minds. No wonder that kid was totally screwed up …."

"Similar to mine…?... Tell me luv…?" Tommy looked confused

Martha went into detail…

"I'll tell you Tom… some of the bile that spilled from Chloe's gob…" Martha pointed her finger at Tommy… "There's a hospital bed with her name on it…!"

"Very similar, you couldn't make it up…" Tommy bit his lip

"I'd say they spent a lot of time around the table colluding, milling it over in their minds, putting it together, making it fit for their purpose…" Martha paused… I'd go as far as to say… its scripted"

"Sounds like they learnt their lines, played the part and followed the script perfectly…." Tommy stated

How did it end up with your discussion…? Martha asked

"That's the strange part, Fred came out with some profound comment about we will never know, he sort of, semi retracted, back tracked… said… maybe none of what he had said happened…!"

"And….!" Martha emphasised…

"And the wig and I couldn't disagree, it's like he mugged us off, but we couldn't disagree…!" Tommy took a breath and a swig… "Even the wig said… give it a go…"

Martha smiled, a wry smile…. Ditto darling, exactly what Chloe did to us… conniving pair of …..
Best actor, best supporting actress… Best actress, best supporting actor… played us… Oscars all round..."

"I agree wholeheartedly... but you know something.... I came up with an idea... from all of this ... our kids keep saying help them, help others... maybe that's what we have to do..." Tommy took a large gulp of scotch... "help others who have lost their kids... somehow..."

"You came up with that not them...?" Martha queried

"Yea, why?"

"The same scenario played out... and Joan came up with the same.... conclusion...!" Martha informed Tommy

"What...?" probed Tommy

"Yea, how strange is that...?" Martha pondered

"Maybe they never played us...? Quizzed Tommy

"Maybe not... but it's strange way of doing it..." Martha squared Tommy straight in the eyes

"Agree, I won't forget that....!"

"Don't you know it...!"

# Chapter 20

"Joanie are you in dearest…?" Geoffrey inquired when he returned from the pub…

"Yes Love, I'm in the kitchen…" replied Joan….

"How did the conversation flow with Chloe and Martha…?" Enquired Geoffrey

"Conversation… I would say it was more like an inquisition…!"

Inquisition…? Echoed Geoffrey
Accusation…! Added Joan
Accusation…? Echoed Geoffrey
Interrogation….! Countered Joan
Interrogation….? Echoed Geoffrey

"Are we living in an echo chamber…?" smiled Joan

"No, merely intrigued … by your description of events…" Geoffrey summoned up
"I would go as far has to say... a combination of all three…" Joan stated

"A…" Geoffrey started

Joan put her finger up at him… forbidding…. "Do not go there…"

"Not pleasant then…?" Geoffrey asked
"No, quite hostile….!"

"I see" Geoffrey stated
"Prey give me a rundown of events...?" Geoffrey quired

"We, Martha and I asked relevant questions, like why did Sophie murder our children…."
Geoffrey nodded

"What was her reasons for such an action…? Joan continued…
"Had they witnessed any significant changes in her words, actions… behaviour in general…"

"And the answer…?" Geoffrey asked
"Categorical No, none…" stated Joan

"And then…?" quizzed Geoffrey
"And then… only that Sophie was heartbroken when Louise and Tommy fell in love… and planned to marry. By all accounts she had designs on Tommy and it was a given that they would marry… of course not missing out that Louise she loved like a sister…!" Joan was becoming agitated

"Did she continue after these exchanges?" Geoffrey paused" how did Chloe conclude my dear…?"

"Chloe became somewhat antagonistic, in her words and occasion stance, she was volatile, slanderous, an indictment of pure purgatory, at what she aimed at Louise and Tommy…" tears rolled down Joan's face… "it was beyond comprehension what she portrayed and outlaid to us… and then changed with the wind ….
Totally unpredictable…."
"There was more… Joanie… a nail in the coffin, so to speak…?" Geoffrey probed
"Yes… Chloe made a closing statement…" Joan's voice became very soft… "that left us with no other option but to agree with her…it was unnerving. Prior to that statement I had anger in my heart. Martha and I,

individually wanted retribution, revenge came easily to mind…!"

"Are you OK Joan…?" Asked Geoffrey with a firm but loving tone…

"Yes, I need to express my feelings" … Joan was sobbing… "Hey I was ok… with revenge, it came so naturally… easily… cruelly…" Joan paused… "the gallows beckoned, depths of depravity.         I wanted vengeance inflicted brutally, as it was to Louise and Tommy by Sophie…"

"Joan, you don't have to continue…" Geoffrey tried to comfort his wife, but she held him off at arm's length…

"My mind was in a state of pure insanity, terminal, squalid thoughts towards Sophie, Chloe and Fred… after all they gave birth to her and there she was, Chloe, defending her. Throwing vindictive abhorrent callous un-substantiating claims of fantasy evidence, to clear or justify her daughters repugnant act…" Joan paused tears rolling down her face… "I might add, that had no baring or connection to the truth, in my mind…!"

"And then Chloe hit you with the statement…?" Geoffrey held his arms out, and Joan fell into them…

"Yes…!" she sobbed... "and both Martha and I agreed with her… Geoffrey I am so ashamed of my thoughts…"

"I have heard the phrase revenge is sweet… my dear... but we cannot take the law into our own hands…"

"I can understand how clients I've defended... and prosecuted, seek and inflicted revenge…" said Joan calmly

"But you agreed with Chloe.? to give it a go…? we will never know the answer…?" Geoffrey quizzed
"YES…!" exclaimed Joan in bewilderment…

"Collusion…cohesive…sub delude…" Geoffrey questioned himself…

"Define…?" Joan was now composed and curious…

"Common denominator…!"

"And…!"

"Frederick mirrored Chloe's behaviour, words indictment… and then had us eating out of his hand… we, Thomas and I agreed to give it a go…"

"You consider there is conspiracy…? For what end…?" Joan countered

I don't know…! I don't know if its coincidence, planned, inspired or Devine… Fred was incompatible
at times and then pure personification, the perfect diplomate, with a profound answer…"

"My God… You have described Chloe…" Joan was bemused… "Tell me all that went on? how did it start? who commenced the dialog? Was it convivial…? No…!" she countered herself, "Divulge Geoffrey…"
Joan was in control
"Well, it was somewhat tentative my dear…"

"Yes, yes…!" Joan was impatient
"I do declare, there were occasions, I believe, that Thomas and Frederick could, quite easily have set about

each other. Fist fight and I doubt Queensbury Rules would be observed…"

"Resonates… continue...!" encouraged Joan
"I'm quite sure urban warfare was imminent; no rules would apply…" continued Geoffrey

"How, Geoffrey, how was you, feeling…?" Joan questioned caringly
"Somewhat frightening, terrifying in fact… like being in the middle of a war zone…" Geoffrey confessed

"My love…!" Joan exclaimed
"But…! Exhilarating…!" he declared… "and I am shocked to admit it…!"

"Geoffrey Childs you're an urban gorilla… my man…" Joan smiled with pride
"A strange mixture of emotions…" Geoffrey offered

There was momentary silence

"How was Tom…?"
"I could resonate with Tom, when he got angry, such strange emotions building up inside of me, when Fred got very bitter, in his slanderous assassination of Louise and young Tommy" Geoffrey had tears in his eyes

"Come here, you, my big hunk…" Joan took him close...
"I must say, to my own astonishment, I would have had no qualms, in biffing Fred myself…" Geoffrey's words were cold

"You could well have been bailing me out, would ripping someone's tongue out, constitute ABH…" Queried Joan… "or would it be considered to be humane in putting them out of their misery…"

"We are all in misery my dearest Joanie… we may well have been sharing a Peter together …" They both smiled and hugged each other

"The strangest of occurrences" shared Joan
"That they both acted and spoke in the same dialogue …" with conclusion… added Geoffrey

"Yes, but more so we all agreed to try, give it ago…"
Joan paused… "and an idea sprung into my mind…
Our kids want us to help others… hence the idea…"

"An idea... mmm you never said…"
"No, got carried away with our conversation" apologised Joan

"This is so freaky… so did Tommy… the same thing happened…"

# Chapter 21

"Chloe you home?" Fred questioned

"Yes, I'm in the living room…"

Fred entered the living room and the first thing he noticed was Chloe holding a large wine glass…

"A good, eventful evening then I see…" he said sarcastically…

"Please Fred don't start, I had a couple at Joan's and this is my first here…"
"How did it go…?"

"As expected, I suppose…!"
"Likewise!" responded Fred

"Interrogation…?"
"Yep, not a scratch on what I went through in training…" Fred said cynically

"No thumb screw and electric shocks then…?" Martha wisecracked
"Na, I expected aggression from Tommy and diplomacy on the whole, but a little bit of tantrum from Geoffrey…"

"How did that go down…?" quizzed Chloe
"I handled it… I could even understand where they are coming from, if the boot was on the other foot… I'd be antagonistic…" Fred paused… "I would demand answers... I would be brutish… I would want to know why…?"

"That is a good analogy of how it went…at Joan's" responded Chloe

"Did you handle it ok…?"

"I believe so…" Chloe took stock… "I could be defensive when I needed to be and then tried to be calm and receptive when the occasion presented itself…

"How did they respond to that…?"

"I think it confused them…" Chloe once again pondered… "They couldn't grasp how I took it all, countered and then responded in a pacified manner…I believe I was defusing the situation…"

"And…?"
"On hind sight I suppose it could have come across a bit psychotic… very hostile and belligerent and then calmness, ok matter of fact… woops" she smiled

"I bet that fired up flames…"

"With the venomous bile spate at me, I couldn't win, accusation interrogation why? why? why…? if I'd replied to anger with anger, it would have inflamed the situation … so I lowered my tone and said consistently, I don't know, we don't know…" Chloe stated calmly

"Yea that rings a bell…"

"So, after all the discussion deliberation, soul searching, punishing ourselves, you and I have done in pursuit of the truth, with all the different connotations that it could be…." Chloe paused… "We came to the same deliberation; we don't know why Sophie murdered them…!"

"And you stated this case…?" Fred quizzed

"In a fashion, I also handed out a few of the connotations, conspiracy theories, what's, ifs, and buts…" Chloe paused… "maybe's, might have been, could have been. That in seeking the truth we have had to endure in the quest of the facts, beating ourselves up relentlessly…"

 A calm silence prevailed

"So, I threw a few, if not all of them out….!"
"And in response…? "Fred replied

"Indignation, they couldn't believe it, how could I be so cruel and spiteful…!" Chloe took a breath and wiped tears from her eyes… "All about their feelings, their loss, their grief…"

"Circumstances are different Chloe…" stated Fred

"I know, the strange thing was, after I made it perfectly clear we didn't know why Sophie murdered them…. Chloe thought for a moment… "They kind of accepted it, Joan then made some statement… There is the answer, Devine destiny…."

Fred raised his eyebrows… "How interesting…." He responded

"But we are still grieving… what about our feelings… for our daughter…?" Chloe paused… "For Tommy and Louise who we loved as our own family, for Martha, Joan, Geoffrey and Tommy…they were, are…?" Chloe took a mouthful of her wine… "like our own flesh and blood, we are grieving for them…."

"Maybe they haven't recognised that fact, that we are grieving for them" Fred paused... "They wallow in their own self-pity, and quite rightly so...!" Fred took a moment, swallowed hard... "Yet they forget we are also grieving for them, we are also in our own state of anguish, compounded by having to live with the stigma... it was our child who murdered theirs.... And a pound to a penny...... they won't be grieving for Sophie..." Fred conceded

"How did it go for you? ... With Geoffrey and Tommy...?" Chloe inquired

"I've assessed the situation and say... a carbon copy.... Perhaps they had a script they worked from..." Fred paused.... "Why? why? why...? didn't you see anything different? did she change...?"

"As if, we had known, seen... considered, do they not think we would have acted...? Responded Chloe

"Quite...!"

"Was it hostile...?"

"Ding ding...! round one, come out boxing, it could have kicked off with Tommy a couple of times..."
"How so...?" inquired Chloe

"Provocation... pushing, niggling, sniping... goading baiting... why...? why...? continuous ..." Fred had poured himself a large glass of wine and happily filled Chloe's glass up ..." I kept my composure by reminding myself... in their world, I'd be doing the same.... So, I bit my tongue..."

"It's a wonder you didn't bite it off…!  it's a wonder you didn't bite his off…!" Chloe smiled at her husband…. "Fred Miller I'm proud of you…"

Fred smiled at Chloe….

There was a peaceful silence….

"And you never retaliated…!" Chloe quizzed with a wry smile

"World War 3 was imminent…!" Fred answered with a wryer smile

Chloe pondered "So, brink of war, dooms day clock… Armageddon… how did peace prevail…? Or didn't it…?"

"I did what you did…" Fred half giggled… "they probably think we had a script… I threw in a number of hypothetical hypotheses… could have…! maybe…!"

"And…? Interrogated Chloe
"They were none too pleased…!" stated Fred

"And…!" Chloe stated impatiently

"And, and like you…Chloe, make no bone about it… I made it quite clear, abundantly clear… no if's and but's… we don't know why Sophie murdered Tommy and Louise…" Fred said calmly

"Reaction…?" Chloe pushed
"That's why I said interesting…" Fred

"Fred you're a cantankerous sod…." Chloe smiled… "Did the tension subside, did you finish on a positive note….?"

"Yes…! It did finish on a positive note…" Fred stated tranquilly

"I swear Fred Miller it's like getting life out of a corpse…" Chloe was looking puzzled

"Yes, I fired back a couple of volleys', they didn't like it…" Fred took stock... "they had their say…" he paused…. "And then as sincerely as I could, I affirmed to them… we will never know…!" Fred paused took a mouthful of wine… "Is there a way we can make peace…"

"Their reaction…?" Chloe was on the edge of her seat…

Fred thought for a minute… "There were words of give it a go" … he paused … "bury the hatchet…

"In no one's back I hope…!" Chloe cut in…

"Bury the hatchet… give it a go… for the sake of what our kids want…" Fred looked at Chloe…

"Sorry… and…? Chloe said and asked...

"And that's when Tommy came out with his statement…" Fred looked at Chloe "And they're my friends... may be the answer and our quest…"

Fred and Chloe finished off a litre bottle of sauvignon blanc… and opened another …

"You know Chloe…" Fred paused… "I've been giving it a lot of thought…"
"What's that soldier boy…?"

"The thing that rankles with me, is… If they hadn't invaded our territory and bought houses here…" Fred took a large mouthful of wine…" our darling daughter would never have met their kids…"
"Where you coming from…?" slurred Chloe…

"If they hadn't bought houses here, our Sophie would never have met Louise and Tommy…!"
"Makes sense…"

"Exactly…! and they wouldn't have become *The Three Musketeers…one for all, all for one…!* they abandoned Sophie…!" he paused and took another large mouthful….
As did Chloe…
 He carried on…. "They took off …they went rouge … traitors... left her out to dry…"
"If they hadn't brought them here…" Chloe garbled

"Affirmative nurse…" Fred stood to attention…

"And we know what happens to traitors…?" Chloe had sobered instantly
"They get shot…!" Fred never minced his words

"And Sophie wouldn't have murdered them…" Chloe took a sip of wine… "If they…" pointing out the room…
"Hadn't brought them here…"

They finished the second bottle and staggered up to bed.

# Chapter 22

"Tommy, luv, theirs someone at the front door, can you get it... I'm in the middle of putting washing out..." Shouted Martha...

"Putting the washing out...! Luv...! all that old moody...!" Tommy bellowed so as Martha could hear him...
"I can hear you...!" She stated...smiling

"I know you can, you can hear a pin drop at twenty paces..." he said quietly...
"I can still hear you..." she responded

"I know sweetest one... and you know I'm watching the game... on the tele... not to be disturbed...! it's our boys playing...!" Tommy paused... "Tommy might have been out there..." Tommy's mood slumped from being jovial...

Martha was standing in the doorway... her eyes moisten as she looked at her husband's demeanour crumble

"I'll get rid of who it is and we can watch it together..." Martha whispered

Tommy put on a half-smile... "Ok..."

As she opened the door, she gasped... "Freddie...!"

"Hello Mrs. Jackson..." he said quietly

"Tommy..." she said with urgency in her voice
"Martha ..." Tommy picked up Martha's tone... "You ok...?"

"Tom its Freddie…." She sounded surprised

"Fred, ok tell him to come in…" Tommy was a bit surprised

"No luv… its Freddie… Tommy's Freddie…!"

Tommy was out of his seat like a ferret up a drain pipe…

He stood staring at him… "Freddie lad… come in, Martha invite the boy in… come on. Come in…" Tommy said shocked but delighted

"I hope you didn't mind me popping round, I know it's been so long…" Freddie questioned hesitantly
"The door will always be open to you son" Martha said her eyes welling up…
"Of course, when she remembers to invite you in…" Tommy tried to lighten the atmosphere

They all smiled

"I thought you would be at the game… I thought you might be playing…?" quizzed Tommy

"I've not been able to… well I've started back, but I wasn't able to play for a while…" Freddie mumbled his words…

"How are you now Freddie…?" Tommy said sincerely
"Would you like a wassa son…?" asked Martha caringly

"A wassa…" he reflected… "that would be nice…"

They were still in the hall way…

"For heaven's sake, let's sit in the front room, do you want to watch the game or…" Tommy dithered… "or the kitchen…?"

"I don't mind...". Freddie hunched his shoulders…

"Take a seat son…" Tommy took control and showed him into the front room…

Martha went to the kitchen and made three wassa's… then returned…

 "I'm sorry I haven't been around to see you, since the funeral, Tommy's funeral…" Freddie blurted out…tears falling from his eye's...
"It's ok Freddie we understand" Martha cradled him

"I just couldn't cope... with what happened...". he shook his head...
"We know son… the club were magnificent in what they did for Tommy… flowers, drape's, flags pictures at the ground..." Tommy was trying to ease the tension… his eyes welling up

"You came to his funeral Freddie; we couldn't ask no more than that. Other players, members of the staff… the manager, coach… even the owners, an avenue of supporters… they showed great respect…" Martha was now crying

"They all loved him, I loved him, he was my best friend…" Freddie was inconsolable

"We know son how close you were... the deadly duo… the newspapers nicknamed the two of you…" Tommy tried to perk him up

"She, that Sophie, she should have killed me as well that day, I'm nothing without Tom…!"

"That's not true, you must carry on and be the best you can be… for you… and achieve what you and Tommy, dreamt about, talked about leading England to World Cup victory". Martha paused… "that's what you two told us you were going to do… so do it for Tommy… do it for both of you…" Martha was passionate and slightly angry…

"I'm sorry Mrs. Jackson, I've upset you and caused you distress...that was not my intention… I'll leave…"

"No, you won't leave son, Martha and I want you to have the life Tommy isn't able to… you can do it for the pair of you…" Tommy was firm yet compassionate

"I think you have misunderstood me… when I said she should have killed me that day… she did… inside of me… I cannot get that vision out of my head … her words… *it should have been me…*" …                  I turned as everyone else did" Freddie paused… "and there we are looking down the barrel of a gun… pointing at us…I was so frightened... terrified… BANG…! There was Louise with her brains scattered all over the vicar... I went numb.  Me next I thought, she loves Tommy everyone knows that… she won't shoot him… and she moved her arm, her aim, I'm standing next to Tommy as he was cradling Louise… I closed my eyes…. I felt tears trickling down my face…Bang…!  When I realised, she hadn't shot me…! I open my eyes and there's Tommy, the back of his scull splattered everywhere… I never knew if she had more bullets…" Freddie's face was distorted… "She should have killed me that day… she all as well did…"

Martha and Tommy had tears cascading down their face's... as they relived that day with Freddie's words... but felt no fury toward him... just sorrow...

They all sat in silence holding hands...

*"Help him... help others..."* They heard the words, they looked at Freddie...

"Did you say something...?" Freddie asked politely

"What happened Freddie, to you, after the funeral, we asked after you, the club said you were in shock, in trauma and were having therapy..."   Martha sidestepped the question...

Freddie pondered for a moment... "Did you hear the words help him." he queried again...

"Did you hear those words Freddie...?" asked Martha
"Yea... I did"

"Do you believe in life after life... Life goes on in a different realm, spirit...?" Tommy asked lightly

"No, do me a favour... Tommy used to go on about this... he believed in all that..."

"WHAT...!" They both exclaimed
"Are you telling me that's Tommy.?" Questioned Freddie
"Yes..."
"No, don't take me there, I'm not going back into that clinic..." Freddie said horrified

"What happened Freddie...?" asked Martha...

"Straight after the wedding day… I was diagnosed with stress and anxiety…I was in shock, numb from the brain down, no emotion, no feeling, I couldn't talk…"

"What did they do…?" Martha asked
"The old favourite, I've found out, anti-depressants… but they didn't work… then they decided to get me back playing…"

"Was that wise…?" queried Tommy

"Not really, I didn't want to kick a ball, it was like my passion for the game was dead… I had no ability left… couldn't make a pass…"

"How did they deal with that…?"
"They were excellent, they encouraged me, supported me, then I was diagnosed PTSD… and went into a private clinic, to process the trauma… different therapies…"

"Did it work…?"
"To a degree, one day I was in the gym hall… and there was a ball… so I started kicking it against a wall… and I felt like Tommy was with me, I turned and I thought I saw him… making a run, like he used to… and I pinged the ball onto his toe…." Freddie smiled… "and then he was gone…"

"Did you tell anyone…" asked Tommy…

Freddie fell silent…

"Freddie did you tell anyone…?" encouraged Martha

"You kidding… I saw my dead mate making a run and I passed the ball to him… do you think they would have let me out…. The main thing was, which was massive. I started kicking the ball about on a regular daily basis and doing skill work… it always felt like Tommy was there. So, they decided I was ok… and let me back to the club… under supervision"

"How are your team mates, patient…?" asked Martha
"They are great, they understand…, they just don't seem to understand, why I pass the ball into empty spaces where none of them are…!"

"What…?" questioned Tommy… "you were one of the best passers of a ball, never waisted possession and such a quick eye and precision..."

Freddie shrugged his shoulders….

"They weren't empty were they…? you saw Tommy running into those spaces… didn't you Freddie…?" Tommy pushed…" Tell us son...?"

"You think I'm going to tell them that… they will put me in that place they put Sophie…the murderer, she should have killed me that day….!" Freddie was nervous and shaking

"No, they won't Freddie…" assured Martha
"No, they won't son… confirmed Tommy
"Yes…! Is the answer to your question… They were runs Tommy would make… and yes I saw him…"
Freddie was calmer… "What's going on…?"

"We hear Tommy… we smell Tommy…. We know when he is here or around us…" Martha stated

"You're just telling me that to pacify me…"

"You heard his voice and words… help him… didn't you Freddie… because we did…confirmed Tommy

"You two are the most down to earth people I know… you wouldn't lie, so you're not lying to me... coz you think I'm nuts…?" Freddie pleaded

"You're not nuts, as you put it… you are hearing spirit, you are hearing and seeing Tommy's spirit, you told us he believed in life after life…" Tommy stated sincerely

"Yes….!" confirmed Freddie
"We never knew that, he never confided that in us, so he must have trusted you enormously…" concluded Martha…

Freddie was composed… "yea he did… and to tell ya the truth… I resonated with it, but it scared the life out of me…"
"That's a good example" quipped Martha…smiling

They all laughed…

"Yea apt…" Freddie quipped

"Don't be scared, don't be frightened, once you're not afraid of something it no longer becomes the burden hanging around your neck… confront it, it no longer has a hold over you…" Tommy stated
"Maybe you need to talk to Tommy, like he's sitting next to you…" Martha said

Freddie looked sideways…
"I'm not saying he is…." laughed Martha…

"Ask him to stop showing himself and making those runs... because it's making you look a plum and he wouldn't do that because he trusted you… and respected you as a player and his skipper…" Tommy injected positively…

"Maybe he's showing you where to put the ball, to improve and educate your team mates…" countered Martha… "Tell them where you want them to run, move to…"

"You think…"

"Why don't you go up and sit in his room… talk to him, see what happens, you know he loved you like a brother, he isn't going to hurt you…" Martha smiled

"Go on Freddie and stay for a bite to eat… you haven't had one of Martha's all-day breakfasts for a long time… you know where Tommy's room is…." enthused Tommy…

"Thank you, I will…".

Freddie took the stairs up to Tommy's room and laid on his bed… instantly feeling his presence…

"Is this how we help others…?" Tommy looked at Martha empathically
"It's a good start, strange how he just turned up…" deliberated Martha
"Maybe meant to be…" Tommy took a mouthful of a fresh wassa… "let's wait and see…"

After a couple of hours had gone by…

Martha said to Tommy… "why don't you pop up and have men's talk or see how he is…"

Tommy climbed the stairs normally to allow Freddie to be aware he was coming up…

Tommy knocked on the door, and then entered… Freddie was sound asleep… peacefully…

"He's putting back the zzzz's" Tommy told Martha when he came back down

"I guess he needs it… let him sleep until the morning…" Martha said...

# Chapter 23

They had arranged to reconvene and meet up at Joan and Geoffrey's…

"I'm pleased we're all here… it would be difficult without all parties present…". opened Geoffrey…
"In my capacity as a judge, I'm not looking to preside over our meetings …. We have spoken openly, honestly, I believe. At times emotions over boiled and at times I'm sure the brutal honest truth was spoken…. The truth must be spoken…!"

There was silence….

"We split up into two groups and I know from our discussions things were said, opinions expressed, hostilities shared…" Geoffrey took stock … "we all allowed anger and emotions to flow freely…."

"May I comment…" expressed Joan…
"Of course, my Dearest, we are not in court…. Please…"
Geoffrey opened his hands up, passing the floor to Joan

"I would like to say… in our discussions, there were some intimidating, antagonistic, aggressive, points of view voiced. It was at times unkind, passionate, frank, critical obscene recriminations… all round….!" Joan paused and looked individually to every one of them…
"And I endorse what Geoffrey has outlined…! I'd like additionally to say … I'm sure behind closed doors, more words were said… it is imperative that we place our hearts on our sleeves…"

"We only said what we felt…" Tommy stated
"We spoke from the heart…!" Martha expressed

"We all took a turn in saying what we thought…!" Fred added
"And we said it… what's wrong with that…" Chloe specified

"Precisely, this is what I'm arriving at…" Geoffrey started
"Exactly my friends….!" Joan cut in… "that was exactly what was needed…"
"Clear the air… we needed to clear the air, expel the elephant…" Geoffrey concluded

"Warts and all say what we felt… even if it provoked" Tommy quantified
"Yes…!" yelled out Joan
"Clear the throat, get it off the chest…to the detriment of others" pursued Fred
"Yes…!" roared Geffrey

"To be honest… to the brink of being ruthless, was that necessary…?" enquired Martha
"I'm afraid so Martha, we all released our inner judgements" Geoffrey sombrely shared

"To be that candid, merciless in thought and speech… we really all had to endure that pain…" Chloe pleaded
"It was essential Chloe; we all demonstrated and remonstrated our own demoniac depravities, of resentment and thoughts of revenge…" Geoffrey articulated gravely

"To release, more so to relinquish ownership… to let go…!" Fred pronounced

"To acknowledge… to respect… to dismiss… …!" Chloe endorsed

"If we are truly sincere in coming together, to achieve, to make something happen…for our kids, to honour our children… that was necessary…!" announced Tommy

"Sure, it's the only way we can move towards our children's desire, to make something grow…a birth, to give a validity to the lives" proclaimed Joan

"This is what was indicated by both of you… an idea… an answer… a purpose… a destiny… depicted by you both in separate locations… In helping each other. So, it bares providence in helping others…"
 Geoffrey concluded

Martha, Chloe, Fred and Geoffrey looked expectantly at Joan and Tommy

"What is it you are asking …?" enquired Joan

"Give us a clue here… What do you want …?" Tommy remonstrated with frustration

"What was it you were thinking when you said those words Tom…?" asked Fred
"Joan what was in your head, when you said our Devine destination...?" asked Martha
 "Joan, Tommy, share your ideas with us…please…?" asked Chloe

"Be in the knowledge of internal strength… Joanie, Thomas… you know the answer to our destination...".
Geoffrey's words were so profound

The room was motionless …The silence deafening…

"Forgiveness and unconditional love, means our pain is not the final word on the matter…for us, then the ripple, to help others…" Tommy's mouth opened and the words flowed…

"We must learn to be compassionate, to trust, to give love and receive love, unconditionally and we will be at peace with the past and have faith in the future… for the benefit of mankind" Joan's word's rolled off her tongue

Tears where in abundance by all present….

*"Help them…"*
*"Help others…"*
*"Forgiveness…"*
*"Unconditional love …"*

The words in unison echoed around and around and around like poetry flowing from a ports mouth…

"I really think we could do with a drink, I could, I'm mentally emotionally fatigued" sobbed Chloe...
"I concur…!" decreed Geoffrey
"I agree with the misses…" agreed Fred
"I agree… I so agree…! Approved Martha nodding her head.

Joan and Tommy looked at each other and smiled…
The others looked at them in wonder and adulation

"I harmonise with that decision…" quipped Joan…
"And I second all of those emotions….!" Tommy jested running his hand through his hair…

# Chapter 24

Supreme isolation in a crowded room... a serene silence prevailed...

They each contemplated in the own space and mindfulness....

Thought and providence of which they had all experienced, within their individual comprehension was coming to fruition....

Ideas formulating...

Pearls of inspiration divulging themselves...

Aspirations...

Innovations...

Revelations...

Little beings chipping away at a rock... chipping away.... chipping away.... Chipping away... within their depths of their subconscious minds.

until ...their subconscious thoughts emerge into a coherent plan of action

Cascades of wonderment exploded into logical thought patterns, that can become reality

The silence was broken.......

"We need a venue...!" Martha stated

"A place of peace, for people to come…!" Joan added

"A place that people feel safe…!" Emphasised Geoffrey

"A place for people to share…!" Chloe said

"People like us…!" Fred said solemnly

"People who are experiencing bereavement….!" Tommy expressed peacefully

"People who are grieving loss…!" Joan stated

"Martha you're a complimentary therapist…!" Tommy said excitedly

"Yes, would that help…? Asked Chloe

"Yes, there are many forms of complimentary therapies that can help…!". Martha stated

"We need professional help…!" insisted Chloe

"We will need a counsellor…!" endorsed Martha
"We will need a bereavement counsellor…!" Geoffrey pronounced

"Can we not do our own counselling, to listen to talk to share…" Fred questioned

"Listening is one of the best therapies there are….!" Chloe said

"We have one mouth…!" Tommy pointed at his own mouth

"Yes, and two ears…!" Martha pointed at her ears

"Yes, listen twice as much as we speak…!" Tommy paused "Martha taught me that...!"

"Let's create our own retreat…!" Chloe said enthusiastically

"A place for people to come dedicated to helping bereaved parent's…!" Fred quantified

Let's buy a premise and create "the sanctuary for bereavement" Joan expressed hungrily

Specialise, "the sanctuary for bereaved Parent's…!" Geoffrey detailed

"All sell up and buy something…?" questioned Martha"

"Or raise the funds….!" Joan stated soberly

"If we can do this… and are willing to promote…. Our own bereavements…then we can show others there is help…." Chloe said empathetically

"That's a journey to share…!" Tommy defined

"To overcome…!" Fred added compassionately

"And help others to cope…" Geoffrey sympathised

"So many ideas….!" enthused Martha

"Where do we start…?" quizzed Tommy

"Yes, we need to do a brain storm and condense it down to an achievable project, to create a facility, a vehicle that will work..." stated Fred

"This is so exciting ...." Joan blurted out

"Your exuberance is compounded by sheer delight...!" Geoffrey proclaimed

And so, to work... allocate ourselves tasks to explore, and to bring together..." Fred decreed

"We will need a project manager...Joan specified

They all looked at Chloe

"Chloe it's not rocket science... You're a qualified nurse with lots of experience in organising under severe duress, expertise in the medical trade..." quantified Tommy shrugging his shoulders
"And Martha... as a qualified physiotherapist who has also worked in hospitals... a match made in heaven...!" Geoffrey accentuated

"I propose Joan to work closely as the advocate" Fred stressed "you have all the qualifications... QC...!"

"And we will be the foot soldiers...!" Tommy looked at everyone individually... "now we all have a purpose, let's go to work...!"

Now, for all of their endeavours, upheaval, conflict, recriminations they had a belief, from the depths of depravity they had found a unity  A common ground was formed.

# Chapter 25

"Good morning, I'm really sorry, I laid down on Tommy's bed and crashed out..." said Freddie

"That's ok son... come on sit yourself down" said Tommy smiling

"Would you like a cuppa...?" Asked Martha

"Yes please..." Freddie replied

"Have one of Martha's famous breakfasts, I know you used to enjoy that..." Tommy assured

"Yea, that would be nice, I always looked forward to that treat..." Freddie smiled

"Did you sleep Ok...? asked Martha

"Like a log....!" Freddie smiled and nodded

"Did you speak to Tom...?" Tommy asked in a matter-of-fact manner

"I laid on his bed and immediately I felt his presence... I closed my eyes and I felt so serene..." Freddie paused" it was a weird sensation, but I felt safe and comfortable... crazy...!"

Martha and Tommy looked at him with interest and encouragement...

"I could hear his voice, carry on Freddie, carry on playing and achieve our dream.... You're my best mate, my brother, do it for you... do it for us...I'll be right there with you…" Freddie was getting choked up and tears rolled slowly down his face…

Tommy leant across the table and held his hands compassionately… Martha stood behind his chair and placed her hands on his shoulders….

"It's ok son…" Tommy confirmed

"It was crazy, it was like I was sitting on top of a cloud…" Freddie paused… "it's the only way I can explain it…" Freddie exhaled… "so surreal…."

"You know you are welcome here anytime…" Martha paused… "you can stay if it helps and we can listen if you want to chat…"

"Are you going to carry on playing Freddie and become the person, the player you were truly meant to be…?" Tommy inquired

"Is it ok if I want, need to, sit in Tommy's room from time to time, it gives me an inner strength… I feel composed, calm, strong, focused…" Freddie was nodding his head as he spoke, his voice was more assertive… "my mind feels clear, logic focus clarity, none of that monkey mind… energised… I can feel a warmth and tingling where your hands are Mrs Jackson and as your holding my hands Mr Jackson, I feel strength, what's happening…?"

Martha and Tommy looked at each other… Tommy had heard of healing energy from his mum… "you would make a lovely healer son and your young lady" was her words, but never experienced it…

"Yes Mr Jackson, Mrs Jackson, I am going to carry on playing... for Tommy, for you, but mainly for me... does that sound selfish...?

"No son" said Martha, tears in her eyes... "that's beautiful, thank you..."

"I'm proud of you Freddie...". Tommy choked...

"Now let's have some brekki...!" exclaimed Martha


There was a comfortable silence and a feast of a breakfast....

"How have you coped with what happened to Tommy and Louise...?" Freddie asked as kindly as he could...

"Very difficultly Freddie..." Martha affirmed

"At times great anger ... remorse..." Tommy admitted

"Remorse...?" queried Freddie

"Remorse we ever came here, moved here... met our neighbours and their children...." Tommy affirmed

"As much as we loved the kids and our friends, if we hadn't moved here, Tommy would be alive...!" Martha shared

"You say that and I can resonate with that emotion..." Freddie took stock... "yet you talk of hearing Tommy's voice, I believe you.... caring and encouraging me. You both appear so assured and calm... at peace even..." Freddie paused aware of what he was expressing... "I'm not ungrateful, please don't think that and I'm not trying to upset you… I don't want to over step the mark or my welcome…"

Martha and Tommy looked at each other and then at Freddie

"You haven't overstepped the mark…"
"Or upset us" Martha injected

"It's taken time… and we have expressed thoughts of hatred, revenge… retribution…" declared Tommy

"But it's not what our kids want…!" Martha stated

"You say kids like its all of them…?" Quizzed Freddie
"Yes, it's all of them…" confirmed Martha

"Including Sophie…?" Freddie asked sternly

"Yes, including Sophie…" Martha stated

"And you accept that…?" again Freddie asked sternly

"Yes Freddie, as hard, as it is to accept…" Tommy paused… "and it's difficult to come to terms with… it's what Tommy wants, they want us to help others…."
Tommy looked at Martha

"And we have, with great deliberation, heated at times, arrived with an idea, a concept, where we believe we can help other parents who have lost their children…".
Martha concluded
"Early stages but we have started to put plans into place… a co-operative, a combined collaboration, with help from the others, all of us, helping each other…!"
Tommy resolved

The atmosphere changed….

"Is that a problem for you Freddie…?" Martha queried

"You say others, may I ask what others…?" Freddie asked

"Joan and Geoffrey…". Martha paused
"And Chloe and Fred…." Tommy concluded

"Sophies parents, Fred and Chloe…!"

"Yes…!" Martha stated assertively

"The Sophie that shot dead, murdered your son and his future wife on their wedding day…, she slaughtered my best mate… why I was standing next to him…" Freddie was in a state of high emotion

"Calm down son, I realise it's a lot to take in…" Tommy affirmed
"It was for us Freddie…  but it's what Tommy and Louise want…" Martha added

"Tommy asked me to take her out a few times, as much as I loved him and Louise … I never could take to Sophie, I always found her on the edge…" Freddie bit his lip…  "Through that bitch, I lost my best friend and brother and Louise who I admired so much, for making my man happy…To top it, she blew me away… screwed my mind…"

"We can understand your hatred Freddie, we were their…" consoled Martha
"We lived it, slept it…" Tommy added

"Then I come here and you share with me that you hear Tommy… I stay, thank you for that… you feed me, you give me hope…." Freddie paused…" and I find solace, belief… consolation… strength, courage, to understand and continue with my life…."

"You can son, you can do it…"
"You can Freddie… you could help us…"

"And now you tell me you're cosying up to the parents of the scum that murdered Tommy and Louise…
Fred was in the special services, SAS, and Chloe a military nurse…trained in action. He's a trained killer any kind of weapon and Chloe was, is, an expert shot in archery… have we ever wondered why Sophie was such a fruit loop….

"Enough son…" Tommy cut in on him
"Freddie your upset and angry, calm it …!" Martha said sternly

"They travel from country to country doing their task and then move on to pastures new… did they ever make true friends; did she ever have friends…one thing for sure… they made her who she was…Dead shot Sophie… that was her nickname wasn't it… well she proved that right… and they trained her…!"Freddie was sobbing…

"Freddie please son, we have thought about all of that … and for the sack of our kids wishes, we have to" Martha was trying to console him

"You thought about it, you know it….!" Freddie bit into his lip… "And now your bosom buddies... setting up together… how can you….!"

"In honour of Louise and Tommy…. And for what they want…" stated Tommy

"In honour…! Dishonour…! she murdered them, they taught her…! you may have to cosy up to them, but I don't… I hope they rot in…
"STOP….!" Yelled Martha…

"Your upset Freddie, angry and emotional, we can speak another time about this…" Commanded Tommy

"I'm so sorry, I so respected you both… but there is no honour here… I best leave…" Freddie headed for the door

"Freddie don't leave like this…" beseeched Martha

"Freddie this door is open for you, we need to sort your feelings out… help us to help other who are suffering. As Louise and Tommy want…" Tommy implored

"You forgot Sophie… I won't forget or forgive…" Freddie strode down the road.

# Chapter 26

"So, how have we progressed...!". Probed Joan...

"My, give the women some authority and a title.... and we have created a ..." Geoffrey was being jovial ... then realised what he was about to say...

"The word you are looking for Geoffrey is monster..." Chloe said with a wry smile on her face...

"Please don't walk on eggshells around us... starting, stopping, what you would normally say..." Fred hesitated and a glib smile came on his face... "we know there are words that could be quite antagonistic in connection or identifying as a label of Sophie..."

"Yes, indeed...!" Geoffrey pondered for a moment... "Joanie, my darling, a monster...!"

"Now we have ejected that elephant... not you Geoffrey...!" Joan adored Geoffrey and they bantered frivolously... "Out of the room, may we conclude on the existing agenda.!" she paused and started again in an air's breath... "So, before any other objectional outbursts... how have we progressed...?"

Paradoxically... there were smiles all round...

"I have approached two bereavement counsellors from the private hospital who are very keen to help out and ironically, both have lost a child, boy and girl... also, I have designed an itinerary, agenda and programme" stated Chloe

"I have spoken to two complementary therapists who would be willing to come and do treatments for anyone wishing to indulge, pamper, and I've emailed another three who I am waiting to hear back from..." stated Martha

"I have spoken to the local radio station who are prepared to do a piece and follow ups, free advertising...and approached a number of stores in town, who are willing to support..." stated Geoffrey

"I have got leaflets, flyers, business cards and a banner priced up, very competitive rates and quick turnaround from ordering...and a number of organisations who are willing to advertise them for us..." stated Fred

"I have spoken to the new vicar..." there were slight looks at each other, given what had happened to the vicar at Louise and Tommy's wedding ceremony... "and he is willing, as he understands the need, given what happened..." more glances... "to allow us to use the parish hall, Saturdays or and some week nights...". stated Tommy

"Wow... very impressed with what you have achieved in such a short period..." confirmed Joan

They all looked at Joan and smiled... then they all looked at Joan in some form of anticipation...

Joan was aware of their stare and smiled back....
"What...!" she declared.... Then smiled....
"I have checked out Trading Standards, Public Liability and Professional indemnity Insurance.
Any Therapist or Counsellor will hold their own insurance and therapy certification.

We will have the appropriate Insurance for us and the venue, in the event the venue does not have its own cover.

Health and Safety requirements…

Laws and Code of Conduct…

CBR, which is now DBS checks for anyone working within the set up……" Joan concluded

They all nodded in admiration and smiled…

"It's becoming a reality…" exclaimed Chloe… "congratulations well done all…!"

"And now…?" asked Geoffrey…

"And now the hard work begins…!" beamed Martha

"We will seek a day of commencement, with much pre advertising… putting your itinerary and agenda programme into practice Chloe…." Joan claimed

 Fred, Geoffrey and Tommy glanced at each other, grinned, then looked at their wives adoringly, with pride flowing from their eyes and hearts…

# Chapter 27

"Geoffrey I'm home dear where are you...?" Joan's dialog was panicky and frantic

"I'm in the lounge dearest... what's wrong...!" Geoffrey stood to meet his wife... he could hear the fragility in Joan's voice "Joan what's wrong...?"

Joan came through the door to meet Geoffrey and cradled herself into his arms... "Hold me...!"

"I have you my love, you are safe... come, sit with me..." Geoffrey cocooned Joan and manoeuvred his wife gently, protectively, to sit down on the settee, he continued to embrace her in his arms...

"Joan, can you confide in me, what is it, that distresses you...?" Geoffrey was calming and securing

"Geoffrey dear I need to speak to you off the record... breaking protocol and confidentiality..." Joan confided

"This is most serious and I feel a grave menace..." Geoffrey pondered... "there for, you have the right to break protocol and I am your confidant, confide with me, calmly, pragmatically..."

"Geoffrey, you know the case I've been working on... Well, the client I was defending, he was acquitted today... not guilty on all accounts..."

"Mmmm that comes as quite a surprise...!"

"For me too, I didn't think I had a cat in hells chance of getting him off, all I could do was to do my best... and maybe there would be some leniency..." Joan paused "I would have no reason to think why that might be, considering the evidence against him.."

"I thought, I've been following the case from within chambers..." Geoffrey paused "the evidence was over whelming and the CPS and the police had great confidence of a conviction and a long sentence..."

"Given what he was charged with... let's see, murder, conspiracy, conspiracy to pervert the course of justice, money laundering, protection, prostitution, drug's..." Joan held her chin in her palm and shook her head... "He is head of a serious crime syndicate..."

"And still he got off... on what grounds...?" Geoffrey quizzed... then continued...
"You must have given a great account of yourself and persuaded the jury to have reasonable doubt..." Geoffrey tried to appease his wife

"There were some minor loop holes, miniscule... to create a doubt, prove the evidence wrong, I was pissing against the wind Geoffrey..." Joan took a deep breath... their evidence was conclusive, I tried, to insinuate, pursue, proposal of reasonable doubt..." Joan sighed... "But not a sniff, their case was watertight..."

Geoffrey shook his head... "and it's this that has left you so unnerved...?" Geoffrey pondered... "there must be more... what has taken place Joan...?"

"After the judges summoning up and he was not impressed with the jury decision.
My client said... "Thank you...You are a beautiful, attractive, clever women and I'm attracted to you, I could certainly show you my gratitude..." "I nodded and

smiled, to be honest I was in a state of disbelief... I wasn't ready, for congratulations, celebrations...or him coming on to me...". Joan looked at the floor shaking her head... "He then said... "I'm sorry for the loss of your daughter, no one should lose their daughter like that... he then paused... as calm as a cucumber... he then said "on her wedding day.... No one should get away with that... it can be sorted..."
Geoffrey looked stunned...

"He got up and walked out, he looked back once and winked at me..."

"My God...!" intimidation in a court room...! This is repulsive, a custodian of the criminal service, an advocate of Law and Order...! In the Mother of all Justice, The Old Bailey...! being accosted and propositioned...!" Geoffrey exploded with disdain

"I went over to the club; we always use near the Bailey. I needed a stiff drink and compose myself..." Joan paused and tears formed in her eyes... "I was sitting alone looking out the window...contemplating what had taken place... then all of a sudden a hand touched my shoulder; his head was firm against mine...! his words were whispered..." Joan dithered... "But menacing... his words chilled me... he said... there's a lot of grateful people, for what you done... great work, you had the jury eating out of your hands.... He paused for no more than two seconds, then he said.... sorry about your daughter... it can be sorted... it should be avenged... and he was gone..."

Geoffrey stood firm... "The jury has been got at...."

"Geoffrey, I haven't finished... I didn't even drink my drink, I went straight to the underground car park, the one we always use… as I approached the car, I could see an envelope on my window screen under the wipers…". Joan again dallied…" I looked around the car, scrutinized it, thinking maybe someone had dented it and left contact detail…" Tears started to roll down Joan's eyes…

"Take your time Joanie… what materialised…?"

"I got into the car and opened the envelope…" Joan burst into tears sobbing…

"What was in the envelope Joan…?"

"A piece of white paper… with a mobile phone number scrawled on it… and the words underneath…
just say…YES…!"

"Did you inform the police…?" quizzed Geoffrey

"And say what, someone said thanks, twice and are grateful… misunderstanding, give me a phone number… they would say it would be claimed… I was being chatted up by an admirer… no name, no face…
so, inconclusive circumstantial...!" Joan was firm and direct…

"I concur…" Geoffrey said

"Besides they have history of our lives, they know which bar I drink in, they know where I park my car…they probably know where we live…!" Joan darted to the front room window… scrutinising the road…

There was silence…

"The jury has been nobbled…! obviously and they have the temerity to approach you and offer a service for revenge…" Geoffrey was furious… "This person as no moral fibre, no respect, in offering you retribution, without fear of recourse…!"

"We are, being offered the opportunity for retribution…!"

"And be in their pockets for ever more…" fumed Geoffrey.

# Chapter 28

"Fred luv, did you see the envelope on the table...?"
inquired Chloe
"No luv, does it look important..." responded Fred

"Why... won't you open it if it does...?" giggled Chloe
"No...! Not if it's my call up papers, re-enlisting
orders... I've done my time..." quipped Fred

"How strange you should say that...!"
"What...!"

"That's spooky Fred, are you gaining the gift...?"
chuckled Chloe
"What...!"

"I know we both hear, but are you now seeing the
future...?".
"What...!"

Cloe laughed out loud....

"Sorry luv... I'm playing with you..."
"Mmmm.... that sounds interesting..." Fred laughed

It had been a long time since there was spontaneous
humour and flirtation in the Miller households...

"It's weird, strange that you said from the service...!"
"Why...?"

"The letter has the regiment insignia on it..."
Fred looked perplexed and looked at Chloe "Addressed to
me or both of us...?"

"Take a look, what do you think, I'm your secretary…"
Chloe paused, Fred took a second take on Chloe… Chloe
smiled "to you, its addressed to you, with your rank…
Captain Miller…"

Fred stood to attention and saluted… Chloe mirrored his
every move…

"How puzzling…!" Fred stated
"Open it then…!" Ordered Chloe
"All right, slow down… remember your rank…" Fred
roared laughing
"Come on I'm intrigued…"

"Yea, so am …I" Fred scratched his head

Fred examined the letter very deliberately, pensively,
feeling every edge, running his hand over it … five
ounces… allowing his middle finger to follow the
contours of the envelope…. then laid it flat on the table.

Fred took a deep breath … placing his chin in his
hand…tapping his index finger onto his lips... staring at
the letter from all angles…

"Fred what's wrong...?" asked Chloe gently

"I don't know…" Fred paused…" it seems strange, I
wasn't expecting any correspondence from the unit…"

 "Do you suspect it's something sinister…?" queried
Chloe
Fred sighed…

"Should we call the squad…?"

Fred again gently runs his hand over the envelope, tentatively...

"Luv what's wrong...? What's concerning you...?
"No one has used my title outside of the service..." Fred pondered for a moment... "I was always a clandestine, no rank... a Mr."

"Fred I'm getting worried..." Chloe sounded anxious...
"Maybe I'm being over vigilant.... There's no obvious defects that stand out...!" Fred stated firmly

He placed a knife tip into the fold and slit the envelope open....

Chloe held her breath and pulled back....

"Are you mad... just a little bit too zealous..." Chloe sighed
"Not mad luv... just calculating..." affirmed Fred

"Calculating...?" quizzed Chloe

"Yes... if, by the slightest chance, if that was a bomb or toxic powders, it would not be addressed to Captain Miller... it would have been Mr. so, leaving me unsuspecting..." avowed Fred

"Calculating, and if, if by the slightest chance someone had indeed sent such a letter, perhaps they would have used reverse psychology and put Captain...." Chloe snarled

"If... If so my luv, we would not be having this conversation..." Fred shrugged his shoulders
"You are so dam blasé at times, Fred Miller... Mr... Capitan..."

"Shall we have a glass of wine…?" Fred smiled…
"Wine… I need a bloody brandy…" Chloe paused…
"What does the contents have to say…?"

"I'll have a brandy with you…"
"It's too early… but we can have a Jackson wassa…"
smiled Chloe

Fred opened the envelope and pulled the contents out….
Slowly…
It was a piece of cardboard, plain white with serrated
edges, he read it diligently… then paused, placing it back
on the table, plain side up.

Chloe hovered expectantly, waiting in anticipation… her
eyes flitted between Fred, then the card, then Fred

"Well…?" Chloe summoned impatiently…

"They are orders, encrypted orders, our presence of
services, have been requested…" Fred said solemnly

"Fred… why us…?" Chloe asked inquisitively

"We have been invited to a regimental reunion in
celebration of honour…" Fred stated proudly

"Celebration of honour … who's honour…!" exclaimed
Chloe
"In honour of us…!" Fred choked…and stood to attention
"we are the guests of honour in appreciation of
service…"
"Ho my god…what a lovely surprise" Chloe screeched…
"you bastard… you bastard…" she laughed out loud…
"you wound me right up… did you know that invitation
was coming…?".

"No…!" …. Fred took a breath… "it's as much a surprise to me … as it is to you…"

"Yet you still opened that envelope…" Chloe stared at Fred

There was a silence…

"We are going… aren't we…?" Chloe smiled

"Of course, it would be rude not to… and incredibly dishonourable… as it's in our honour…" Fred stood firm

"What an honour Fred…" Chloe glowed

"Undisputedly…!" Fred was so gratified

"Will we tell the others, Martha, Joan, Geoffrey, Tommy… of our invitation…?" Chloe reflected

"We have nothing to be ashamed of… yes we will, with our heads held high…" declared Fred.

# Chapter 29

"How exciting…" said Chloe jubilantly

"Yes, but extremely nerve racking…" stated Joan sombrely

"It's a mixture of elations, I'm ecstatic that the day as arrived, yet as nervous as a kitten…" confessed Martha in her very down to earth manner

"Summed up perfectly… quite exhilarating…!" pronounced Joan

"Yes, I am excited, bubbling up inside with anticipation, like a cat on a hot tin roof…" giggled Chloe

"It's a whole new responsibility…we are dealing with people who have experienced bereavement of their child…children…" stated Martha

"Emotions will be raw at times; we can expect that…" shared Joan

"Many emotions will rise up and hopefully they will be able to be released…" Chloe said caringly

"Hopefully their grief will be released and relinquished in time… their own time…" Martha paused, sniffled, then cleared her throat… "Yet their love and memories will still go on and live with them…forever…"

"Something we have experienced, so we are not living blind

"I remember when I joined the service as a nurse, I was nervous but excited, frightened yet determined to be there when I was needed...to do the best I can..." Chloe paused... "and this, what we are doing, is bringing all those feelings, emotions, desires, rising up inside of me. This isn't a battle or a war zone, we are entering into... it's no man's land, where we can come together with compassion..."

"For all the years I was at university learning law... I knew what I wanted to do... help those in need. To fight for their rights and I was determined, forthright, strong, blinkered to achieve my goal..." Joan stopped and looked at her two friends... "Then I remember the first day in court, my first case I was representing. I was like mush... terrified, falling apart at the seams...couldn't put two words together in my mind. How I won I'll never know... and this is how, this feels, from adversity we grow... stronger, to help those we can..."

"How do I follow those experiences..." Martha quipped with a hint of humour... "I can't, all I know as a mum and wife, all I wanted was to do my best for my family. When I trained to become a physiotherapist, I did it with heart and soul... when I saw the improvement in people's lives, wellbeing, quality of life... and I could help them achieve their wants and needs... I knew I found my second calling... this feels like the third..."

"We are not in a competition...!" Joan advocated smiling

"Care and Consideration should be our motto...!" Chloe chimed in smiling

"Come along ladies our journey has just begun...!" Martha bellowed smiling back at them

"Well, the hall is all set up…" Tommy said feeling satisfied
"Exactly how we were directed to do it…" Geoffrey stated proudly

"Ordered to do it…!" Fred specified jokingly

"Is the banner up outside and the posters on the notice boards…" interrogated Geoffrey

"Yep…!" Tommy affirmed

"Kitchen supplies in place…" Fred questioned

"Yep…!" Tommy affirmed

"Leaflets and paraphernalia on show on the tables..." Geoffrey quizzed

"Yep…!" Tommy affirmed

"A bit chilly outside is the central heating on…?" Geoffrey paused… "We don't want people coming in for help and comfort and walking into a chilly environment…"

"Yes, it is, the timer was set, there's a comforting warmth in here…" Fred affirmed

"Also, the chairs are in place in the discussion area, the therapist's couches are in the therapy designated area …" Tommy paused... took a breath … "counsellors chairs are in the counselling areas... quiet and set apart for privacy…" Tommy paused again… Geoffrey and Fred were in limbo …. Animated suspension… "Geoffrey you're the doorman, concierge, matradee…! … Fred, you and I are kitchen staff…serving assistants, gofers, cleaners and bottle washers…" Tommy laughed…" our pinafore and tea towels are waiting for us…!"

Geoffrey and Fred stared at Tommy…

"And the therapists will be arriving in 30 minutes…!" added Tommy

"Pip… pip… tally ho… all ready to go…" Geoffrey enthused

"All present and correct…." Fred teasingly saluted Geoffrey and Tommy

"All we have to do now is wait for the ladies…" Tommy stated

"Anyone for a cuppa…?" quizzed Fred

"A positive outcome… for all concerned…" Geoffrey enhanced

# Chapter 30

"Martha…!"

"Yes luv…" answered Martha

"I'm going to a spiritual church on Friday…! I've been checking them out and theres three I'm drawn to…" stated Tommy

"Ok…am I invited to join you…?" she enquired

"Do bears shit in the woods… pope kiss tarmac… of course… if you wanna come?"

"I want to come… do you think we will get a message from Tommy…" quizzed Martha

"Who knows… hope so…" Tommy smiled… hopefully

"Tommy don't forget, it's the birthday bash at the old haunt back home on Saturday, so don't go making any plans…" Martha stated

"Ok luv… so who's not having a drink…" asked Tommy

"We both are, we deserve it…" Martha pointed with her index finger up

"Right...!" retorted Tommy

"I've booked us into that swanky hotel on the corner, that used to be that old pub we used to go to for a late'n…" Smiled Martha

"That one that you got patted down when you went in, n if you weren't carrying a weapon, they'd give you something…" laughed Tommy

"Hahaha…" Martha laughed… "Slight exaggeration Tom… but yea proper rough, all the faces, in pecking order... yet rarely any trouble…!"

Saturday arrived…

"Wow…! this is proper nice… do you remember the old days…" asked Martha

"Yep rough as guts... but we felt safe... the old East End... now it's all high rise and posh wine bars..." Tommy turned his nose up...

Martha and Tommy arrived at the pub they all used to drink in...
They entered through the door .... "Martha you're here...!" all of the wives greeted....
"Tommy" ... "Tommy" ... "Tommy" ... his name was shouted by a number of his friends...

One of the ladies passed Martha a large scotch ...
Martha and Tommy looked at each other nodded and smiled...
Tommy made his way through the pub...
Seeing friend after friend

"Tom mate sorry about the news, let us know we will sort it..."
"Tommy, you know where here mate, just say so and it's done..."
"Tom... dog n bone... and it's put to rest..."
"Just say the word Tom..."

Time after time Tommy nodded, smiled... "Thanks... but..." And moved on

"Ah no problem... wink wink... we understand..." and all the guys winked and nodded at Tommy... understanding...

Tommy came to a group of six...

"Hello Tom, sorry about young Tommy... just let us know when Tom..."
"Give us the word mate..."

"Tom give the word… and we will take their eyes out with a cork screw…."
"And feed their bodies to the hogs…!"

"Tom, the travel agent can go to work mate… a trip can be organised…"
"Delivery service is sorted Tom…"
"Tom, one-way tickets can be arranged, to a very hot location… a furnace… by the bay…"
"There's a couple of building sites Tom, they have very deep foundations… that need filling… concrete overcoat…!"
"Tommy you only have to say the word…"
"Severe pain needs to be inflicted Tommy… give us the nod…!"
"Good bye from us… goodnight to them…!"

They all shook Tommy by the hand…

"Fellers, thanks, but let it go…" Tommy bit his lip… "I don't want nothing to happen… I don't want nothing done…"

"Ah… ok got the drift…"
"Course Tom…we understand…"
"Got yea… clever that …"
"Nothing to do with Tommy…"
"Right out of it…"
"Perfect alibi…"
"Sorted Tommy…"
"You know nothing…"

And they all howled with laughter

"No Fellers I mean it…!" Tommy affirmed

"Yea…" "Yea…" "Yea…"

"No sweat Tom…"
"No conversation took place…"
"Nothing will happen…"
And again, they all howled with laughter

Tommy smiled nodded and excused himself…

There was a gentleman sitting in the corner, in a three-piece suit… clean cut and sharp…
The font of all knowledge, an entrepreneur, who never did a day's work in his life… the designer, orchestrator of business development and enterprise. Putting lots of money into colleagues' pockets and being hugely rewarded himself…
As Tommy approached him, he stood up… early sixties… six foot two inches, fifteen stone, more fat on a butcher's apron…
Deep eyes… high cheek bones square chin… a face like granite. He held his hand out and Tommy took it, a double handed clasp….

"My hand, my heart Tom…" he said firmly
"Thanks Jack, rightbackatya…" Tommy replied

"Two large single malts and two pints of Guinness Mary… please" he ordered

Mary was the manager and never moved far from Jacks snug, as he called it… situated in a corner next to the bar, facing the door in one direction and stage in the other…

"Sit down son…" Jack motioned
"Thanks Jack…"
"So how are you and Martha, ah Martha the beautiful lady, she will be joining us presently…Jack stated politely
"Martha knows the routine Jack…" Tommy smiled

Jack took a puff from his cigarette and stumped it out, Jack never got a visit from the ol' bill he had obtained.... a special licence...

"So how are you dealing with the situation...?" Jack said quietly

"Day by day... we plod on day by day Jack..." Tommy said solemnly.

"Bad business what happened to young Tommy, on his wedding, and his bride... bad business, that boy was going somewhere..."

"Yes, it is... Yes, he was..." Tommy sniffed

"I understand the perpetrator of their passing also met her demise... but the family live on...? quizzed Jack

"Yea...!"

"I understand the parents of the perpetrator are again your neighbours and moved back...?" queried Jack

"Yes, they have Jack..."

"I understand they were in the services... he was... He Who Dares...!" Jack paused took a swig of his scotch...

"They can be served Tommy...!"

"I want it left Jack..." Tommy stated firmly

"We know you go to... normal work Tommy, but your old school son and your family were old school son..." Jack paused "and you are well respected... you have helped a lot of these out, with being on the periphery with your wise words, as for me..." Jack affirmed

"Please Jack, me and Martha want it left..." Tommy reiterated

"There's a lot of the team, substitutes that want to make the team and young guns... who are all making noises Tommy" Jack took a deep breath.... "They all respect

you, all they want is the word Tom…" Jack paused…
took a swig… "your losing respect Tommy…!"

"But I… me and Martha have self-respect…" Tommy
took a swig of his scotch… "and we're doing it for
Tommy…"
"For Tommy…?" Jack interrogated
"Yea, he's asked us to leave it alone… and help
others…!" Tommy stated
"You've heard voices…?" Jack stared coldly…
"Yes, both of us have…" Tommy said firmly
"You've got the gift, like your mother… bless her heart a
wonderful lady…" Jack declared joyfully

"Yea, by all accounts…" Tommy paused… "you knew
my mum had the gift…?"
"Yes, your mum was known as the messenger…" Jack
smiled… "My mum, my aunts, most of the old school
would go visit her… behind closed doors in the old days
they called it…"
"You believe in it, Jack…?"
"Of course, son… absofuckinglutely … I went to see her
many times… she told me… from above…" Jack took a
mouthful of his Guinness… "I think it was me grandad…
to call a bit of work off, because there was a talker in the
team…"
"Did you…?"
"Yea… well suspended it… until the grass…. Was less
green, quite a mouldy brown actually…" Jack smiled…
"And was propping up daisies…"
"So, what happens now… I'll tell them if you want…?"
Tommy enjoyed a mouthful of his Guinness and
smiled… "I'm not ashamed…!"
"And neither should you be… I'll put the word out
Tommy... to let it be…" Jack paused… "But some of
them are head strong…" Jack paused… "Young Tommy
was a working-class hero to some of them…" Jack took a

swig of his scotch… "And they feel cheated, deprived if they don't get vengeance…"

Tommy pondered... that's no reassurance…

"We feel cheated Jack…!" Tommy's eyes welled up…
"But we are doing what Tommy wants…"
"Two large single malts and two Guinness's please Mary…" Jack requested
"I'll get them Mary and send one round to Martha please…" Tommy interjected

"So, what's the plan Tom…?"

"We, and you aren't gonna like this, Louise's parents..."
Tommy started
"Ah the Judge and QC… she did a good job recently…!"
Jack cut in
"Is their nothing you don't know…?" Tommy smiled
"It pays to know Tommy…! Jack responded... "carry on…"

"And Sophie's parents are setting up a bereavement group, to help grieving parents who have lost their kids… and kids have lost possibly brothers and sisters…"
Tommy felt proud when he made that statement

"A noble sentiment… why the killers kin… that's macabre …. "Jack stared at Tommy

# Chapter 31

"Martha" … "Martha" … "Martha" … her name echoed around the pub…. People saying hello…
"Martha's here…."
"About bleeding time…!"
"Didn't think you was coming…!"
"Been having a bit of ours your father…darling…!"

She stood with a group of wives and partners…
All enjoying a drink…

"How are you coping…?"
"So sorry about the loss of Tommy…"
"How are you dear….?"
"Oh Martha… you poor dear…"
"Martha if there is anything I can do…"

Martha accepted all of the platitudes with dignity…
nodding and smiling
Although she was breaking up inside…

"Thank you, we are taking day by day…" Martha said sincerely

"Don't let anyone tell you in time Martha…it gets better… it doesn't…!"
"Time is a great healer, is another favourite…"
"Pull yourself together now…"
"Oh, it's been long enough…"
"You have to get on with your life…!"

"Ladies, my dear friends…" Martha paused… "trust me… I've heard every one of them… many times…"
"How did you react Martha…?"

"I… I, bit my lip… I clenched my fist…" Martha sipped at her scotch and pondered for a second or three… "and I wanted to smash their faces in… to break their jaw…!"

"I bet you did…"

"It wouldn't have taken a lot to pick a bar up and bury into their skulls…" Martha shared

"Did you…?"

"No… I looked at them with the contempt they deserve… I felt sorry for them really…" Martha sipped at her scotch… "Emotionless vessels with no compassion or brain waves to make a valid point…!"

"You always had that inner strength Martha…"

"If you can't say something with real feeling of sympathy…" Martha took a mouthful… "then its best to say nothing…!"

"Smile and nod…"

"Yea…" "yea…" "yea...". was the collective response…

Martha stood at the bar talking to her close friends…

"Was, there any signs…?"

"No… none..."

"Was she insane…?"

"Not that we were aware of …" Martha paused…

"although she was locked up in a mental hospital…"

"How are you coping Martha, in respect of what are you doing to keep going…?"

"We never not talk about Tommy…" Martha stated

"It would have broken me…"

"Yes, it did, but the love Tom and I have for each other and the love we have for Tommy" Martha paused and took a mouthful of scotch… "will never die and it keeps us going… it keeps the memory of Tommy going…"

"That takes some strength..."

"Yes, we are strong…"

"You and Tommy always were…"

"Lovely boy young Tommy…"

There was an eerie silence, only a minute or two…

"Martha is it true the parents of … of…"
"Her name's Sophie…" Martha said as a matter of fact…
"How are you so calm…?"
"Is it true they have moved back into their house, as your now neighbours?"

"Yes...!"

"That takes some temerity…
What does that mean…?"
"Gall…!"
"Audacity…!"
"Nerve…!"
"Flaming nerve…!"
"Bloody cheek…!"
"Boldness…!"

Martha waited until the name game was concluded…

"I think they have got some fucking balls and they are taking the piss…!" One of the friends spouted out

"Martha, you know if you want to inflict damage in a physical way…" the lady looked around… "you only have to say…!"
"To be honest Martha, we obviously speak and all of our men are only waiting for the right word..."
"Any inclination Martha…"
"Obviously, you and Tommy would be sunning yourselves… in the Canaries or somewhere far away…"
"You aren't going to let them get away with it…?
"Are you Martha…?"

"She may have been the culprit… but the family live on…!"
"And had the front to move back in… I'd burn their fucking house to the ground…!"
"With them in it…!"
"Break their fucking legs first, so they can't escape…!"

The atmosphere was getting pithy… and hostile….

Martha ordered a round of drinks… for the group… the same time as she received a drink from Tommy…

"Cheers to the sweet smell of revenge being inflicted …!" one of the ladies raised her glass and they all charged their glasses…

Martha did not indulge…

"Martha are you ok…?"
"Are we being to insensitive…?"
"It makes my blood boil…!"
"It makes my piss boil…!"
"Sorry are we being too obvious…"
"Have you already got a plot growing…?"
"Have seeds been sown Martha…?"
"Has a plot been hatched Martha…?"
"Has Tommy organised a little retribution Martha…?"

Martha took a mouthful of scotch… shook her head… then took another mouthful….

"You're keeping it close to your chest dear aren't you…?"
"Your being very secretive…
"Clever is the term …."

Impromptu: "We… Tommy and I asked them to move back in to their house… as you say our neighbours…" … Martha paused… "we are not seeking revenge… nothing is planned… no retribution…"

"What…?"
"Why not…?"
"Martha you cannot be serious…!"
"Martha, she killed your Tommy and you're not going to have revenge on the family…!"

 Martha shot a look across her bowl…

"Sorry…"

"There has been enough violence… so we seek revenge… they seek revenge… and so it continues... until no one is left… No…!" Martha paused and took a large gulp of scotch… "It stops now…!"

"Clever… very clever… keep your friends close…draw your enemies closer… what a wonderful alibi… why would you seek revenge; towards people you forgave… I raise my glass to you and Tommy…" and the lady winked at Martha…

"No…! We are doing it for Tommy…" Martha emphasised
"For Tommy…?" the lady queried…
"Yes, we have heard Tommy's voice asking us to forgive them and help others…"
"You and Tommy have the gift, like Tommy's mum...?"
"Yea, I guess so..." replied Martha… "Did you know Tommy's mum…?"
"Jack and I used to visit her… as did Jacks mum and family…"
"So, you believe…?"

"Aww, I think we all do dear… it just frightens some and they don't want to admit it…"

"I think I should go around and meet up with Tommy and Jack…" Martha shared
"I'll come with you dear…" the lady said…

As they excused themselves from the group… a few murmurs went up…

"Martha it's only a phone call away…."

Martha looked back, smiled and nodded….

They edged their way through the crowded bar…

# Chapter 32

"Hello Martha..." ... "Mrs..." ... "Martha..." ..."
Mrs..." ... "Martha..." ... "Mrs..." ... "Martha..." ...
"Mrs..." all of the men acknowledged and nodded in
respect...

"Tommy..." Martha kissed Tommy.... "Jack..." Martha
learnt forward and kissed Jack on the cheeks...
Jack greeted Martha... "Are... here you are Martha...
such a beautiful lady... I've been having a very
interesting conversation with your Tommy...". Jack
paused... "Mary please... a round of drinks here
please..."

Mary was on hand...

Tommy stood up to greet Martha and the lady...

"Hello..." Tommy held out his hand...

"So, you two have met..." pointing to Martha and the
lady... "and you two haven't..." pointing to Tommy and
the lady..." Jack paused... "Let me introduce you, this is
Martha and Tommy Jackson... but you know that,
because I've told you about them..." Jack smiled... "and
this beautiful lady... is Mrs Jackson my wife... Glenda"

"Your wife...? Mrs Glenda Jackson...?" stated Tommy
startled...
"Mrs Glenda Jackson...?" said Martha also startled...

"Yes, she seldom comes out... to mix..." Jack paused
took a mouthful of Guinness... "she never gets
involved... but my rock... she wanted to come tonight...
so consider yourself... honoured..."

"I never knew you was married Jack…" assured Tommy
"Mrs Glenda Jackson…?" sort of queried Martha
"I never knew your surname was Jackson… Jack…"
enquired Tommy

"Everyone calls me uncle Jack… because I'm everyone's
uncle…." Jack laughed

"Are we sort of related…?" quizzed Tommy
"Yes son… we are…" Jack replied

There was silence…

"So, my darling… you and Martha have become
acquainted…?"
"Yes Jack, we have… charming and very resourceful
under pressure…" she smiled
"Have you discussed young Tommy…?"
"Yes Jack…!"
"Have you discussed revenge…?"
"Yes jack…"
"Have you discussed…" Jack paused…
The spirit story of young Tommy talking to them and not
seeking revenge…" Glenda paused "and wanting to help
others…?"
"Yes… and your thoughts Glenda…?"

Martha and Tommy looked at each other bemused… and
then at Glenda and Jack

"It's plausible… Tommy as the gift of his mother… as
does Martha…" Glenda paused…. "As do I…
It's either the truth…" Glenda pondered… took a
mouthful of scotch… smiled…
They all waited with baited breath…...

"Or it's a unique ruse… a covert deception…" Glenda paused took a mighty swig… smiled broadly….
"An open disguise… a masquerade of mammoth proportion… shockingly wonderful…!"

As Martha and Tommy left the pub, a taxi was waiting for them… Tommy opened the door and let Martha get in… From the darkness a shadow appeared and moved menacingly forward… Tommy turned….
The figure and Tommy shook hands and words were exchanged….

# Chapter 33

Chloe, Martha and Joan entered the hall...

"Oh my... it looks very spic and span...!" Chloe exclaimed
"Doesn't it just..." Martha voiced
"So professional..." Joan paused.... "Nicely set out....!"

"As ordered Commander..." laughed Fred...
"Every detail exact..." Geoffrey added
"Instructions followed to the letter..." Tommy stated...

"Excellent...!" Chloe nodded with approval
"The therapists and counsellors are right behind us..." Martha advised
"We will escort them to their areas..." Joan informed them

"Come in... please come in..." Geoffrey welcomed them
"Great to see you...." Tommy nodded
"Thanks for coming..." Fred said sincerely

"You're welcome..."
"Anything to help such a worthy cause..."
"Please point us in the right direction..."
"Nicely set up..."
"Lots of space for privacy..."
"Very professionally thought out... congratulations..."

"This is the discussion area with seating... for our initial chats..." Chloe advised and pointed smiling
"Reiki, Indian head, Reflexology..." Martha paused...that area is over here, please join me..." Martha pointed and led the way... "you each have an allocated space for privacy. Enough room as you asked for, to put

up your couches and chairs without encroaching on each other's space… is it adequate…?"
"Counselling area for one to one or couples are over here…" Joan led the three Counsellors to the allocated area… "with lots of room for privacy…Ok…?"

"Yes, it's great…"
"Excellent…"

Lots of nodding of approval….

Each of the Therapists and Counsellors inspected their space and set about putting together their own area of expertise…

"So now we wait…!" Joan looked at everyone individually… with a smile on her face…
"We could do no more, than that we have…" Geoffrey said proudly

And at that point….

So, Parents…Mum, Dad, Parents with children, started to walk through the door… 1, 2, 4, 6, 7, 10… 11

On edge, a little apprehensive… some maybe even scared, what did they know, that was waiting for them…
How would they be greeted…
How would they be helped…
How could they be helped…
"Please come in… tea, coffee, soft drinks… are available… right over there at the counter…" Advised Geoffrey… with a welcoming smile…

Chloe, Joan and Martha approached and welcomed each and every person…

They introduced themselves and invited the visitors to sit down…. Passing out leaflets to each…

"We are here to share our losses …"
"To help each other…"
"No one is here to judge…"
"Please feel freely to speak…"
"We are here to listen…"

These statements were shared by the counsellors….

"It may help if our hosts share their stories… to start…"

"We would like to share our stories with you…"
"This may help you to feel comfortable in sharing yours…"
"You may find what we are going to share, quite a shock…."

All the visitors sat in the chairs and nodded in approval…

"I had a son… who…." Martha told the story of Tommy…
"I had a daughter… who…" Joan told the story of Louise…
"I also had a daughter… who…" Chloe told the story of Sophie…

The audience of bereaved parents and siblings sat in awe and shock…

One of the parents asked… "You have each individually told us of your child's journey, aspirations for their future, their love for each other…." She paused… "and the betrayal of that love… and… I'm sorry I can't put it into words the finale at the end… of how they died…"

Another said "I'm amazed, in admiration... that you can share this with us...!"

"I'm shocked... that considering the events..." One of the dad's said... "you are able to work together...!"

 "I don't think I could do what you are doing as a team..."

"It's mind blowing what you have told us..."

"We understand that..." Martha shared... Chloe and Joan nodded in agreement... "and to begin with it was hard for us to come to terms and be able to set this up to help others..."

There was a silence...

And then one parent shared only a little... but a start...
Then another...
Then another...

"If anyone would like to have a complementary therapy...please feel free..." offered one of the counsellors

"Or we can offer you one to one... or one to family group..." Stated one of the others...

# Chapter 34

Friday Evening....

"Tommy I'm so anxious, nervous..." admitted Martha...
"To be honest, me to..." Tommy countered...

They walked into the spiritual church... in anticipation...

"Come in please, your most welcome..."
"Thank you..." said Martha
"Is it your first time...?"
"Yes... is it that obvious..." shared Tommy
"Please take a seat..."

There were a few regulars... and volunteers, chatting and laughing... a very warm atmosphere...

More and more people came in... couples, singular ladies, men on their own... friends...

The Chairperson welcomed everyone and read the notices... then introduced the Medium....

The Medium said a few words "should I come to you...I would like you to respond" pause...
"Please speak up... spirit need to hear your voice.... yes... no... not sure... I can go back and ask for more information..." a pause... "smiles are good..."

The Medium went to a number of those who were attending... direct... individual... giving evidence of life after life... most of the people could take what was given as a message... some couldn't... some bit's...

"I'd like to come to you Sir…" pointing at Tommy….
"Are you two together, as in a couple…?"
"Thank you… Yes, we are…"

"I have a young man… six feet… ish… don't shoot me
for an inch or two…" the medium pondered… "I'm sorry
that was inappropriate…" a pause…" a very athletic
young man around 18/19 in age… can you take him…?"
"Yes…" said Tommy nodding his head... Martha
nodded…
"He is saying how much he loves you…"
"We love him…" they both said with crooked broken
voices…
"He is saying he knows…" a pause… "he is bouncing a
football… he played football, he was good… a
professional…!"
"Yes…!"
"I have a name of Tommy being shouted… please does
that mean anything to you…"
"He is Tommy…" Tommy choked…  "I am Tommy…"
"He is your son… he is saying mum and dad… I love you
so much…." a pause… "who is Martha…sorry does
Martha mean anything to you…?"
"I am Martha and yes Tommy is our son…"

Both Martha and Tommy had tears rolling down their
cheeks...

"Would you like me to stop…?" the Medium asked
"NO…!" they both said emphatically

"I don't know how to say this…" the Medium was aware
of a given responsibility he has to the congregation
"Just say it…" stated Tommy… "please…!"
"He passed over on a very special day for all of you…in
such awful circumstances" the Medium held his head…

"I have such a pain in my head…" he paused "now it's gone…"

"I know what happened and I'm not prepared to share that in an open forum…" he continued….
"I have a young lady coming in… in such a beautiful dress…" a pause… "she is standing very close to Tommy…" a pause… "she is saying she loves you… can you tell mum and dad I love them…"
"We love you… yes, we will pass the message on…" said Martha…

"This should never have happened; this should never have happened… there is so much love between them… and both of you… so much love…!" the Medium said…"
I can feel it…!"
"Yes…!" Martha and Tommy nodded…

"There is another young lady just standing back… oh…oh…! do you want to accept her….?"
"Yes…! we will…" still both having tears rolling down their cheeks…

You could hear a pin drop in the church… not a murmur…

"She is saying she is sorry… so sorry for what she did…". The Medium paused… "she is standing back… Sophie….! Can you take Sophie…? she is saying sorry… I do love you…" He paused… "please tell mum and dad…. I'm sorry …I love them …"
"We know…!" said Martha… "we can take that and we will pass the message on…."
"Louise… I have Louise…" he paused… "can you take Louise…?"
"That is the young lady standing close to Tommy…" Tommy stated sobbing…

"They are saying forgive… please forgive… help others…" a pause… "can you take that…?"

"Yes…! … we understand that" they said in unison… wiping their eyes…

"They won't let me finish…"

"They are saying it's going to be hard… times will get tough…" the Medium paused… "Very tough, testing, but please… Don't give up, don't give up on what we asked you to do… don't be put off …."

"We appreciate that… we won't…" Tommy confirmed

"Don't walk away… They are saying…"

"Are you a Medium Sir … may I ask…?"
"No…!"
"You should be up here…" a pause…
 "Are you a Healer…?"
 "No…!"
"You are…! … have you ever thought about training in becoming a healer…?"
"No…!"
"I've got news for you…" the Medium smiled
"What….?" asked Tommy
"If they want you… you will work for spirit… perhaps you could consider it…" said the Medium
"Maybe… although I can't see it…!" said Tommy
"I can…" and he pointed to his side… "so can Tommy… he is smiling…" … a pause… "Tommy… may I call you Tommy…?"
"Of course, you can…" Tommy smiled
"Tommy, I believe from what I'm being told… and your Tommy is nodding…. it's your calling…"

"And now I must finish…" pause…
"No, one last thing… you must both know, that both
Tommy and Louise…" a longer pause… "they both are
and look in their prime… be aware of that fact… both
look as they did on the morning of their wedding
day…beautiful and handsome…." a pause and big
breath… "I'm so sorry for you, for them… in what
happened… and I think you are special people, in
accepting…. the other young lady… very special…"

There was silence…….

"Now I must end…."
"God bless…"

The chair person and the congregation clapped… as did
Martha and Tommy…

The Medium then closed the service with a closing
prayer….

They stayed behind for a cup of coffee… as did many
others including, the Medium…

Inevitably Martha, Tommy and the Medium started to
talk….

"To be honest with you, I can't recall what I say… its
spirit giving the message, I'm just the vehicle that passes
it on…"
"How do I become a healer…?" asked Tommy…
"You can train with one of the associations... recognised
Healing groups… I believe this church has recognised
teachers… ask one of the people who runs the
church…they will help you…." the Medium paused…
"it's your calling…".

"Thank you… I will…" Tommy smiled

"Thank you for the message…" Martha smiled

# Chapter 35

Tommy was pointed into the right direction by one of the church committee, toward the healing teacher…

"Hi my names Tommy Jackson… I would like to learn about spiritual healing and if possible, train to become a recognised healer…" Tommy paused and took a deep breath…. "Apparently, it's my calling…"
"Hi Tommy, yes I heard the message that you got… and it would be rude to ignore such a profound message…" he smiled…

The healing teacher was a very down to earth bloke, who didn't put himself on a peddle stool…

"How did you get into spiritual healing…?" Asked Tommy who was curious…
"Same as you, something happened in my life, I was drawn to come to a Spiritual Church, a Church isn't the obvious expectation... a Church can be in a hall… Church is the people, a gathering of people, an assembly of people…" He paused…" sorry I'm teaching…!" and paused again…
"No, it's interesting…!" Tommy cut in… "please continue…"
"And like you I got a message that I should be doing healing… it's my calling, as it is yours…" He paused…
"I was fortunate to have had a very special Teacher… and eventually here I am now… Teaching…"

"How do I start…?" asked Tommy
"It would be nice if you attended the Church…" He paused… "We do teach on Tuesday night…and after the message you got… I'd say…. please join us…"

"When do I start…?" Tommy knew, a gut feeling, he had found his Teacher… although he would attend other Churches to explore…

"Tommy… Tuesday sounds good…!" He laughed and winked… "I would advise you… please attend other Churches for experience…!"

Tommy laughed… "Yea Tuesday sounds good…!"

They shook hands… warmly…

# Chapter 36

"Fred will you be wearing your formal dress uniform…"
Chloe looked over at him… "or a civvy suit…?"
"It's a Regimental Honouring… a celebration Chloe….
Of us…" Fred stood upright and swallowed hard…
"Formal uniform please…and you my love… what shall
you be wearing…?"

"I've picked a three-quarter length evening dress with
shawl…" Chloe smiled…
"I'm sure we will do each other proud…" Fred smiled.

They had booked into an hotel near to HQ where the
function was being held…
Chloe had packed enough clothes for a week…

"Come on then if we leave now, we can have a light
lunch and then have a rest, it will be a long night…"
stated Fred…
"Ok, I'm ready, all packed…" said Chloe…
Fred took a second look, "yea I can see…" he smiled

As they left the house and packed the car…. Martha and
Tommy, Joan and Geoffrey joined them…

"Have a great time…" Joan smiled
"Don't drink too much…" Geoffrey… wishing the
ground had opened up…
"Don't do anything we wouldn't…!" Tommy winked
"Don't get drunk and get shanghaied into resigning…"
Martha giggled

Martha Tommy Joan and Geoffrey all saluted as Chloe
and Fred got into their car and drove off….

"Do you think everything has been put to bed Fred…?"
"It's a very precarious situation dear… who knows what lays dormant beneath the surface…" Fred chose his words carefully…
"Everything seems to be so convivial…. now…" Chloe said softly…
"Yes, and let's hope that it remains the status quo…"

They had a pleasant drive and arrived at the hotel… in time to book in…
They spent the afternoon preparing and pruning…. Slick, classy and elegant….

"Are you ready madam…?" Fred stood to attention… looking very dapper…
"I am indeed Sir…" Chloe responded…
"Our carriage awaits…!" Fred pronounced

Their taxi took them to HQ…
The main dining hall, in the main building… had been decorated to perfection…

Chloe and Fred entered the hall and were welcomed by senior officers…

The PMC announced Fred and Chloe…
"Captain Miller and Mrs Miller…"

"Welcome Captain…" …. Mrs Miller…" and Chloe's hand was kissed a number of times…
By High-Ranking Officers…

Fred manoeuvred his way over to his squad in the regiment ….

"Hello lads… you know the wife…" Fred said

"Yea, hello Mrs. Miller…"
"Hi Mrs. Miller…"
"Mam…"
"Madam…"
This went on and they all smiled touching their forehead
with their index finger…
A round of drinks was ordered…

"Would your good lady like to retire to the ladies
table…"
Chloe didn't need asking… "I know the way… go and
play, boys will be boys… just as well I know you all…
and your better halves…" Chloe smiled and nodded her
head …

"Chloe come on sit down…"
"How are you dear…?"
"I'm so sorry… poor Sophie…"
"How are you and Fred coping…?"
"You always coped under pressure Chloe…!"
"Not all that meets the eye Chloe…!"

"I really appreciate your friendships and your concerns…
Fred and I are dealing with it…" Chloe paused… and
took a mouthful of her brandy… "with help from
above…"

"You have turned to God…?"
"Or spirit dear…!"

Chloe smiled and took another mouthful…

"How are you Cap…?" Fred's Sergeant enquired
"Captain…. you know we are all on standby…" one of
his men stated
"Something went on skip…" another quantified

"On that holiday something took place… something happened for Sophie to retaliate…

"We have all had a conflab boss… you, we, can't let this go…"

"Honour of Sophie Sir…"

"Gentlemen I respect you all, wrong time, wrong place…" Fred surveyed them all, one by one with his eyes… "I will take into consideration what you have said…"

The Mess Sergeant announced; "The Ladies and Gentlemen, Distinguished Guests…. Dinner will be served…. kindly take your seat's..."

"But skip…" one of Fred's men remonstrated

Fred's Sergeant immediately intervened "Squad… Attention…!"

The men fell in…

"This is exquisite…" Fred sighed
"The food is absolutely amazing…" Martha enthused…
"I'm puffed…" Fred confessed
"Blotted… good job this dress wasn't tight…" laughed Chloe

The CO of the regiment and camp stood up… silence prevailed

"This Mess Dinner was ordered, by me and my peers… who shall remain anonymous…" He paused… "as you are. In order to honour one of our own!" He paused… "For service above and beyond his call of duty. To show homage for a man, a soldier, a special soldier… a covert soldier. Who put his life on the line… who stood in the

174

line of fire…! Who infiltrated extremist groups, placing his life in extreme jeopardy...!
In fear of being caught, interrogated and tortured…killed… many, many times…For Freedom… for Democracy… For his Queen and Country…!
Honoured guests I ask you to stand and raise your glass to Captain Fred Miller…"

To a soul everyone stood up… "Captain Fred Miller…!"

Fred was awarded a medal….

And a big cheer went up….

Fred saluted back….

The CO stood up again…

Silence prevailed

"I have an additional award to present. In honour of service beyond the call of duty, in the fiercest environment's… He paused… again putting life and limb on the line. Being prepared to go where others not necessarily want to. Taking care of, looking after, saving lives. He paused… Helping to keep our soldiers fit. More than all of that… much more…". He raised his glass…. and paused…………

To a soul everyone stood up….

"Our very own Florence Nightingale… Mrs. Chloe Miller … for putting up with Captain Fred Miller…!"

"Chloe Miller…" every Officer, including Fred, Soldiers and Soldiers wives… stood to attention and saluted….

Chloe blushed....

Then a massive cheer went up....

# Chapter 37

The ladies congregated around the table…

"Chloe what are you going to do about Sophie…?"
"Something took place to drive Sophie to react the way she did…!"
"Something happened Chloe, you have to sort these people out…!"
"If you don't want Fred to know… we can sort it…!"
"It's all connected to that holiday… what took place…?"
"We can put an operation underway … to be honest it already is … just the word…!"
"We would never let the enemy get away with this Chloe…?"
"Their parents must be held responsible… Those two are the product of their parent…!"
"Chloe, you want these people taken out… don't you… yes…?"

"Fred and I have no evidence anything untoward went on… conjecture yes. But no proof…
We cannot allow you to take this action…" Chloe paused… "We have heard from Sophie… and she wants us to help others, who have experienced their own children's loss…"

"What…?"
"You have heard from Sophie… as from Spirit…?"
"Yes…!" declared Chloe
"Ahh got it…!"
"Go to work at close quarters…"
"Clever… the covert operator, has put an operation into practice…!"
"NO…! we don't want revenge…" Chloe pleaded

"Sure...!" "Sure...!" "Sure...!"
"If anything happens, how could it be you... too obvious..."
"Clever...!"
The ladies all agreed...

"We are working together with the other families to help people in our position..." Chloe emphasised

"We understand ..."
"Cryptic..."
"All clear and understood..."
"You're all clear... out of the frame..."

"Please we really don't want anything to happen... we just want to get on..." Chloe beseeched

"Of course, Chloe" ... "We understand..." "We totally understand..." "Everything will turn out ok..."

"Leave it with us..."

"Captain... whatever happened, the truth has been covered up... someone has to be held responsible...!"
"We know where they go, we know what they do...!"
"Boss we can take them out, one foul swoop... gone...?"
"Cap... you have just received a medal for bravery and honour... what about Sophie's honour..."
"We saw Sophie grow up... let us do our job...?"
"No one will ever know...!"
"Pain must be inflicted... Sophie was one of our own...!"
"Don't you want revenge Captain...?"

"What you are suggesting is murder... that gentlemen, is unlawful, it is, against the Law of the Country we served to protect..." Fred took a deep breath and a mouthful of his brandy... "I honour and respect my Medal... I honour and respect my Sophie… I have no proof; I have no evidence. I do not condone what Sophie did…"

"We can get you the evidence, those two would have confided in their parents… we can screw the evidence out of them…!"

"I cannot condone that…" Fred paused and took a mouthful… "we have heard from Sophie and she wants us to work with the other parents, in helping others who find themselves in the same position as us… and that is what we are going to do….!"

"Heard from Sophie…!"
"Like you mean heard her voice Cap…?"
"Yes….!" Stated Fred

They all stood nodding their heads…

"Heard from Sophie…"
"Keeping close…"
"Working together…"

They all nodded…


"We will obey orders Captain…"
"We will obey the Laws of our Country… Sir"

"Any covert operations, that may take place… will remain covert…"

 They stood to attention and saluted Fred…

Fred stood to attention… took their salute… and saluted back….

As Chloe and Fred were leaving… A tall lean man came up to Fred… Fred greeted him…

"Fred you only have to say the word… I'll slip into both houses, five minutes…tap tap… tap tap… slip out, not seen…job done…"
"Leaving us in the frame…!" Fred stated…
"No, I'll come into you… tap one into your pillow and tap one into your shoulder… we have a tussle, I drop the piece and I have it away… you frightened me off… no prints on the gun… it's clean, never been used…"
"What about Chloe…?" interrogated Fred
"Fred… You want me to tap tap Chloe…!"
"No…! she would be laying there…!" Fred said exasperated
"One tap… flesh wound into her arm… she won't know a thing… looks convincing… job done…!"

Fred got into the taxi… next to Chloe….

"No…! leave it…" Fred touched his forehead with his finger…. And shut the door….

# Chapter 38

"It's so difficult…!" one of the parents shared… "we, you, I should imagine…" The lady paused… "we never expected to be laying to rest, my child, never before my life time was over…"

"No, we never, never crossed our minds that we would be burying our daughter, at such a young age…"

"Our daughter was in her prime, nineteen years old... At University, a beautiful young lady… struck down…!" the mum had tears in her eyes... tears cascading down her cheeks…" to have to witness the curtains closing at her cremation…" … she wiped her face… "It broke my heart…!"

"It doesn't seem right that a young life… with no life experience, no life as such, to have experienced… cut short… it's so wrong…!"

"Why…? Why… does this happen…?"

"It's heart breaking to be burying your own child…."

"At such young ages to be struck down with such cruel diseases…" A dad spoke up… "if they have to take someone…" He paused… wiping tears from his face… "why didn't they take me, at least I've lived some…"

"My son was taken by some gutless coward with a knife….!" His dad stood up… "I'd rip his heart out if I get hold of him…!"

"My baby…!" the mum placed her head in her hands… "seventeen years young… committed suicide… depression… he could have spoken to us…" she paused… "but he never… he bottled it up inside… why didn't he speak to us….!"

"One doesn't expect… when you give birth to your child… you love them… you nurture them… you think you are there to protect them…" The mums voice chocked… "the next thing you're arranging the funeral…"

"You never expect to be burying your own child, you bring them into this world, providing life, to see us off…!" the dad paused… "and then we experience their death…!" He sobbed

"My daughter got in with the wrong crowd, wrong boyfriend… we didn't know, we saw changes and thought it was her growing up, hormones… having tantrums…!" The mum wept… her husband put his arm around her, consoling her the best he could… "she died of a drug over dose… we didn't know….!"

"That's quite ironic…" the dad started… "my son got webbed up with the wrong crowd, wrong girlfriend, she used him, got him on drugs… broke his heart…" He paused… grimaced… "he topped himself… overdosed…!"

"My son and daughter, twins…were having a night out with friends… celebrating their eighteenth birthday…!" the dad gritted his teeth… his wife held his hand… "they were mowed down by a drunk driver… also eighteen…!"

"My daughter was bullied at school, we didn't have the money to buy her the posh, fashionable clothes, she was smart… she was clean… but didn't wear the right clothes…!" The mum clenched her fist… "to be in with the in crowd…." Her husband swallowed hard and held her clenched fist… "she hung herself…. She was Fourteen….!"

"My baby passed over at one month…" The mum wept… her husband wept….
"My twins passed within a week of each other … ten weeks old…." The mum slumped and her partner cradled her in his arms…

"My son was bullied at work… his first job… because he wasn't as strong as the others… he cut his wrists... and bled to death…!"

They shared… they all shared… their loss, their grief, their bereavement…

The Counsellors listened…

The Therapists listened…

"Some of us can say we understand… because we have had the same loss, our children passed away…" One of the Counsellors shared…. "But we cannot say we know how you feel… every loss, is the individual loss, of those who have lost…" … she paused… and said softly… "we can be here and share with you…!"

"We don't have the answers… none of us do…" the other Counsellor paused… "I have never had such sorrow in my life… I can only listen and share with you, if you allow me… your loss…"

"Would anyone like to have a private consultation…" enquired one of the Counsellors…

A few of the mums and dads took advantage of the offer…

"Would anyone like to have some Reiki…? Indian head…? Reflexology…? One of the Therapist enquired...

"The Therapy won't take away your grief... your grieving… your loss…" The Therapist paused…" but they can help you… to relax you… des-stress you…re-balance you…re-energise you…" she paused… "if nothing more… it's a little bit of you time… some solace…"

A few of the mums took the chance to experience the different treatments… and enjoyed their time, their space… the peace… even if only for the moment….

"None of the men are taking up the offer of the Complementary Therapies… we need a male volunteer...!" stated Martha… agreed…!" echoed Joan and Chloe

Fred, Geoffrey and Tommy looked at each other…

"You're interested in all that Thomas…!" pushed Geoffrey…
"Yes, Tommy you have been talking, all about that sort of business…!" Fred added…

Both taking a step backwards….

"Our Hero's…!" Joan ridiculed
"On the front line…!" Chloe derided
"What are you suggesting… Geoffrey defended…
"What...!" Fred said innocently…

"Tommy… please…" Martha looked at him… "We need someone to make the guys feel at ease with it…"

"I'll give it a go… I'll give that Reiki business a bash…!" Tommy smiled at his wife… "Des-stresses… Re-balances… Re-energises… luvly jubbly…". he paused… "I was reading the leaflet… I could do with all of that… and apparently, it helps with many physical ailments that are manifested through mental stress and emotional trauma…" he paused again…. "I read more of the leaflet…". Tommy smiled…. "With me two compadres over there… sticking me in the frame… I need all of that…" and burst out laughing…

As did they all….
Tommy lay on the couch… and the Therapist began….

"Blimey Martha, that was out of this world…!" Tommy had a smile on his face like a Cheshire cat…. "I went out like a light… and feel magic… Tommy paused again… and contemplated… "I might look into training in that…!"

"Does she teach….?"
"Yea, she's a Master…"
"Ok …. Go for it… between us, when you have completed your training… Spiritual Healer… Reiki Therapist… and me a qualified Physiotherapist…. We could set up of own business…!" Martha smiled


The evening started to draw to an end…

People started to leave….

"Thank you for organising this….!"

"Yes, it's been very helpful and we will be back…"
Yes definitely… is it once a week…?

"Yes…!"

"Thank you for sharing your stories… it must have been difficult…"
"By you sharing, it actually encouraged me to share…!"
"And me…"
"And me…"
"It doesn't take the pain away… but by being able to share my grief and talking, I have found some comfort…"
"Yes, me too…"

"You are also very welcome..." said Chloe
"Yes, we hope you come again…" stated Martha…
"You are welcome…thanks for joining us…!" enthused Joan

The hall emptied quickly… Leaving the Counsellors, The Therapists, Martha, Joan, Chloe, Geoffrey, Fred and Tommy….

# Chapter 39

"How do you think it went…?" Chloe asked the Counsellors…

"Considering it was the first time… it went better than I expected…."
"Yes, very pro-active…!" the second Counsellor added

"How did the Therapies go…?" Quizzed Martha…
"I did two ladies and one gentleman…" said the Reflexologist
"Three ladies…" shared the Indian Head Therapist
"Two ladies and one gentleman…" answered the Reiki Therapist….
"You mean Tommy…?" giggled Martha…
"Yep…" was the response… "very responsive…"

"That's very encouraging…!" Joan bloomed…
"Absolutely….!" Exclaimed Chloe

"They all asked if we are back next week…!". The Therapists enthused
"Wonderful…!" enthused Martha… "so positive…!"

"I think Tommy was quite taken away with the Reiki Treatment…!" Martha was thrilled…
"Yes, I believe he was…. He has asked me, if I would consider training him…"
"And…!" Martha was impatient…

"I explained to him that the true essence of Reiki dates back to 563BC to India, the first Buddha Shakyamuni, also known as Siddhartha … The Eastern Teachings. It takes many years to learn this on every level and you basically give your life to it..." She paused, took a deep breath and smiled.... "Then Reiki was Re-Discovered by Mikao Usui...!" The Master paused and smiled broadly....

"The true essence, the Eastern format in the 1890s."
"In 1923-25 he started teaching the simplified form, made plausible to the West and accepted by the West. Today known has Western Reiki. He seemed very keen, not daunted and I have agreed to Teach him Western Reiki..."

"Oh, that is wonderful, bless you... thank you so much... my Tommy a Reiki Therapist...!" Martha had tears streaming down her face... "Oh my and a Spiritual Healer..."

# Chapter 40

"Geoffrey dearest… Don't forget this Saturday, we are attending your Lodges, Masonic… Ladies night…"
Joan prompted
"Yes, my love, I am fully aware of this Saturday's events… and you will…. My Lady… be in your element… the perfect demonstration of a Lady in her true essence…!" Geoffrey articulated

"Oh my, you're such a smooth talker, did you swallow the blarney stone…?" Joan teased him… "prey continue…!"
"No, my treasure, diamonds that glitter, stars in the sky, will never compare what I see with my eye…!" Geoffrey enunciated

"Judge do you speak to all your prosecuting and defence council in such glowing sensual terms…"
"Hardly my beauty, you're the only one I sleep with…."
"I should hope so… otherwise your testes shall be dangling from the tower…" Joan smiled so innocently…
"So, have you booked the suite at the hotel…?"
"Yes, I so love it when you speak with such vigour…"
Geoffrey pronounced

They looked each other square in the eyes… and burst into laughter…

"Saturday… Saturday… it's Saturday… ladies' day and night… Geoffrey Childs…" Joan sang out…
"Are we ready to leave…?" Geoffrey enquired…
"Oh yes…!"

The hotel they booked was a five-minute drive from the Lodge in London…

"Joanie, you look stunning… my princess…!"
"Geoffrey my prince charming, shall we vacate…!"

They arrived at the lodge for pre-drinks….
They were welcomed by friends and colleagues…

"Good evening, Judge...
"Your Honour…"
"Your Worship…"
"Ma Lady…"

All the pleasantries … where observed and adhered to…

Geoffrey stood with their regular associate at such venues…

"Geoffrey old chap… we need to discuss policy…" one Senior Official appealed
"Yes, my dear boy a word in your shell…" a Top Ranking Official motioned
"Childs great to see you…let's chew the fat…" Geoffrey was manoeuvred
"The library is discreet dear fellow…" This Official pointed in the direction

"Excuse me your Honours... one moment if you please…"  He took Joan's arm… "This after all is Lady's night…" Geoffrey led Joan to one side…  "Joan excuse me dearest… I am being railroaded into stormy waters, for a clandestine meeting no less…" Geoffrey always thinking of his wife…


Joan consoled herself in the company of other Queens Council and waited patiently for Geoffrey's return…

"Joan, what does one say… Louise… your poor Louise, how utterly devastating… dreadful goings on…"
"Goings on…!" responded Joan… "mmm goings on...!
I'm conscious that is one way of describing my Darling Louise having her scull…. Joan's voice got louder….
"Joan my deepest apologies… not very tactful alas…"
Joan was cut off abruptly
"No…! it was without taste or diplomatically…!" Joan was terse…

The lady excused herself…

"Great start…!" Joan said
She never was delicate…" One of Joan's peers had witnessed...
"No not one of her merits…" Joan took a mouthful of her gin and tonic
"Without thought or discretion… a time bomb waiting to explode…!"
"Perilously close to the wind…" Joan smiled…

"What's to be done Joan…" another two female Judges, wives of Masons had approached
"How do you mean…done… in what context are we using the example of done…?" Joan crossed

"You know people in high places can make things happen… without them ever happening in the light of day…… if you get my drift" she paused…. "It's available as a matter of request…"
"People in high places… people in subordinate positions of usability, would like to see Justice Joan…"
"It's wrong Joan, that people with the knowhow and ability to delegate, without recourse… should suffer…!"

"Subservient minnows are available to enact and colluding to perpetrate Justice…!" Stated Joan
"Yes, in a nut shell…!"
"Who's Justice…?" Paused Joan… "Justice by the Law and the Court of the land… or the Masonic ability…? Joan smiled… "If we are discussing hypothetically…!"
"Don't be naive Joan…"" she paused… "don't you burn up inside at the thought of those killer creators… walking, talking, smiling…living next to you as neighbours…!"

"Justice was seen to be done in a court of Law…!" Quantified Joan… "Maybe not your Justice… but Justice of the Country…" Joan paused... and deliberated… "when I qualified for the Bar… and became a Barrister… QC… I took an oath… to uphold the Law of this Land… and I stand by that oath…!"

"Your weak Joan……!"
"Just give the nod…"
"It can be dealt with…"
"Quickly and quietly…!"

"We don't want your kind of help…!" Joan paused… we don't need your kind of help…!
We are doing, whether you approve or not… whether you can accept it or not….!" Joan's shoulders went back and she grew… "We are doing what we are doing for Louise, as Louise wants it… likes it… and that's all that matters…."

"Geoffrey… Brandy… everyone for brandy…?" asked one of the officials…
"Yes please… so my learned friends… what do I owe the pleasure of this… assembly…?" Geoffrey looked around the room…
"How have you been…?" He paused… "we don't get much chance to discuss issues of grave importance whilst on the circuit, now we are present, in confidentiality, with our code of conduct…. we can…!"

"We are ok… we wake up every day… we do our job… we cope… we are endeavouring to move forward… we are on the right track…" Geoffrey stated his case

"Geoffrey… you are highly thought of, on the circuit… a man not without friends, colleagues, brothers…!"
"Thank you, that's nice to hear, I'm obliged…!" Geoffrey smiled and took a mouthful of his brandy….
"Sorry we never made the funeral… your Louise's…"
"I understand… busy lives…" Geoffrey was polite...

"You know ol'boy… there are positions in life filled by likeminded folk, who have a moral fibre of what's considered… accepted in fact… of what's right and wrong…!" he paused… "not always what we see as the Judicial right and wrong… or the penalty…"

"Are we debating the mind set of superior beings…?" Geoffrey questioned…
"Some may consider that a prime example…"

"Establishment beings, cloak and dagger beings…"
Geoffrey mused…. "Facilitators of the whims…!"
"Are you mocking us Childs…!"
"No, your Lordship…" Geoffrey bowed his head…
"Worshipful Master"

"We are not on ceremony Geoffrey…!" he lowered his voice… "we are trying to help, to offer a service… a benefit… to help in condolence of your loss… and Justice fulfilled… that some feel as not been purged…!"

"Sufficient time has lapsed old man, what's to be done…?" a question from the corner came…
"Words in dark corridors are being spoken Geoffrey…" a pause…. "Some feel there was not sufficient punishment… handed down, with the early demise…."
Another corner spoke…

"You're a pillar of the Judicial system… no one has the right Geoffrey… to take the Law into their own hands… not against one of our own…!" a voice in another corner…
"Some consider the killer got off lightly, dying so conveniently… too lenient … the punishment should be passed on to the killers' originators… who spawned it…" and another corner with a voice spoke…

Geoffrey cleared his throat…. "Gentlemen, your Honours…I am surely at a loss, not only for the loss of my beautiful child…my Louise. I have to say I'm also at a loss in respect as to what is being offered…" Geoffrey took a breath and a sip… "So as not to misinterpret what is being said, or indeed as a matter of transparency, so to avoid misconstruing what is being said…  What are you, is, actually being offered…?"

"You are not a simpleton, you are one of our own, so a favour, a gift, action in recompense, for your loyalty…" The main man put to him…

"So, please explain to me how this would take place….?" Geoffrey asked

There was silence… then a voice came from a highbacked leather chair… that was facing away from the desk and room towards the patio doors……

"The East Enders would be eliminated…" a pause… "Quickly, painlessly of course…" another pause… "then overwhelming, comprehensively, compelling, conclusive evidence would be found, hidden, of course, at the home of… he who dares and the nurse. Their finger prints would be all over the two guns, …obviously the murder weapons. Conveniently, as it turns out, these had been allocated to them, whilst on active service… and then retrieved when service came to an end. You never know what can be found in the stores…" a pause… "additionally the reason would be apparent, when further evidence would be found conclusively showing that the young lad, had taken advantage on a number of times, the daughter… whilst on holiday. Mobiles with incriminating evidence on them, technology, amazing what can be done with it" a pause… "Which had indeed driven her into killing him and your Louise…" a pause… "in disgrace… a sad case of suicide…" a pause… "wrapped up in a nutshell, would you not say….!" All said as a matter of fact

Silence….

"You are offering to take care of, in a manner of speaking… to dispose of the Millers…. by disposing of the Jacksons…." Geoffrey paused… no evidence, no connection to us…neat and tidy… we are all clear…!"

"By Geoffrey… I think you've got it… welcome to the club… ol'chap…" and a few cheers went up..

"You… Bast…" Geoffrey cut short and bit his lip…. "So, without now reading between the lines, listening to

195

hypothesis, inuendo, you are actually instigating with insinuation and action, taking the Law into your own hands…murder…!" Geoffrey growled… "exactly, what you have abhorrently made clear…"

"Careful Geoffrey, one doesn't want to burn bridges…" A soft voice from the corner… "you are being granted an honour…" a pause… "to give your wonderful wife and you, a conclusion of reprisal, as of righteousness…!"

"You're buying us… you are…" Geoffrey stood firm…. "Colluding mercilessly, to take the Law into your own hands and by a matter of course, you have us in your pockets, for your future impulses…!"

"You've misunderstood our meaning Childs, it's all hypothetical debate…" the corner spoke with menace… "We are offering you bond-ship…" a softer voice, in another corner…
"Support and backing…!" a pause from the corner… "you never know when you may need it…"

"Are you threatening me…?" Geoffrey kept his composure…
"You have had too many Brandies' Geoffrey" ….
"Watched too many crime thrillers…!" The main man smiled

"No…! but I have a claw in my throat…" Geoffrey put his half-filled glass on the table… and walked to the door… then looked back…
"I'm at a total loss, in how you have, are, treating the Law and the People of this Land, that…!" he paused… "the law is supposed to protect… with…!" he paused…. "Total disdain…!"

"It doesn't end here Geoffrey... it cannot be seen to be...!"
"You will thank us in the end..."
"We will speak again..."

"Not on this subject...!"

"Why...?"

"For our Louise... For her.... For her Honour... For her Moral Fibre... Her wishes....!"

"Geoffrey...!"

"I say No...!"

They all congregated into the middle of the room... and looked at each other... shrugging their shoulders... swallowing their Brandy's ... "Lets join the party...!"

# Chapter 41

Geoffrey joined Joan....

"Are we staying dear...?" Joan asked...
"Yes...!" Geoffrey smiled ...
"How was it...?" Joan quizzed
"Hostile, intimidating, threatening, sly...!" Geoffrey said
"Nothing unusual then..."
"How was your time...?" Geoffrey quizzed
"Hostile intimidating threatening, sly...!" Joan said
"Nothing unusual then..."

"Why are we staying then...?"
"Dinner... then we will leave with dignity" Geoffrey
smiled... "It's my Ladies night...!"
"Thank you... I'm hungry..." Joan held his hand..."is
that the only reason...?" she commented...
"WE won't be chased away...!" Geoffrey paused...
"There are many good people here...!"
"Good... I haven't got my trainers on..." Joan smiled...
"there are... none more than you... my big lovely
hunk..."
Geoffrey's cleared his throat... "oh I say..." his eyes
welled up... "Joanie... my rock...!"

# Chapter 42

"Tommy, look at the view from the window… City
Airport… in the heart of the old East End…"
Martha beckoned him…

Tommy placed his arms around Martha's waist and they
shared the view…

"The old East End with an Airport… I remember when
we had an outside loo and a tin bath…!"

"How do you think it went tonight…?" quizzed Martha…
"It was like walking on broken glass and having nails
stuck in my eyes and hands…!" Tommy sighed
"Yea… really that bad…?" Martha queried…

"Well… no… it's what we were brought up with… you
know, I love the people; I respect them in my own way…
they're like family…" Tommy hugged Martha closer…
"I didn't want that life then… I don't want it know…!"
"That I understand… we never did run with the crowd,
know the crowd, love the crowd… but it never was our
life…" Martha confessed

"They knew that and still respected and liked us…"
Tommy confirmed
"Still do by the offers we received…!" Martha raised her
eye brows

"Some of those offers were frightening…!" Tommy
nodded his head
"Hostile, intimidating….!" Martha stated

"Yea… do you think we made it clear we don't want no
reprisals…?" Tommy asked

"Clear as mud Tom… They respected and loved our Tommy…as Jack said…" Martha paused…. "He can have a word…!"
"But some saw him as a working-class hero… and don't listen…!" Tommy injected…
"Theres the dilemma…!" Martha turned and hugged Tommy

"Didn't know Jack was married…?" Martha stated
"Me neither… all those years…" Tommy paused… "and I didn't know he was a Jackson…!"
"And your related… sort of…!" Martha pulled a face...
"And he knew my mum…!" Tommy pulled a face…
"Visited her for advice…!"

They pulled apart and looked at each other….

"How long has Jack and Glenda been married…?" asked Tommy

"By the way Tom…" Martha paused… "Who was that bloke who you were talking to…?"
"Which bloke…!" quizzed Tommy
"The bloke lurking in the shadows… who came up to you when we were getting in the taxi…" Martha paused… "you shook hands and talked a while…?"

"That was one of Jacks equalisers...!" Tommy told her
"Equalisers…?" Martha gasped
"Yea, Jack don't like the name Henchman… Body Guard…Minder…" Tommy smiled

"Equaliser…!" Martha expressed
"That's what he calls them..." Tommy countered
"Them…! ….. What's his name…?" Martha asked
"Martha what's all this… with names…!" Tommy queried

"What's he known as…?" Martha pursued

"Ahh… Boof Boof…!" Tommy responded

"Boof Boof….!" Martha gasped

"Yea …!" Tommy said

"Why is he called Boof Boof…?" Martha enquired.

"That's what he does…" Tommy held his hand in the

position… "Boof Boof…!"

"So, what did he say…?" Martha paused and looked puzzled… "how do you know him…?"

Tommy looked at Martha… "He works for Jack…" he paused… "he said Tom… can I have a word… you can't allow what happened to happen…  give me the word… and I'll be around, do the business…  Boof Boof… job done…"

"Job done…!" Martha repeated… "For our Tommy…?"

"Yep… as easy as that… drive by… day out… wrong place wrong time…!" Tommy stated…

"That easy… no come back…?" queried Martha taking a deep breath…

"None…!"  Tommy confirmed… "That easy…!"

There was silence…...

"What did you say…?" Martha questioned

"I said No…!" Tommy paused… "don't get involved…."

"And…!" Martha asked

"Boof... Boof… shrugged his shoulders….!"  Tommy paused…. "Smiled and winked at me…!"

"What does that indicate…?"  Martha exclaimed

"It indicates no one can control Boof Boof..." Tommy took a deep breath... "if he makes up his mind... unless he has a change of mind... by a prang of conscience... coz I said No...!"

"Does he ever have a prang of conscience...?" quizzed

Martha

Tommy looked at Martha... "I have never delved into the mind of Boof... Boof...." He paused... "it's a dark place Martha... it's not a place I want to go... to question him.... or for me to be in his mind....!" Tommy paused again.... "For him to be thinking about me... no thanks very much...!"

# Chapter 43

"So, thought I'd let you know..." Tommy paused... "me and Martha went to a Spiritual Church on Friday evening...".

Geoffrey Joan, Chloe and Fred all looked at each other...

"Why...?" quizzed Geoffrey
"Didn't you want us to come with you...?" asked Chloe
"What made you do that...?" Fred enquired
"How interesting... could we not have come...?" questioned Joan

"Wow, slow down..." Martha grinned... "Spanish inquisition or what..."

"Just wondered why we never got invited...?" Joan stated
"You didn't mention your intentions...?" Geoffrey negotiated
"Was it a spur of the moment thing...?" enquired Chloe
"Was you out and saw it advertised...?" Fred asked...

"I told Martha it was something I wanted to do..." Tommy paused... "I'd been doing some research and wanted to experience it first-hand...!" Tommy stated
"And I asked Tommy if I could accompany him or did, he want to go alone...!" Martha added
"We weren't being secretive or not wanting you to join us, I, then we, wanted to go alone..." Tommy confessed
"No mystery... Tommy wanted to go, I tagged along..." Martha replied

"Sure, no problem...!" Fred confirmed
"Quite right...!" Geoffrey nodded
"Was it good...?" enquired Chloe

"Was it scary…?" asked Joan

"It was good… very good… very informative…!"
Tommy shared
"Not scary in the least, Joan… very calm, very
peaceful…very welcoming…" Martha assured

"Informative…" Geoffrey question…

There was silence….

"Yes informative…! there was a medium working, giving
evidence that life exists after life…" Tommy stated

"Evidence…?" crossed Joan…
"Yes…!" Martha paused… "pure evidence, precise,
exact, spot on…"
"How so…!" beckoned Geoffrey

"Messages from loved ones, friends… in spirit….!"
Tommy took a breath… "That… Could not be
disclaimed…!"
"What he told us could not be misconstrued, as general
information, not repudiated…!" Martha swallowed… "it
was beyond a shot in the dark… it was evidence, that
only the person… spirit, could be telling him…
sharing….!"

Silence prevailed….
"Who came through….?" Chloe asked coyly
Tommy to start… Tommy answered
Followed by Louise…" Martha added softy

"Sophie…" pleaded Chloe holding her hands to her
chin…
"Yes Chloe…" Sophie came through

They were all in tears... cascading down the faces...

Geoffrey cleared his throat.... "What was shared... did they pass on any words....?"
"Yes, Geoffrey they did..." Tommy wiped the moisture from his eyes...
"Louise shared words...? Joan was weeping
"Yes, Joan, Louise passed on a message of love to you and Geoffrey..." Martha sobbed...

Geoffrey and Joan cradled each other... sobbing

"Sophie... Did Sophie pass on any message...?" Fred stammered
"Please, did she...?" Chloe pleaded

"Yes... Sophie said..." Tommy wiped his face with his hand, it was wet with tears... "She is sorry for what she did... she loves us..." Tommy choked......
"And she is sorry and she loves you, mum and dad..." Martha choked and wept...

Fred and Chloe collapsed into each other's arms... wailing....

They cocooned and cuddled their respective partners... sobbing... really heart felt sobbing, wailing, groans of pangs of pain... grieving... from their hearts... the pits of their stomachs churning, the depths of their souls ... tears flooding...

Can we go...? Chloe pleaded to Fred
Yes of... course...!" Fred consoled Chloe

"Geoffrey..."
"I know dearest Joanie... we will attend..." Geoffrey answered Joan's plea before she finished it...

"Tommy....!" Martha looked at Tommy solemnly
"Would you all like us to go together or to make your own plans..." Tommy asked.

"Together...!" Chloe stated
"If that's good...!" Fred quipped
"Oh yes together...!" specified Joan
"Please Thomas all together...!" confirmed Geoffrey

"Then its together... we go...!" Tommy smiled

# Chapter 44

"Well, that was a beautiful event…!" Chloe said sitting
on the double bed in the hotel, as she removed her shoes
"Yes, it was, very respectful and we got a medal
each….!" Fred expressed
"I knew you were getting one, I didn't expect to be
receiving one…!" Chloe confessed
"I knew you were getting one, I didn't expect to be
receiving one…!" Fred confessed

They looked at each other and laughed…

"A covert operation was put into action…" Chloe giggled
a bit tipsy
A ruse….to mislead, confuse and surprise…" Fred
smiled…

Fred poured them both a glass of wine

"Everyone was so charming, weren't they…?" Chloe
commented
"Everyone was… on the surface…" Fred countered

"Did you have a bad time…?" asked Chloe
"No not bad, but there was a lot of inuendo flying
about….!" Fred shared
"Inuendo… I'd say dam right warfare on the horizon…!"
Chloe countered
"You experienced it…?" asked Fred
"Yes, did you…?" responded Chloe
"Yes…!" Fred stated

"Some of the ladies, our friends, our comrades in arms…
are hell bent on revenge…!" Chloe stated
"Really…" Fred nodded

"Yes, they have a plan in place, just waiting for the word...!" Chloe said

"Really..." Fred nodded

"Yes, they also believe we have contrived a plan for revenge... a covert operation...!" Chloe informed him

"Really...! Fred continued nodding

"Yes, they also think Sophie's actions where manifested by what took place on the holiday...." Chloe said

Fred nodded.... "Was it...?"

"Fred....!" Chloe queried... looking puzzled...

"It's ok let it go...!". Fred took a mouthful of wine...

"I told them we were doing what Sophie wanted...!" Chloe paused... "they all thought it was a part of the plan..."

"So, you said you came under fire...?" Chloe questioned

"Yes...!" Fred said shortly

"Revenge indicated....?" Chloe questioned

"Yes, but it's just some of the chaps... getting overzealous..." Fred submitted

"Oh yea...!" Chloe said

"Yes, hot under the collar...!" Fred countered

"Oh, yea...!" Chloe nodded

"Yes, actions planed...!" Fred informed her

"Oh, yea...!" Chloe nodded

"Yes, waiting for the word, to be hatched...!"

There was silence....

Fred poured them a glass of wine each....

"And...?" Chloe asked bluntly

"Some of them think revenge should be implemented...!" Fred shared

"And…?" Chloe nodded

They have it in their heads it goes back to the holiday…. Fred told her

"And…?" Chloe continued nodding

"They think for Sophie's honour, there should be retribution… passed down…" Fred stated

"And…?"

"They have a covert operation set up and waiting to be implemented…." Fred took a mouthful of wine

"What was your response…?" Chloe question Fred

"I categorically said no…!"

And….?"

There was discontent in the ranks…

And…?"

"I gave a direct order nothing was to take place, happen in an act of revenge…." Fred stated

"And…?"

"Some, said if a covert action took place… it would be covert…" Fred held his chin…

"Oh, dear…" Chloe sighed

"I told them we were doing what Sophie had asked us…" Fred sighed…

"Fred…. Who was that, tall lean chap, who spoke to you as we were leaving…" Chloe paused… "you spoke quite intimately, then you saluted him with your finger…?"

Fred paused…

"That is a gentleman who I have shared many a close encounter with…"

"How close…!" Chloe giggled

"Not that close…" Fred paused… "but deadly close at times…!"

There was a silence....

"You had close encounters with him... undercover...?"
Chloe quizzed...
Fred looked at Chloe with that... "are you sure you want
to know the gory details...!"

"What's his name...?" Chloe asked
"He is known as Tap...Tap..." Fred smiled...

"Tap...Tap...!" Chloe echoed...
"Yes...!" Fred confirmed
"Why... Tap...Tap...?" Chloe questioned
"It's his line of work...!" Fred said
"His line of work..."
"Yes, he goes in where others fear to tread... a very silent
worker...." Fred paused..." in...tap...tap... out and
gone..."
"Why tap...tap...?" Chloe queried
"It's the noise it makes, when a silencer is applied to a
pistol..." Fred stated

"Did he offer you Tap...Tap..." Chloe was cottoning
on......
"Yes, he did.... He said they cannot get away with it..."
Fred paused... "He would go into the two houses...
Tap...Tap... Tap...Tap...."

"And leave us as prime suspects...!" Chloe exclaimed...
"No, he is a professional... had the remedy for that..."
Fred paused... "He would come into us... tap...tap...
you...
"What...!" Chloe exploded
"Just a flesh wound... one in my pillow and one in my
shoulder..." Fred paused... took a swig of wine... "we
would have a tussle, he would drop the gun and have it
away into the night... no prints on the piece... looks

convincing, we are the innocent party, frightened him off... we got away with it..."

"He would shoot me... just a flesh wound...!" Chloe paused... "Fred Miller... you would let him shoot me...?"
"A flesh wound, you get off lightly..." Fred paused...
"I've got one in the shoulder...!" Fred paused again...
"think about the others... they're brown bread...!"

"You would allow that to happen..."
"I said No...!"

"And...?"
"Tap...Tap... is a Law unto himself...." Fred stated in a manner of fact way....

# Chapter 45

Friday evening came around....

"Ok, all set...?" Tommy asked

They piled into Martha's people carrier....

"I'm very excited....!" Chloe paused... "but very nervous..."
"We were like that, that first time..." explained Martha
"I'll be a bag of nerves when we get there...!" Joan said excitedly...
"My Joan a bag of nerves... I object..." Geoffrey paused... "nerves of steel..."
"I'm going to confess, I'm on edge..." Fred said
"Me to old chap... but can't let on...!" Geoffrey shared

And they all laughed...

"You are funny Geoffrey..." giggled Martha...

"Oh Oh.... I say....!" Geoffrey cleared his throat..." I'm funny ... oh jolly good.... Still a tad on edge...!"

They all roared again....

They had chosen to try a different church from the one Tommy and Martha had visited....

The rest of the journey was in silence...

They were warmly welcomed...

"We would like to extend a warm welcome, be it regulars or newcomers..." the Chairperson said....

"A warm welcome to our Medium for tonight..." she paused..." if the Medium comes to you, please speak up, to be heard.... with a yes, no, not sure... and the Medium can continue or seek further information...."

The medium did an opening prayer.... "Welcome ladies and gentlemen... as, has been said, if I come to you it helps if I can hear your voice, then so can spirit...! and they need to hear your voice...!"

The lady Medium went directly to a number of people in the congregation...
"Yes, I can take that..."
"No, I'm not sure..."
"No..."
"Yes... that's...."

It was a varied response...

The three families had decided to sit together in one line....

The Medium scanned the congregation....

"I would like to come to... you...." she pointed at Geoffrey....

Geoffrey gulped
Joan grabbed his hand....
"Sir, may I work with you...?" she asked smiling...
"Oh Oh...!" Geoffrey cleared his throat... "Oh my... yes ... delighted...delighted...."

The medium started to put her hands out and as if.... balancing them... "Scales...I'm seeing scales... robes, grandeur... very grand building... a court, The Old

213

Bailey…" The Medium paused… "this is a place of
work… can you take this Sir…?"
"Yes…. yes… most definitely…" Geoffrey mumbled...
"Clearer Sir…please…!"
"Yes…I can…!" Geoffrey replied
"I see a gathering… within the Court… oh… dear…
there is an individual female, standing alone...in the…
who…!" She paused… "Do you know what I am talking
about Sir….?"
"I believe so…!" Geoffrey confirmed in a clear voice
"Is this your lady wife…?" pointing at Joan…
"Yes, she is…...!" Geoffrey re-affirmed…
Joan nodded…

"I have a very difficult situation going on here… a
tragedy… I can't share this with the …" and she waved
her hand out over the people…" I can't share the details
with the congregation… I have responsibilities…"
"I'm grateful…!" stated Geoffrey….
"Can you take the name Lou…?"
"Yes…!" Joan and Geoffrey shouted and tears cascaded
down their cheeks…
"I have a young lady… standing close … mum, dad…
she is calling out… is this your daughter… Louise…!"
The Mediums voice raised
"Yes… it is… my baby…!" Joan expressed
"Louise darling…!" Geoffrey sobbed…

"She is saying how much she loves you… oh my… the
feeling of love for you two is overwhelming…" She
paused…. "Are all six of you related… she is saying…
tell them I love them all….!" She paused again…        "I
don't know why she is saying forgive… help them…"
"Does that make sense….?" She asked
"Yes, abundantly clear…!" announced Geoffrey…
"Yes, it does... bless you darling… we love you….!" Joan
sobbed her heart out….

All six were in tears…

"I… I can't come away from that line…"

"Madam…!" She pointed towards Chloe… "I have…
Oh….!" She stopped….
I… I…I Know… what happened…!" She paused….
"Do you all wish me to carry on…?" the Medium
asked…

All six nodded…

"Yes … we do…" was stated by all…

There was silence, you would hear a pin drop……

"I have the first young lady … she is standing very much
alone…" The Medium paused….
"She is saying sorry… I'm so so…sorry … for what I
have done… for what … I have put you through …. All
of you…!"
"We know…" said Chloe…. Sobbing…
Fred nodded… "We know…"
"Is this your partner, husband….?" She pointed toward
Fred…
"Yes…I am…" he paused sniffling…
"Who is Soph…?" the Medium asked
Fred held Chloe's hand….
"Sophie is our daughter…!" Chloe wept as she said her
words

Tears flowing down Chloe and Fred's faces…

The medium nodded her head…

"She is saying she loves you… I can feel this love...! she truly does…"
The Medium paused….
"We love you Sophie…" Chloe wept tears of pain
"We love you Sophie…!" Fred wailed in agony…

"She again is saying sorry… and she loves all of you… please forgive me… please, please forgive me…
She paused again… "and help others…!"

Chloe and Fred nodded… weeping…

"I'm not sure what she means by this… then I'm not meant to…" She paused… "can you take this…?"

"Yes… we can…!" affirmed Fred
"We can…we will Sophie…!" added Chloe


All six where wiping their eyes….

"Madam may I come to you…?" pointing at Martha…
"Yes… please…" Martha stated
"I have a young man…standing close to me and close to Louise… Sophie is also their…!" the Medium paused….
"Is this your son…? …. Don't answer…!" the medium cut Martha off….
"He is saying he is your son… Mum Dad….!"
"Yes, he is…!" Martha confirmed
"This is your husband….?" pointing at Tommy…
"Yes, he is…" answered Martha
"Two Toms… who is Two Toms…?" …. "I have Two Toms being shouted at me…. Stop shouting….!" The Medium said
"Tommy is our son…" Martha sobbed her words…
"And my name is also Tommy…". Stated Tommy… wiping the tears from his eyes….

"Ahh Two Toms…!"

There was silence in the Church…

"He was a very athletic young man…!" she paused…
"what's this badge on his chest…?"
"It's…" Tommy got cut off….

"Three lions… he played for England…! Mmmm…
Little sod… woops sorry…" the Medium smiled…
"He's just kicked a football at me…!"

Martha and Tommy smiled… "Sorry that's Tommy…!"
Martha said…

"Tommy is saying help to heal them Dad…".
"I will try son…" Tommy's eyes welled again…
"You are a Healer …" The Medium paused… "You do
know that don't you…?"
"So, I've been told…I'm starting my training soon...…"
Tommy sniffed
The Medium smiled… "So was your mum… she also did
this… she is telling me…!" She paused…    "She is
very proud of you…!"
"Love you mum…!" Tommy shouted out…

"Tommy is saying he loves you both, so much, so so
much…". She paused…
"Forgive them… help them… help others… that's his
words…." She said… "You understand…?"

"Yes, we do Tommy…!" Martha expressed… sobbing
"We do son… we will…!" Tommy added wiping the
tears from his face…

There was a hush in the church….

"I have to say…. I admire the way you six can come together for the greater good….
The love of you children… and you can forgive…. Bless you…"

The Medium closed the service in prayer…

# Chapter 46

"I must say Geoffrey, that was a splendid idea…. dinner was exquisite… and leaving at our pace was so, a up yours's moment…!" Joan was glowing…
"And you did it sublimely my dearest Joanie…" Geoffrey crowed

"Do you think the Grand Master and subordinates would be horrified, contemptuous that we left after the toast honouring the lodge for Ladies night…" quizzed Joan
"We drank the toast did we not… we honoured Ladies night for the Ladies….?" queried Geoffrey
"In honour of the Ladies not the Lodge…!" crossed Joan
"After tonight we may not be welcome in the Lodge… we may be outcast… burnt at the stake…" Geoffrey stated poignantly

He poured them both a brandy… and sat on the bed next to Joan…

"Lovely hotel dear…?" Joan said nonchalantly
"Yes, it is my dearest…." Geoffrey replied casually…

They both took a large mouthful…

"Do you want to do opening statement for the prosecution or defence?"
"Analyse and dissect…?
"Debrief the events…?"
"Conclusion of the evidence presented before us….!"

"Sorry I had to leave you…" Geoffrey paused… "how did your evening proceed…?"
"Rude, discourteous, insulting… hostile…. Joan paused…. Disparaging….

"Would you like to elaborate…?" countered Geoffrey
"Well basically no one was playing blind man's bluff…
cards on the table…" Joan elaborated

"Define…!" Geoffrey pushed gently

"It was on a plate Geoffrey, it was offered, without any
concern of reckoning…" Joan paused… "it will be taken
care of…. just say the word… like ordering fish and
chips…! There was no fear of the law coming after
them…!" Joan paused and took a mouthful…" these
people are a law unto themselves….!"

"Mmmm….!"

"I was called weak…! there was insinuation, of
misgivings, character assassination, intimidation… and
the Gaul of these people…!" Joan was getting irate…
"They say in the name of the Law and Justice… revenge
must be applied…!"

Silence…. Joan poured them a large brandy each….

"I wouldn't be surprised if the blighters didn't already
have a plan in obeyance…!" Joan paused and took a
small swig… "that's conjecture…" She corrected
herself…. Paused again…" but I wouldn't be
shocked…!"

"Were you tempted Joan….?" Geoffrey paused took a
large mouthful… "when they remind you, regurgitate the
emotions, hurt… pain… when they get right under your
skin… and it burns like smouldering embers…" Geoffrey
paused… "that ignite into a rage…!"

Joan looked at Geoffrey… and tears fell from her eyes…

What happened, when you went for your clandestine meeting....?

"Brandies all round ol'boy..." Geoffrey smirked...
"How many of you in there...?"
"I walked in with four...but there was more...!"
"More...! how many more...?"
"There was one in each corner of the room..." Geoffrey took a mouthful... "very discrete, keeping in the shadows...!"
"Very cloak and dagger..." voiced Joan
"Mmmm very daunting.... voices coming out of the darkness...!" confessed Geoffrey

"What was said....? ... were you interrogated or intimidated...?" pressed Joan
"I was infringed... trampled on..." Geoffrey stated

"Geoffrey...!" ...exclaimed Joan
"Rapid fire... examined, cross examined..." shared Geoffrey
"My love...!" Joan cried out
"Insinuation, inuendo.... Allusion... interrogation... intimidation...From men in dark corners..."
"The Grand Master was their...?" Joan quizzed
"A superior puppet...!" Geoffrey expressed

"Geoffrey....!" Exclaimed Joan

"Many things where stated, accusation, slander menace...!" Geoffrey paused... "then the ol'boys act... your one of us Childs...!" ... Geoffrey eyes narrowed... "the Law must be seen to be upheld... minnows must pay dearly for the crimes...!" He took a large swig... "and if sufficient sentence is not served... by unfortunate death..." Geoffrey took a breath... "then the makers of the perpetrators must suffer the consequences and pay the penalty.... Punished ultimately..."

"Oh my god...!" Joan sighed

"Pillows of the establishment must be protected... and punishment must be seen to be enacted....!" Geoffrey poured himself a large brandy.... Then offered Joan a top up....

"As you so eloquently stated Joanie... it was put on a plate...". He paused...

"Who...?" Joan pressed...

"Well cross-examined Barrister Joanie..." Geoffrey bit his bottom lip.... "There was one more person in the room... a voice hidden in a chair with his back to me... that was protected..." Geoffrey took a small swig and breathed deeply... "He offered ... and their would-be overwhelming evidence and reason..." .... Geoffrey paused again shaking his head.......
"The Millers would eliminate the Jacksons... and then, oh so conveniently commit suicide... with their own service weapons... so conveniently dug up from the stores... covered in their finger prints..."
Geoffrey by now was so agitated... "in a nut shell as it was sold to me....!"

"And where does that leave us...?" Joan took a large mouthful.... "If we agree...!"

"In their established pockets forever and a day... to be played like puppets by the puppet masters...!"

"Was you tempted to agree...?" Joan returned the question...

Geoffrey squinted... tears began to form....
They sat on the bed and cried...

"No..!... I said No... I took my oath... but ...!" .....
Geoffrey paused.... And took a large gulp....
"For my Louise... I told them... No...!"

"I knew you would tell them to stuff it...!" Joan learnt
forward and kissed Geoffrey on the forehead...

"Were you tempted....?" Geoffrey posed the question...

Joan took a small sip... "I told them as a QC and
Barrister I would always uphold my oath... the Law...!"
Joan paused... "I told them for my Louise... we don't
want their help...No...!"

"My Rock...!" Geoffrey kissed Joan's forehead...

"Geoffrey my treasure..." Joan peered toward the door...
"What's that envelope on the floor, by the side of the
door...?" she said inquisitively... pointing....

"How long as it been there...?" Geoffrey got up from
the bed... "I shall investigate..."

"I never noticed it love..." Joan said

Geoffrey picked up the envelope...

"There's no name..." Geoffrey looked puzzled
"Open it...!" Joan stated looking inquisitively

Geoffrey opened the envelope...

Pulling the contents out....
His eyes widened....

"Well...!" exclaimed Joan...

"There's a piece of white paper..." Geoffrey took a breath... cleared his throat.... "With a mobile phone number scrawled on it... and the words underneath..." He paused... "just say...YES...!"

"My god... they know we are here...!" Joan's voice never quivered, to the contrary it was strong, determined, with a hint of anger...

"My god... are they all embroiled into this web of corruption, conspiracy...!" Geoffrey paused... "assassination...!"

# Chapter 47

"Tommy are you genuinely taking up Spiritual Healing…
has the Medium said…?" Geoffrey inquired…
"Yes Geoffrey, I am… I genuinely feel it's what I'm
meant to do…" Tommy paused… "it's now been said
twice, by two different mediums…." Tommy smiled…
"In two different Churches…" … he paused… "and our
Tommy has also confirmed it twice…!"
"And your mum did it…!" Fred added…
"Apparently… yes, that was also confirmed by a very
reliable source…." Tommy looked at Martha…. "Who
she gave some very valuable advice to…!"
"On more than one occasion Tom…!" Martha injected…
"You are also going to train in Reiki Tommy…?" Joan
asked
"Yes Joan…"
"Are you nervous Tommy… dealing with spirit…?"
Chloe asked

"No Chloe… I felt comfortable and feel I have the right
person to teach me Spiritual Healing… apparently that is
important…!" Tommy paused… "and I am sure… it feels
right… we meet people for a reason… that the Reiki
Master who came to the Bereavement group… was meant
to be…!" He paused again for a second… "that applies
in both cases…!"
"Devine intervention… Tom…?" Joan quizzed…
"I don't know about that Joan…" Tommy paused…
"maybe it was always on my pathway… always going to
happen…"
"Are you chosen…?" enquired Fred
"My understanding is… Tommy paused… if spirit want
you to work with them… you can…you will…" he
smiled… "I've heard this has happened on many
occasions…" Tommy paused again… "I might add you

225

have freewill…! You have the choice…and you can train in both... one or the other… or none…"

"Can anyone undertake such training and learn…?" Geoffrey queried

"Yes Geoff…!" Tommy smiled… "are you going to train with me…?"

There was a silence….

Geoffrey coughed in his usual manner and cleared his throat……

"I admire and respect your course of direction Thomas… and will support you wholeheartedly… Geoffrey paused…

"I do believe I will leave that to you… the only spirit I will be working with, is a large brandy… if that's ok…?"

They all giggled and laughed….

"Oh oh… have I been amusing again…?" Geoffrey beamed…

"Does anyone else want to accompany me on this journey…" Tommy opened his hands

"I'll certainly give it some consideration…" Fred said pulling a face… "mmm probably not… I'll leave it to you…!"

"You gave that a lot of reflection…" Martha smiled… "grass never grew under your feet… did it." Martha giggled

They all giggled…

Geoffrey cleared his throat… "Martha… I do the amusing…" they all laughed… "Ok...!" nodded Martha

"I think I'll be too busy with work and the Bereavement group…" Joan confirmed

"Same for me Tommy… Nursing and the Group…"
Chloe added
"Same for me my lover…" Martha winked…
"Physiotherapy and the Group…"

"How do you know you have picked the right
Teacher…Master…?"
"Again… My understanding is…" Tommy mused….
"When the student is ready…The Master will appear…!"

# Chapter 48

At the following Bereavement Group meeting… many parents attended…

"Martha the Therapists are ready to receive anyone who would like to try a treatment…" informed Chloe
"Ok Chloe I'll go and ask them…" Martha replied

Martha approached some of the parents who were having a welcome cupper…
"The Therapists are ready and waiting for you, if anyone wants one…?" She asked
"Yes please…I'd very much like to have reflexology…?"
"Can I have that Indian Head treatment…?"
"May I go to the Reiki lady….?"

"Yes, come along, they are waiting for you…." Martha led the way….

"Would it be possible to have a one to one with one of the Counsellor's…?" one of the mums asked
"Yes, please come with me…" Joan took the mum over to the Counsellor

"Would we be able have a chat with that Counsellor we spoke to last week…?" and the man pointed
Of course, come along… and Chloe led the way…

The rest of the group sat and chatted… some cried…. Sharing their many experiences of bereavement...

After the success of the week earlier, they had spoken to another Counsellor that they knew and invited her to join the team……

"Good evening, ladies and gentlemen… children…" She paused…. "You are most welcome… we know why you are here…. We would like to say a massive thankyou to the three ladies and their partners for organising and running this facility…" opened one of the Counsellors…

"We cannot say we know how you feel, we cannot say we understand how you feel, we cannot tell you we can feel or heal your pain… She paused…. "No loss compares to another's loss, for those who have lost… but we are here to listen…" added another one of the Counsellors…

"We are Bereavement Counsellors, but that doesn't make us immune to losing children, we have, all three of us, have lost a child…" She paused… "we can listen, we will listen if you want to share your grief. We are here to support and help you… mainly by listening…" continued the third Counsellor

More of the group had the Therapies on offer… and many had one-2-ones…. Counselling…

They all shared their bereavements, their grief… many tears… and some light laughter…. By all…

"We will be here next week… please come and join us…" Chloe closed the evening…

"See you next week…!" shared Joan

"Thank you, this is so helpful…"
"Thanks for listening…"
"Thanks for being here…."
"Thanks for caring…."

"Good night… see you next week…." Martha concluded.

# Chapter 49

At the end Tommy approached his to be Reiki Master....

"When can I commence my training...?"
"You're eager...?"
"Yes, I want to start my journey...!"

"I have a Reiki Training, scheduled next weekend, there is a space if you would like to have it, interestingly the person cancelled yesterday...!" The Master bowed......
"Gassho..."
Tommy had learnt and bowed back... "Gassho..."

She smiled...

"Yes...!" Tommy said without hesitation...
"OK ....! ... I will put you in... and give you the details before we leave..."
"Can you inform me of the criteria and Training Levels...?"

"You will attend this Level 1 training course, on the Level 1..." She paused... "and I believe it is the most important... like building a house... what's the first thing you do when you build a house Tommy...?"

"You put in the foundations, strong foundations.... From which you build..." Tommy replied
"Exactly...!" the Master placed her hands in prayer position "Gassho" and bowed...

"Then Level 1 is vital to be taught from the true essence..." Tommy stated... and mimicked her, placing his hands in prayer position... "Gassho" and bowed...

"This position is called "Gassho" Tommy… it represents many things of which Respect and Discipline are two…"

Tommy nodded… and smiled…

"Your Level 1 is the foundation, that you can always fall back on …. On this Level you will be taught the history, the morals, principles and techniques, such has the hand positions, in a chair and on a couch…
self-healing…. And much more…." She paused…took a breath and smiled… "Also, on this level you will receive four attunements to connect you to the Rei energy…the highest source… It's over two days, on each day you will receive two attunements… the first three open you up the Rei energy… the fourth will open you up permanently and you are connected…"

"Wow…!" Tommy Paused… "what does Reiki mean…?"
"Rei… is Universal Energy… Ki… is Life force Energy… Reiki… Universal Life force Energy…"

"Wow…!"

"Wow indeed… you will then undertake a 21-day self-healing process… as did Mikao Usui… on mount Kurama -Yama…in Koyoto Japan…" she paused and bowed in respect… "If you miss a day… you start your 21-days again… it's a hard 21-days Tommy…!" She took a breath… "self-healing, cleansing… purifying... Mind, Body, Soul… all the toxins…" The Master stopped and looked at Tommy……
"If you lie to me… you lie to yourself… where is your self-respect and discipline…"

"I won't lie…!" Tommy assured her…

She smiled… "I believe you..."
"I'm also learning to be a Spiritual Healer… is it the same…?" Tommy asked…

"No…! Spiritual Healing is what it says… you are a Medium, an instrument that allows Spirit energy to use you as a vehicle. To give healing... you have guides and so forth…that help you…" She paused… "Your Spiritual teacher will teach you this…" She paused… "That is not Reiki…!"

"I understand…."   Tommy instinctively bowed in Gassho…
The Master mirrored him…

"Reiki taught in the traditional way of Usui… there are no guides and the like…" She paused… "it is accepted and recognised as an Ancient Science… accepted in many Hospitals, Hospices… Clinics and Private Practice… She paused again…
"Des-stress… Re-balance… Re-energise…" She took a breath…. "Many Doctors acknowledge that many physical ailments… are manifested by stress….!"

"Wow…!" Tommy exclaimed…

"You have much to learn Tommy… Grasshopper…"

# Chapter 50

"Tommy when can we go to another Spiritual Church for Mediumship…" asked Fred

"Oh, yes Tommy can we go again….?" Chloe added

"Who would like a tea or coffee, show of hands…?" Martha asked as they all sat round Martha's kitchen table…

"Ok… that's six… Including me… Tommy…!" Martha smiled… "That's three teas… three coffees'…"

"Would be a jolly good venture to go again Thomas…!" Geoffrey enthused …

"I would like to go again, apart from the messages…" Joan paused… "I got a lot of solace just sitting in the church…"

"Funny you should say that… I felt very much at ease…" agreed Fred

"Me too…" added Chloe

"You don't have to only go, with me and Martha…" Tommy passed over the coffees…

"Don't you want us to join you Thomas…" Geoffrey prodded…

"Tommy…?" pushed Joan…

"Martha…!" Chloe looked at Martha…

"Tommy…?" Fred opened his hands…

"Tommy…" Martha looked at Tommy

"Jesus kangaroo court… string me up…" Tommy smiled at them… "I'm not saying we won't be going together…" he paused… took a sip of coffee…. "I think I need a wassa with you lot…! … I'm just saying… you can if you so choose, go individually, on your own… by yourself… on your tod… in Cognito……………"

They were all staring at him… cold stony faced…

"Alternatively…!" He stroked his chin… took a sip of his coffee… "I think what might be a great idea… is…. We all go together…!"

"That's settled then….!" said Martha… "who wants a Martha special brekki…!".
"Oh… jolly dee… brekki for me…" chimed Geoffrey
"I'm pleased that's settled…" Fred smiled… "Be rude not to… please…"
"I've regained my appetite…" Joan winked at Martha… "please my dear…"
"That's a taste idea…" Chloe grinned at Martha… "scrummy… chow time…!"

"Like feeding time at the zoo…!" Tommy roared smiling… "Please my lover…!"

# Chapter 51

"How was your reunion and presentation….?" Martha asked Fred and Chloe…

They looked at each other….

"Our hotel was lovely….!" Exclaimed Chloe...
"Yes, it was… the banquet was beautiful…. As was the venue…!" added Fred…
"The presentation was humbling and joyous…!" supplemented Chloe

"So, you had a good time… meeting up with your comrades and friends…?" enquired Tommy…

"Yes…!" confirmed Chloe…
"Yea…!" Fred stated

"Somewhat unconvincing, a little vague…and apprehensive…in your demeanour…!" Geoffrey proclaimed
"So now divulge the true events, if you please…?" questioned Joan…

"What…?" Chloe smiled...
"What do you mean…!" Fred defended

"Fredrick… Chloe…" Geoffrey paused… "I have spent to many hours in courts… watching blagging criminal elements, lying to pervert the course of justice…" He paused… "to be deceived… when the truth is being concealed…!"

Martha and Tommy looked on… concerned

"Chloe… Fred we know something is being concealed… we can only help, if you tell us the truth… confide in us…!" Joan stated sympathetically…

"Ok… Ok… you want a full debrief…?" Fred relented
"It was awful … we were like lambs to the slaughter…" Chloe declared and tears formed in her eyes…

"What took place…?" Geoffrey said compassionately…

"Firstly, we arrived and was greeted in formal military protocol…" Fred opened
"We got separated as happens, at such events… boys talk… girls talk…!" Chloe injected…

"We both basically got a few snipers to duck, across the bowls…!" Fred paused… "testing shots… to see how the defences coped…"

"It was hostile fire… probing... digging… interrogating…" Chloe wiped her eyes… "we thought they would be there to support… care, consideration, sustenance… understanding… they have all lost love ones in combat.".
"We believed we had squashed the revolt…!" Fred took his hand to his chin… and looked at the floor…

"The food was beautiful…. the presentations of our medals was very emotional and applauded with great enthusiasm and cheering…" Chloe was stronger

"Wanna wassa…?" Tommy asked as he opened the whiskey and Martha filled the cups with tea and coffee… No one answered …. They were just handed out…

"Then the onslaught began, a firefight… a crossfire … a bombardment…" Fred took a mouthful of his wassa… "a terrain of vocal firepower of aggression, vengeance…" he paused… "a barrage of revenge…!"

"Divide and Concore…. Into two camps, separated…" Fred took another swig… "two assaults… Chloe and myself…!"

"We defended our cause, our children's wishes… with valour… it's what we believe in… isn't it…?" Chloe stood up… and took a mouth of her wassa….

"We firmly held our ground….!" Fred stood up and took a mouthful… "and defended our post… I mean our post…!" and pointed his finger in a circled direction at all of them…. "And cause…. With belief and honour…" He squinted his eyes… his face went stern… like granite…

"How was that received…?" asked Joan

"I believe we were perceived as weak…" Chloe admitted
"Traitors to the cause…!" Fred acknowledged
"And pissed a few people off…!" Chloe stated

"No more…?" Geoffrey quizzed

"I don't think they are all accepting my order…!" Fred mused… "or wishes…"
"Tell them…!" Chloe instructed Fred…

"I'm going to share something with you and this isn't meant to frighten any of you…" Fred took a large mouthful… "there was an operative I shared many a close call with… we did what we had to do and saved each other's lives… on a number of ops… Fred paused…. "He approached me and offered to pursue, intent on executing revenge…"

"On who…?" Geoffrey interrogated

"All of you…!" Chloe paused… "they believe collusion…between Louise and Tommy….!"

"I stated No…!" … Fred was firm… "I told him no revenge…"

"For what…?" Demanded Tommy…
"He has it in his mind that something amiss took place on the holiday…!" Fred said bowing his head

"No, I ain't having that…!" Tommy paused… "that old filthy chestnut is raising its head again…."

"We know… nothing happened…" Fred paused…

"That's bollocks Fred…!" Martha exclaimed… cutting in…

"Martha, we know…!" affirmed Chloe…

"Oh… sorry…" Martha said

"The kids wouldn't be coming through with their messages… if there was anything wrong…!" Chloe said softly
"But some don't believe it…" Fred stated… "No matter what we say… people always want to put their slide on others affairs…!"

"Fred, you need to tell them about tap tap….!" Chloe told him…
"Tap Tap…" enquired Geoffrey…
"Yea…!" Fred pulled a face… "tap tap… he is called that because that's what he does…!" Fred created the shape of a gun from his hand… "we were undercover and saved each other many times, he believes he has an allegiance

to me… he is a maverick…" Fred took a swig of his fresh wassa… "and he has offered to do what he does best…" Fred paused… "I ordered him not to, under any circumstances… to seek revenge….!"

Silence took over……

# Chapter 52

"So, Joan how did lady's night go…?" Martha broke the silence

Joan looked up … "It was a splendid venue… and an exquisite meal… lots of toasting… "she said unemotionally

"Oh…!" said Martha … that's it…?"

Joan and Geoffrey shared a glance….

"Geoff…" Tommy looked at him…

"Opening gambit…niceties …!" Geoffrey expressed….

"You two as well…?" questioned Fred…

"We have been in many courts and witnessed atmospheres that could cut through diamonds…" Geoffrey composed himself… "Hostilities between the judicial verses criminal, violence, battling out deliberation…deliverance of justice…!"

"Geoffrey where is this leading…?" Asked Martha caringly

"We were deliberately parted…" Joan looked at her husband… "Geoffrey was ushered away to a private meeting…"

Tommy and Fred looked at each other…

"You ok mate…?" Tommy asked

"Geoff what did they say? ... or do...?" Fred squared up...

"Crossfire, cross examination, subliminal threat, their belief to uphold justice..." Geoffrey paused... "psychological rekindling in opening wounds... pure hatred... elitism... psychology, reverse psychology..." Geoffrey stopped.... "The O'l boys act, we are on common ground... join the puppet club...!" Geoffrey looked sad... "the purchase of our souls..."

"My god...this goes to the very top...!" Chloe held her chin in her hand gravely

"Fragrant abuse of power...!" Joan stated as she stood up.... "re-lancing opening our... segments of sealing emotional discord...!" Joan stood tall.... "To install fuel and fulfil their pleasure... their power trip..." Joan thought deeply... you could see the concentration in her eyes... the wheels turning... "Conspiracy and corruption at the highest level... power and control....!"

"The very top and the underground...!". Geoffrey announced with some vigour

"A combination of power and control... at the top levels and underworld, I take it you mean...! Martha shook her head

"Top level, establishment... underworld... underground... they use each other..." Joan shared... "for their own agenda... of, balance...!"

There was silence...
Joan continued to inform them of her encounters during the court procedures, at the court case conclusion... what

was presented to her... by her client.... without breaking client confidentiality...... in addition, afterwards in the bar... and the envelope on her window screen in the carpark ... then the second envelope appearing on the floor of their hotel room....

Again, there was silence.......

"I have something that you need to see....!" Geoffrey showed them the two envelopes...and contents...

They all in turn read the words....

Again, there was silence....

"My Joan, defended with valour...and grit...." Geoffrey paused... cleared his throat... wiped his eyes of moisture... "And quelled prosecutions endeavours.... And pressures...!"

"I myself ..." Geoffrey cleared his throat... "I refused to be taken in, to be privy of this fraternity... highlighting their intentions and offers...". He paused... "dismissing all approaches... a closed case...!"

"You hope...!" affirmed Tommy....
"Yes...! ... Thomas.... I pray..." Geoffrey quantified
"So, what do we do know...?" asked Chloe

"We all pray...!" emphasised Martha

"We carry on...!" Fred stood up, stating doggedly

"As we told them we would do so, for our children's wishes..." Geoffrey paused and wiped his eyes... "to be endorsed and granted...!" He cleared his throat.... "And to leave our friends alone...!"

"And to establish… maintain and counter equilibrium… right and wrong…. Good and evil…!" Joan paused and took a mouthful of her wassa…. "Love must and always will win ….!"

# Chapter 53

"Martha, please tell us you had a great time......?" asked Chloe

"Yes, please do...!" pleaded Joan....

"It was great going down to the old manor..." ... Martha obliged... "we stayed in a plush hotel that used to be a drinking club...". She paused... "now overlooking City Airport......"

"Yea used to be as rough as guts..." Tommy joined in... "but ironically you felt safe...!"

"How was the birthday bash...?" Geoffrey enquired

"Blinding, great to see all the old faces and some of the younger ones that knew Tommy..." Tommy shared

"Sounds like you had a more receptive homecoming..." Joan urged

"Sounds like you had less hostility..." added Chloe

"More friendly hugs..." Geoffrey supplemented smiling

"Rather than friendly fire... of hostile fire...!" Fred complimented

Martha and Tommy looked at each other....

"One should never assume it appears..." Joan specified

"I ain't going to beat around the bush..." Tommy started... "I am afraid to say the same reception... friendly welcoming..." He paused.... "But it didn't take long before comments were being thrown around like confetti at a wedding...."

"Comments…?" …. Geoffrey quizzed

"Comments Geoffrey… questions, insinuation, offers of revenge… and that was from the women...!" Martha made it clear…

"So, it begins… all round…!" Fred remarked

"Everyone I spoke to… put it on the table… no qualms, no hiding the point…" Tommy took a swig of a fresh wassa… "all what you were offered…" He paused... "no hiding place, like your people, for the same, different, ideologies, they have…!" Tommy shook his head
"Just say the word we were told…" Martha concluded

"No one to stop it Thomas…?" Questioned Geoffrey

"I sat for a long time and spoke to a man who has influence… a man I know well…" Tommy began
"Not has well as you thought you did…!" Martha jumped in

"A man I've known all my life and respect…" Tommy continued…" a man let's say… others respect….!"
"And his response Tommy…!" Joan quizzed

"He questioned my motive for not wanting revenge, for us not wanting revenge…!" … Tommy admitted

"And it turns out he knew Tommy's mum… who had the gift… she was known as the messenger….!" Martha added… "and respected her knowledge…!"
"He thinks it macabre that we are still associated… But when I told him we are doing it for Tommy… all the kids… because we have heard Tommy asking us to…" Tommy paused… "working together because it's what

246

Tommy… all of them want that, to help others… Tommy took a mouthful… "he was ok and said he would put the word out…"

"Young guns Tom…!" Martha injected
"Yea, there's the young guns… wanting to prove themselves, to make first team…" Tommy mused… "who aren't always controllable… but words would be had…"

"Boof Boof Tom…!" Martha nudged him…

"Oh no… Tap Tap… Now we have Boof Boof…!" Geoffrey sighed… "took a mouthful of his fresh wassa…. God save us…!"

"Geoffrey…!" exclaimed Joan…

"Who is boof boof… Tom…?" queried Fred

"Boof Boof is the equivalent of Tap Tap…" Tommy held his hands out… "He's an enforcer, minder…. for the man…. the equaliser… as he is affectionately called…!"

"Affectionately…!" … exclaimed Chloe…

"Chloe…Please…!" Fred said quietly

"I told him in no uncertain terms, as nicely as I could, to let it go… no revenge…!"

 Silence… engulfed them….

They sat digesting and pondering the events of what had been shared…...

# Chapter 54

"We have a Bereavement group tonight…!" Joan took stock… "we cannot allow our anxieties and stress to show through…!" Affirmed Joan…
"Agree, this would be transferred to the parents and children…" said Chloe
"Even though they will have no idea why or where it's coming from…" added Martha…

During the course of the day… the three families tried to get on with their everyday tasks….
But… becoming paranoid… looking over their shoulders, is that person following me… he looked at me strangely…what did she mean by saying that…. who's that looking at us….

# Chapter 55

"What are we going to do Fred...?" Asked Chloe

"We will take care... keep vigilant... hopefully it was all bravado... and trying to impress...". Fred was aware it could be anything but....

"You don't believe that Fred... if not military, the establishment, if not the man... and his team... let's not forget.... affectionately boof boof....!" Chloe spoke with clarity...

"We will have to devise a counter offensive..." Fred was rekindling many a sortie.... "Put our brains and experience to work... and come up with an incursion exploit and counter protection...!" Fred was deep in thought as he spoke the words....

"I have often waited for you to come home from a foray...." Chloe blew Fred a kiss.... "Please Fred come home with a full proof strategy...!"

# Chapter 56

"Geoffrey, how do you think we can get out of this awful dilemma…?" Joan asked…

"I am giving it a lot of consideration Joan…!" Geoffrey had the wheels turning in his head…. "Analysing what's before us and looking for a defensive approach with a loose loophole in their armour, as a counter protection…"

"And you think considering that there are, a number of fractions…" Joan waited… "that this prosecution could instigate from….   An Achilles heel… can be found….!"

"I believe using my years of experience in unravelling complex states of affairs…" Geoffrey deliberated… "and delve into the dark chambers of my mind… I may well achieve the solution to our collective impasse…!"

"I love the dark chambers of your mind…" Joan winked at him… "So, Geoffrey dearest…. get bloody delving…!" ….. "I'm here if you need me…!"

# Chapter 57

"Tommy… this is deep shit…!" Martha hesitated… "Is there a way out… apart from emigrating…?" she said sarcastically…

"We ain't running away Martha… we have a job to do…!" Tommy was stern…. "We need to come up with a plan... a concept… a strategy… something to take the wind out of their sails… to put a stop to this…!"

It isn't just Jacks team… and they are on our side……" Martha sighed… "there are elements of revenge coming from many quarters who are blind to us…in positions of power… military expertise…!" Martha emphasised…

"There is always a weak link Martha… when your opponents, believe they are unbeatable… arrogance is a weakness Martha…. We use it against them…!" Tommy contemplated… placing his chin in his hand….
"In every business negotiation, there is always a way, an ace up your sleeve…to win the day… to make the opposition… take a backward step… and walk away….!"

"If my lover…" Martha beamed at Tommy… "you are going to play three card brag….!" She took a moment and smiled…. "Make triple sure… you have three threes… in your hand…!"

# Chapter 58

"Ok... are we all set up...?" asked Tommy
"We are..." Fred confirmed
"Everything is sorted ...!" Geoffrey endorsed

"We must get through this without showing our own anxiety's..." Joan assured
"Yes, we can...!" Chloe affirmed
"Stay strong... we can cry later...!" Martha stated

They all looked at each other...

"Come in ladies... your therapy area is the same as last week..." Joan pointed the way
"Please set up your couches..." Martha instructed

"And the counselling area is in the same place as well...." Chloe directed

"People are queuing..." Geoffrey stated
"Ok let them in..." Chloe instructed

"Welcome...!"
"Hello...!"
"Please come on in...!"
"You're most welcome....!"

"Tea and coffee, soft drinks are available...."

"May I have a chat with one of the counsellors... please...?"
"Of course, come along...!" answered Chloe
"Can I also...?"
"Yes, they are waiting for you...." Joan confirmed

"May I have an Indian head massage please…?"
"Is the Reflexology available…?"
"I'd very much like a Reiki treatment…?"

"Please, they are all available and ready…." Martha
advised

Many of the bereaved parents and siblings sat discussing
their feelings… with the other counsellor…
Sharing… expressing feelings of deep remorse…
Crying….
Shedding tears and anger…

"Why…?"
"Why… my baby…?"
"Why didn't she talk to me…?"

"We don't know the answers…."

Questions…? Questions….? Questions….?

With no answers…. To pacify their souls….

# Chapter 59

"Tommy don't forget the Reiki Level 1... that you have signed up to... is this weekend...." The Reiki Master smiled

"It's in my diary... I'll be there..." Tommy smiled and performed Gassho...

Martha smiled in the background....

"Tommy how are you getting on with your Spiritual Healing training....?" asked Fred

"It's great Fred.... And I have an excellent teacher... a guy called Charles...". Tommy paused... "and the others there are so friendly and helpful..."

"How does it work Tommy...?" quizzed Geoffrey
"It's early days Geoff..." Tommy paused... "so I'm still learning and don't want to talk out of turn..."

"Keeping it close to your chest..." Geoffrey winked and smiled
"Na, just don't want to spiel bullshit...!" Tommy smiled... "with no basis of knowing..."

"Talks cheap, money buys houses..." Fred put his best cockney accent on... smiling...
"As me mum used to say... "Don't piss up my back... and tell me it's raining outside...!" Tommy winked

The three gentlemen all grinned, noddingly... there unity, camaraderie, bond, was growing, entrenched, as before....

# Chapter 60

"Geoffrey dearest… am I mistaken…" Joan aimed her ear to the living room door… "no I am not… the house phone is ringing…!"
"I do believe it is…" Geoffrey looked at his watch…" Its five minutes past midnight…".
"Oh dear…!" Joan touched her brow… "is that bad news…?"
"Worry not my Joanie… I'll go and answer it…" Geoffrey stood up and walked through the door to the hall way… "it certainly is persistent…!"

"Hello the Childs residents…". Geoffrey spoke clear… "Hello…" … "Hello…!" … "Hello…!"
"Who is it Geoffrey…?" Joan was standing in the doorway…
"Hello…!" … "Hello…!" … "who is this…?" … "who's there…?" Geoffrey demanded…
"Geoffrey…!" Joan looked puzzled…

Geoffrey replaced the hand set… turned around to face Joan… shrugged his shoulders….
"No one there…!" He stated...
"How bizarre…!" Joan looked at her wrist watch…

They returned to the living room… and sat in the preferred chairs…

"Do you think its contact from Louise…?" Asked Joan quite calmly
"If it was my dear…" Geoffrey cleared his throat…" she didn't speak…!"

They continued to watch the programme they had recorded earlier…

"That was spiffing…!" Geoffrey declared…

"Most enjoyable dear… Time for bed…" Joan smiled at her husband

"Quite so…" Geoffrey smiled back

"What time is it…?" Geoffrey quizzed

"12 past one my dearest…" Joan informed him…

They stood up and walked to the door… Geoffrey checked the front door was locked… he then turned… Joan started to climb the stairs… Geoffrey was behind her…. half way up the stairs…. The house phone rang… loud and clear… startling both of them… Joan turned and stared at Geoffrey….

"I will get it…" Geoffrey nodded and trod down the stairs…

The phone rang out …...

"The Childs residence…!" Geoffrey stated… "Hello…" … "Hello…" … "Hello…!" … "Who's there…?" … "Who is this….?"

 Silence…...

"Bed my Dearest… not to concern ourselves…!" Geoffrey specified…

"Geoffrey… Geoffrey… Geoffrey, wake up dear…!" … "please Geoffrey, wake up…!" Joan sounded concerned… "The house phone is ringing again….!"

Geoffrey woke in disconcert…

He looked at the clock on the bed side table…

"Its Two Thirty... in heavens name... 2.30am...!"
Geoffrey exclaimed...

He climbed out of bed... put on his dressing gown and
walked down the stairs....
By the time he got to the bottom....
Joan was sitting on the top stair... watching intently....

The phone continued to ring......

"Good morning...!" Geoffrey stated... "The Childs
residence..." He waited... "Hello...!" ... "Hello...!" ....
"Who is this...!" ... "Who's there...!"

"Geoffrey...!" Joan looked at him

Geoffrey looked up at his wife...

Joan looked perplexed...

"No one there...!" He stated...
"Mind games Geoffrey...?" Joan raised her eyebrows...

# Chapter 61

"Chloe... I'm going up for a bath, before bed..." Fred glanced at Chloe
"Ok... give me a call and I'll be up...."

Fred went upstairs and run a hot bath......
Lazily soaking...
Whilst Chole sat watching the tv....
The phone rang....

"Fred are you expecting a call...!" Chloe shouted up the stairs
"No love... it's a bit late to be phoning people..." Fred shouted back...

Chloe looked at her watch...

"Yea its 24.05..." she shouted back...

Chloe picked up the receiver

"Hello...." She said... "Hello..." ... "is someone there..." Chloe waited.... "Hello can I help you...." "Hello...".

"Who is it love...?" shouted Fred....
"There's no one answering..." She replied...
"Must have realised they had phoned the wrong number..." Fred laid back into the water... for another 20 minutes

Fred dried himself off... and went downstairs

"Bit late to be phoning people...!" Chloe was drinking a glass of wine...

"Yes...! I think I'll have a night cap..." Fred poured himself a glassful and topped Chloe's up...

"I'm going to bed Chloe... its late...!" Fred looked at his watch...
"Oh, my its 1.15 am...!" confirmed Chloe...

The phone rang and startled them...

"I'll get it...!" Fred stood up and walked to the house phone...

"Hello...!" Fred was stern... ... "Hello...!" ... "answer me..." ... "Who is this..."

Fred walked back toward the doorway...
Chloe was staring at the doorway...
She looked at him knowingly, by the look on his face...
Fred's face was stone like granite...

"No answer...?" Chloe quizzed...
"No answer...!" Fred answered...
"Wrong number...?" Chloe queried...
"We will see...!" Fred placed his chin into his hand...

"Do you want a drink...?" Chloe asked
"Yes please..." Fred held his glass up... "Fill it up..."
They sat in the living room... in silence...
The cogs turning in Fred's mind....

"Ok there's nothing more to do..." Fred swallowed the last of his drink... "let's go to bed..."
"Yes..." ... Chloe swallowed her drink... "it's 2.30....!"

The phone rang again...

Fred sprung out of his seat... and strode to the phone....

"Hello…!" … "Hello…!" … Fred waited… "Hello who is this…!" … "what do you want…?"

Silence…

"What's happening Fred…?" Chloe said timidly

"I don't know…!" Fred looks at Chloe caringly……

"What are you thinking…?" Chloe questioned
Fred cocked his head to one side…. "It could be the start of the games…"

# Chapter 62

Tommy pulled the car into the driveway….

"What a lovely meal…."  Martha smiled… "Thank you…!"
"Yes, lover it was… nice to be home…" Tommy paused… "early night is on the cards…!" he winked
"Yes, I am quite tired…" Martha smiled…
"Tired…!" Tommy exclaimed… looking at Martha… pulling a face…

Martha winked and smiled… "You animal…!"
Tommy growled…

They got indoors…

"Open up a bottle of wine babe… and bed…!" Tommy blew her a kiss…
"The corkscrews in the bottle…!" Martha raised her eyebrows and twitched her nose…
"Feline…!" Tommy howled…

The phone rang…

"Who the….  At this time…!" Tommy snarled…
"Tommy it's 5 past twelve…!" Martha frowned…
"It must be important…!" Tommy said
"Make it quick…!" Martha pointed…

Tommy picked up the phone…

"Hello…!" He barked…. "Hello…!" … "Hello…!" …
"Answer otherwise I'm hanging up…" he waited…
"Who is this…?"

"Who was that Tom…?" enquired Martha
"No answer…" replied Tommy
"Oh well, no problem…" Martha said….
"Let's go up…" Tommy smiled
"Are you going to run the bath….?" Martha asked smiling
"Yep, you open the wine…" Tommy smiled back…

They had a round sunken bath… Tommy lit some candles and put a CD on…

"Come on lover the water and bubbles are ready for you…" Tommy giggled… "so am I…!"

Martha got in and they soaked for a while…

"Wine…?" Tommy asked
"Be rude not too…" Martha joked…
"This is so lovely and relaxing…" Martha sighed…
"Yep, sure is…" Tommy took a mouthful of wine…
"What's wrong…?" Martha enquired...
"Just that phone call…" Tommy answered

They soaked in silence…

"More wine…?" asked Martha
"Yea, why not…!" Tommy put his glass forward…

"Tommy the phone is ringing….!" Martha stated
"I hear it…!" Tommy said as he clambered out of the bath….

Tommy picked up the phone…
"Hello…!" … "Hello…!" … Tommy growled… "Who the fuck is this…!" … "Hello…!"

Martha was sitting on the side of the bed….

"No answer…!" She looked up at him….
"No, no answer…" Tommy walked to the window and looked out…

Martha walked up behind him and placed her arms around his waist… snuggling her head into the nap of his neck….

"What's happening Tom…" she paused… is this the start… the intimidation…?"
"I don't know…" Tommy turned and hugged his wife… Maybe…!"
"Come on go to bed and finish our wine…" Martha took Tommy by the hand

They finished their bottle … and snuggled up… beginning to doze…

"Tommy… Tommy… the phones ringing again…" Martha shook him…
"Yes, love I've heard it…" Tommy said… "I'm going to leave it…"
"And it will continue to ring…" She paused… "until its answered …. I'll answer it…"
"No…!" Tommy pulled himself out of bed…

"Hello…" … "Hello…!" … "Hello…!" He said in a tune…

Then went back to bed….

"Fun and games ah…!" Martha was sitting upright… Tommy nodded his head…. "All the fun at the fare…"

# Chapter 63

"Good morning...."
"Good morning..."

The pleasantries continued...

"Is it...! too many disturbed night's sleep...!" yawned
Fred...
"Waiting now for the dam phone to ring...!" Chloe
sighed

"We turned it off...!" Joan moaned
"And...?" ... queried Martha
"The mobile started...!" confirmed Geoffrey
"Same as..." continued Chloe
"Same here...!" affirmed Tommy

The three families sat in Martha's kitchen.... Around the
table.... Sipping their drinks

"So...!" ... Geoffrey began... "we have had these phone
calls at various times...!"
"Actually Geoffrey...!" .... Joan interrupted... "they are
consistent...I've monitored them, with the help of Martha
and Chloe..."

"We applied for itemised bills...!" Martha added
"Showing the times of incoming calls...!" Chloe
confirmed

"12.05am .... 1.15am .... 2.30am .... First night....
11.00pm ... 12.25pm .... 3.00am the Second night....
12.15am ... 1.30am ... 2.45am ... the Third night..."
Joan pondered... "then reverted to First night and

continued… until the Seventh night… 10.30 pm …
12.05am … 1.30am …2.00am … 3.15am…!"

"Then we have had two nights free of disturbance…"
Tommy yawned… "then it's started again… the past two
nights…".
"And so, we wait…!". Fred looked at the floor…

"How do they phone all three of us at the same time….?"
requested Geoffrey…
"Technology…" Fred answered
"One person…" Tommy paused… "three individual
phones…"
"One person…" Fred paused "one machine…"
"One machine… pre-set timer…" Tommy added

"Who is it…?" Geoffrey quizzed looking at them all…

They all shook their heads…

"Thomas… is it the East End…?" Geoffrey grilled …
"your people…?"

"Na… it's definitely not our firm… it's too subtle for
them…" … Tommy deliberated… "they would just go in
bang crash wallop…!" he paused… "especially boof
boof…. and he wouldn't have anyone treading on his
toes….!"

"Must we remind ourselves of boof boof…!" exclaimed
Chloe…

"It's a women thing…" Fred caressed his chin… "sort of
thing a woman would do… catty… feline… feminine
manoeuvre…!"
All the lady's looked at him…

"Sorry… years of being in the job…" Fred defended himself…

"Fredrick…!" … Geoffrey interrogated… "You know exactly how they would conduct themselves in combat…" He paused… "Is it your covert colleagues…?"

"I could not imagine the elite force… SAS…!" Fred looked stony eyed… "phoning in the middle of the night to intimidate…" he was thoughtful…. "it's not their style… it's not my team…. they are trained to complete their task…ultimately….!" he thought… "not play girlie games….! And Tap Tap would make it known… to stay out … its mine…"

"Must we…! … Tap Tap…!" Chloe paused… … "Boof Boof…!" and threw her arms into the air…

"MMMM…!" Geoffrey cleared his throat… "I want you to be perfectly clear on this issue…. You must trust me…" he waited… "I'm not being sexist by no means my lovely ladies…" he paused and cleared his throat… "it is rather a feminine trait…!"

"I must say from past experience…" Joan added… "I do concur with Geoffrey's appraisal… female… womanlike action…. It's not masculine is it….?"

"So, it's not from the gangster moles…!" stated Martha…
"And it's not from any female SAS…!" Chloe echoed…

Geoffrey looked slightly puzzled … "Define please…?"

"Because they would be like their men…!" Martha looked stern…

"Ruthless…!" Chloe nodded…

"Then who…?" growled Geoffrey…

"Psychological mind games….!" quizzed Joan
"Pointing fingers…!" Martha stated
"Divide and conquer… inner fighting…!" Fred affirmed
"But we have all received them…!" Chloe pointed out…
"Perfect alibi…!" Tommy countered
"Perfect reverse Psychology… to get fingers pointing…!"
Geoffrey added
"Creating mistrust… in the ranks…!" Fred injected
"Mind games…!" Chloe stated
"Internal suspicion… eroding from within… team
member with self-agenda…!" Tommy snarled

"And if we are sure it's a female action…?" quizzed Joan
"Could be more psychology…manufacturing a false
trail…?" stated Geoffrey

"You think it's more of an establishment ploy
Geoffrey…?" asked Fred

"Frederick…!" Geoffrey cleared his throat…
"Establishment… underworld… military usage,
involvement, manipulation…  all colluding… Who
knows…?" He paused… "where the orders come
from…" Geoffrey cleared his throat and pondered…
"who signs the death warrants … or terrorist
harassments… as long as they win…!"

There was silence….

"How do we stop this…?" Joan looked at them all…
"This is only the beginning…!" Geoffrey nodded his
head…

"How can you be so sure…?" Chloe said startled
"You say that with some conviction…!" Martha looked at him questioningly
"You say that knowing…?" Tommy pushed

"No… its logical… all the intimidatory subliminal offers… outright threats…!" Geoffrey waited… "I'm just using my years of putting my analytical mind to work and clarity of thinking… on a logical level…"

"So, it's the beginning…!" Fred nodded

"And we must stand firm…!" Martha insisted
"Together…" Chloe urged…
"For the kids…!" Tommy asserted…

*"You must help others…!"*
*"You must stay united…!"*
*"Love…. unconditional love…!"*


The words echoed round the room….

# Chapter 64

"Tommy, Tommy…" Martha glowed…as she welcomed him through the door "Did you complete it…? Did you enjoy the weekend…?"

"Yes, Martha…!" Tommy was also gleaming…. "It was brilliant…!"

"Did learn all about Reiki… Did you have your initiations… attunements…!"

"No…!" Tommy smiled… and yes…! yes…! … yes…!"

"Say what…!"

"No….! … I didn't learn all about Reiki…" Tommy pondered… It was Level 1… the foundation…"
"Foundation…?" Martha questioned
"Yea, like when you're building a house… you put in strong foundations, the strength, the core… that you can always fall back on…" Tommy smiled…

"But you are now attuned to Reiki…?"
"Yes…" Tommy mused for a moment... "it was amazing… there were four attunements over the two days… Two on each day"

"Wow…!" Martha beamed
"Yea first three open you up to Rei energy..." …. "The Highest Source… Universal...!" Tommy smiled again... "The Fourth one opens you up permanently…!"

"Sounds like you enjoyed those…" Martha smiled
"Martha it was incredible…" Tommy grinned… "it was so peaceful… yet exhilarating … so serene…" Tommy

paused… "I saw colours, visions… it was truly amazing…"

"Can they bottle that…?" Martha Smiled…
"Yes… By having a Treatment…." Tommy glowed…
"Only one…!" Martha questioned
"Everyone is different…" Tommy looked at Martha… "It depends on what level…"
"Level…?" Martha questioned
"Yes, emotionally, mentally, physically…" Tommy shrugged his shoulders… "But there are those who feel or see nothing… yet it is still working…".
"Working…?"

"Yes, sifting through…we, once attuned, are like vessels, conduits… that allow Rei energy… to flow through us… and connect… like a set of jump leads… to the Ki energy that is inside all of us…" Tommy smiled… "Life force energy" Tommy took a breath… "De-stresses… Re-balances… Re-energises…."
"Who can you give Reiki to…?" Martha quizzed…

"Anything that as Innate energy… energy within… Ki… Prana… Chi…" Tommy stopped for a second… "So, adults… children… animals…. Any living object… out to the world…!" Tommy smiled… "sounds wonderful doesn't it, Martha…?"
"Yes…!... wonderful…!" Martha's eyes welled up; she was so proud of her Tommy…
"And…!" He added…. "Self-healing… in aid of personal development, wellbeing and growth…."

"So, what happens now Tom…?"
"Well, I have to do a 21-day self-healing process… and do 10 treatments on anyone, who will let me give them a treatment… filling out the paper work… consultation form, treatment form…" Tommy stated

271

"Then…?" Martha asked

"Then I present those to my Master… Then continue with CPD…" Tommy explained….

"Whoo, don't you know…" Martha smiled

"Continued Professional Development…" Tommy explained

"Then…?"

"Then, in three to six months depending on my progress and at my Masters discretion…" Tommy paused…

"I will be invited to do my next Level… Level 2…"

"You must explain more to me this is so interesting…… but we have to go out now…!" Martha paused….

"I am so proud of you….!" and tears formed in her eyes….

"Look Martha…!". Tommy presented her with his Level 1 Certificate….

"This is to Certify that Tommy Jackson has received the necessary attunements and instruction in Level 1 Usui Shiki Ryoho"

"May I have a treatment…?" Martha smiled… "every day for the rest of my life….?"

"It will be my pleasure…!" Tommy's eyes welled up…

"Tom…" Martha looked puzzled… "What does Reiki actually mean…? "

"Rei, is… Universal… Ki, is… Life force energy" …
Tommy smiled and nodded …
"Universal Life Force Energy…!"

# Chapter 65

"So how does the land lay…?" asked Geoffrey….

"All quiet on the western front…" answered Fred….

"Since the last call… there's been none…" Tommy
stated… "to us anyway…!"
"Us either…!" Joan said

"Peace, we have actually got used to getting a good
night's sleep…" Martha added

"So, how long is it now…?" Geoffrey quizzed
"It must be seven nights…" Martha said… actually I've
lost count…!"
"No actually if they all stopped on the same night its ten
nights…." Chloe intervened… "I've been counting…!"

"So, have they got bored…?" Geoffrey
"Calm before the storm…?" Fred stated
"Ten nights… someone picked us out at random…"
Chloe said
"What all three families… same times…" Joan paused…
"now there's a coincidence…!"
"Someone was having a pop at us…!" Tommy specified
"Some malicious individual…" Martha said sternly…
"Jealousy…!"
"A good point of view…" Geoffrey cleared his throat
"please define Martha?"
"That we have been able to overcome our conflicts and
move on… for the sake of our kids…" Martha
quantified…
"Bigger people…" Chloe stated

"We have been able to put to one side our own pain, anguish, resentments…" Joan swallowed hard… "in coming together to help others… directed I must say by our children…"

"Jealousy is a disease…!" Geoffrey stated

"So, do we carry on…?" Fred smiled wryly

Tommy looked at Fred… and got his drift…

"Dam right we do…!"" Tommy winked at Fred… "after all the hard work these lovelies have put in… pointing at the ladies….

"I have never been one to succumb to intimidation…" Geoffrey cleared his throat… "and never let the blighters win….!"

# Chapter 66

"So, are we all set up for tonight…?" Joan perused everyone

"Yes Joan, we are…!" Chloe stated firmly….

"Then we go to work as usual…" affirmed Martha…

Tommy, Geoffrey and Fred wandered into the garden….

"Do you think that's the end of the hostilities…?" asked Geoffrey….

"Who knows…!" Tommy paused… "we don't know who it was…."

"It could have been some jealous individual…!" Fred took stock… "or someone playing psychological games…!"

"The old fishing trick… wear us down….?" asked Geoffrey…

"Possibility…!" Tommy answered… "but we stay strong for the girls…!"

"I guess its wait and see… and continue…" Fred added… "for the kids…"

"Do you think it's all over…?" Joan looked at Martha and Chloe….

"I sincerely hope so…" Chloe said… "We don't want to stop what we have started….!"

"I think the boys are putting a brave face on…" Martha paused… "For our sake…"

"Then we will do the same…!" Joan confirmed

"We support and back them… all the way….!" Chloe stated firmly

"We continue in our quest…" Martha nodded…. "For the children…!"

The evening group continued to attract more bereaved parents and siblings....

# Chapter 67

"Martha, Thomas…" Geoffrey welcomed them…. "Please come in…." he cleared his throat…. "Everyone is in the kitchen…".
"Thanks Geoffrey…." Replied Tommy…

Martha smiled….

Tommy walked into the kitchen….

"Congratulations Tommy…!" the chant went up….

And they all clapped….

Tommy's eyes welled up…

He shook his head and looked at Martha…. "You organised this…" and he smiled….
"No Tommy it was a collaboration…" Martha paused… "it was mutually agreed whilst in conversation…".

"Have a drink mate…" Fred passed him a glass of champagne…

Tommy downed it in one and shook his head….

"I'd rather have a Guinness…" He smiled
"I knew you would say that…!" Joan passed him a freshly poured pint….

"Cheers Tommy…" Chloe held her glass high…
"Cheers my dear friend…" Geoffrey followed her lead…
"Cheers Tommy…" Joan raised her glass
"Best of luck… cheers Tom…" Fred touched glasses…

"I am so proud of you…!" Martha wiped her eyes… and kissed him

"We all are…!" …. They roared in unison

"How did you know…?" Tommy asked…
"A little bird whispered in our ears…" Joan smiled…
"A very proud little bird…" Chloe added smiling….

And they all looked at Martha….

"Thank you… thank all of you for your encouragement and support…". Tommy raised his pint of Guinness to all of them nodding… "Thank you…! …. What a lovely surprise…."

"By the by Thomas there is something…" …. Geoffrey cleared his throat… "I need a little word… in the lounge… if you would oblige me…"

Geoffrey beckoned him to lead the way….
Tommy led the way….

"Is everything OK Geoff…?" Tommy asked concerningly

"Please… the lounge…!" Geoffrey pointed
Tommy entered the room….
There was a Therapy couch ready for use in the middle of the room…. With a big purple bow around it…

Tommy looked back…no Geoffrey…. An envelope with his name was on the couch…. He opened it and the words…. "To Tommy …. To Thyself Be True…! … Love from All…"

He turned around to face the door… and they were all standing there in a line….

"I don't know what to say…! …. Tommy sounded shocked
"That's a first…!" giggled Martha…

"That's a mystery of life…!" Geoffrey stated…. smiling

And they all laughed…

"You are funny Geoffrey…" Martha bellowed
"Oh, I say… I'm funny…!" Geoffrey cleared his throat

They all continued to laugh

Tommy held his hands out…
"Who…?" … He paused… "Why…?"

"All of us…" Joan declared
"We clubbed together…" Chloe smiled at him
"Like birds of a feather…!" Martha winked…
"I'm so proud of you Tom…!" Fred held his hand out…

Tommy took Fred's hand… both doing a double clasp…

"Why…?" Tommy asked

"Why…? Why…? … Dear chap…!" Geoffrey exclaimed… then cleared his throat… "We all want a treatment…!" He paused… "Bagsy I'm first…!"

# Chapter 68

"No….! No….! No….!" Chloe screamed

Fred bolted into the kitchen….
Chloe was slumped over the table sobbing her eyes out….

"Chloe what's wrong…?" Fred asked
"Chloe what has happened…?" He pursued…
"Chloe talk to me…?" He paused… "Love what is the matter…?"

Chloe was sitting in the chair, bent over the table, face down on the surface… her arms and hands clasping her head…

Fred scrutinised his wife…. Then scanned the room… his military service kicked in… nothing amiss…

Fred sat next to his wife, embracing his arm around her shoulder…

"Chloe what's happened…?" He asked in a softer tone…
He could hear her mumbling….
"No… No… why…"
"Why... what Chloe…?" He paused… "No … no to what Chloe…?"

She continued to mumble…
"How could anyone be so cruel…"

"Cruel… Chloe love… who's been cruel to you…?"
Fred asked caringly

Fred continued to cradle his Chloe…

Chloe mumbled
"Why ... how ... could anyone be so cruel..." and she
sobbed uncontrollably

Fred again scanned the room... nothing...

Fred saw the post on the table... and sifted through it...
nothing ... a couple of statements...

"Chloe love please tell me what has happened...?"
"So cruel..." She mumbled

As he did so, he took her into both of his arms and
cuddled her close to him...
He then noticed an opened envelope addressed to Chloe
and Fred Miller...
He took it with one hand, no contents ...

"Chloe what has come in this envelope...?" He
whispered into her ear... and kissed her...
"Why so evil..." she sobbed

The he saw the crumpled piece of paper on her lap...
It had fallen as she collapsed onto the table....

Fred took the paper and began to flatten it out on the table
with one hand, as he comforted Chloe with the other...
As he read it, rage erupted inside of him....

He took Chloe closer to him and held her tight...

"Why Fred...?" She howled
"I don't know Chloe..." He paused... "but when I find
out... I will rip their fucking hearts out...!"
"Who could be so heartless... if they had a heart..."
Chloe cuddled into Fred

"We will get to the bottom of this…" He paused… "and if they don't have a heart… I'll rip their fucking throat out… with my bare hands….!"

"I need to phone Tommy and Geoff……."

He pulled his Mobile out of his pocket… and rang them both….

# Chapter 69

Joan was sitting in the kitchen having a cup of coffee…
The post popped through the door…
She looked up the passageway toward the door and there
was one envelope on the floor…

"So, what is that…?" she paused… "another bill… or
advertising material… it should be against the law to
obtain peoples private details….!"

Joan went to the door and picked it up….
"Mrs Mr. Joan Geoffrey Childs… mmm interesting…"
she said

She walked back to the kitchen made herself another
coffee…

"So, what have we here…?" She smiled

Joan opened the envelope and pulled out the contents….

She read it... time after time…

Her eyes welled up and tears cascaded down her face…

"How in heavens name can any human being be so
macabre…" then the bile spilled out… "Evil… Evil…
Evil…evil bastard people…!" she bellowed

She sobbed…
She went to the toilet and was sick….

"Why would anyone be so evil…? She yelled out…

"Joan …. Joanie… Darling… where are you…?" Asked Geoffrey as he entered the house…

Geoffrey searched the downstairs… out the garden…. No Joan…

"Let's have a coffee…" He said aloud
"So, what's this…?" he saw the envelope on the kitchen table…

Geoffrey opened the envelope… no contents…

"How strange…!" Geoffrey began to ponder…

Geoffrey started to climb the stairs to change his clothes…

He could hear sobbing coming from Louise's room…

"Joanie what's wrong my dearest…?" Geoffrey asked delicately….

Joan was crumpled up on Louise's bed… sobbing…

Geoffrey sat on the bed… "Joanie what's happened…?" Geoffrey cleared his throat… "Talk to me darling, please share with me….!"
Joan flung her arms around Geoffrey's neck… quivering…

"How can human beings be so evil…?" She paused… "Why do people want to hurt others so…!" she was sobbing relentlessly

Geoffrey clasped her in his arms… "What has happened…?" He took a moment… "what have we received…?"

At that moment her saw a piece of paper on the pillow….

He laid her down and picked up the paper….
He read it….
His eyes filled with tears….

"Who could be so malicious in sending this…!"
Geoffrey's tears flowed…
"I can't fathom who would do this…" Joan sobbed
"I will find the culprit…responsible for this…!" Geoffrey cleared his throat… "and the wrath of the law will come down on them…"

He stared at the paper…

I must phone Fred and Tommy….

# Chapter 70

"Tom… I think that was the postman…" Martha pointed out…
"Was it…?" Tommy looked up from the table…
"Yea...! can you get it…?"
"Postman you say…" Tommy smiled
"Yea…!" she affirmed
"Postman Pat…?" Tommy grinned
"Postman whoever…!" She giggled… "can you get it whilst I finish preparing this pie…".

Tommy stood up and started to the door…

"What's the rush … it's probably a bill…" He said…

Tommy picked up the letter…
He returned to the table and dropped it on top…

"I'm having another coffee…" He looked at Martha…
"Would you like one…?"
"Yes please…" She smiled.

Martha joined Tommy at the table…

"Who's the letter from…?" Martha asked
"I don't know…!" Tommy winked

Martha picked up the letter

"It's addressed to Mrs Mr Martha Tommy Jackson…!"
Martha looked puzzled
"That's unusual…" Tommy looked up
 Yea…!" Martha pulled a face

Martha began to open it…

She pulled the contents out and read it…
Her face contorted and she began to cry…. Tears dropped
down her cheeks

"What is it…!" Tommy enquired…

Martha's eyes were glued to the contents…

"Martha who is it from…?" Tommy stated

She began to sob….

"What kind of sick minded people are out there…?"
Martha growled
"What…?" Tommy exclaimed

She threw it across the table…
Martha got up and walked to the work top…
Tommy picked it up and read it…
His eyes moisten up and his face twisted…

"Martha…!" Tommy looked at her… "This is sick… I'll
fucking kill them…!" he raged
Martha picked up the plate with the pie on… and threw it
across the room…

"Not before I will….!" She screamed

She went to pick up another dish…
Tommy stood up and grabbed hold of her….

"Stop… stop that…!" Tommy held her… pulling her into
him

She was bawling…
As was Tommy…

"Find out who it is Tom... and put an end to this...". She paused... "Before I do...!"

"I will...!" He said...

"I'll rip their fucking heads off with a claw hammer...!" Martha held on to Tommy...

"I will... I promise...!" Tommy said calmly... but boiling inside

They held each other tight...

"I need to phone Fred and Geoffrey....!" Tommy said...

# Chapter 71

They all sat around the table...
Their faces where blotchy from crying...
The atmosphere could be cut with a knife.... tense...
The silence was deafening...

Fred was the first to cut the ice.... "Do we all have what we received...?"
"We do..." Declared Joan...
"Yes... we have ours..." Tommy held Martha's hand

"Do they all have the same contents of writing..."
Geoffrey spoke up...
"Who knows...!" stated Martha

"Should we read them out..." asked Chloe
"Why not...!" Joan said...
"Do you want me to read them all out...?" Asked Geoffrey...
"No..." stated Martha...
"No..." added Fred...

"Ok Then I'll go first..." Geoffrey went to stand up...
"No..." Joan said... "I'll do it..." She paused...

"Mr. & Mrs. Childs you are cordially invited to The Wedding of..." She sobbed... "Louise and Tommy..."
"Chloe is requested as Chief Bridesmaid..."

They all looked down...

Fred spoke next... "I'll do ours..." He paused...
"Mr & Mrs Miller you are cordially invited to The Wedding of..." He choked... "Sophie and Tommy..."
"Louise is requested as Chief Bridesmaid..."

They all looked up…

Tommy picked up the piece of paper…
"Let me do it Tom…" Martha took it… she paused….

"Mr & Mrs Jackson you are cordially invited to The Wedding of…" She wept… "Louise and Tommy…"
"Chloe is requested as Chief Bridesmaid…"

They stared at each other….

"So, it starts again…!" Fred clenched his fist…
"This is beyond phone calls…" Geoffrey stated
"This is evil…" Joan quantified
"Spiteful and vindictive…" Chloe affirmed
"They are scum and heartless…" Martha growled
"This has got to be stopped… now…!" barked Tommy

There was silence….


"This is very personal…" Geoffrey specified
"The way the invites have been changed… is purposeful… to inflict as much damage as possible…" Joan said
"It's designed to create a split…". Fred stated…
"To break us up…" Chloe said
"Yes… to cause conflict within…" Martha scowled
"That's their agenda…" Tommy stood up… "They don't win…!"

"How do we stop it…?" asked Chloe
"We have no idea who is behind this…!" Joan said
"This has to be stopped…" Martha pointed her finger
"We do not know who is orchestrating these actions…" Geoffrey quizzed

"Then we find out…!" Fred said coldly…
"Maybe visits are in order…!" Tommy's voice was soft but icy….


There was silence.

# Chapter 72

The following day…

"Thomas… How are you progressing with the Spiritual Healing Training…?" queried Geoffrey
"Yea…! … good thanks Geoff" Tommy replied
"How does that work Tom…?" quizzed Fred…
"We learn to connect to the energy, allowing it to flow through us… we are taught pacific hand positions… and the code of conduct" Tommy stated…

"Pacific hand positions…" posed Joan…
"Yea …. Regulated hand positions… It's important to know them, where to touch… where not to touch….!" Tommy paused… "after all one doesn't want to be known… as a Feeler… not a Healer…!"
"Oh dear…!" Chloe looked concerned…
"Yea and we ask if we can touch… those pacific positions… some people for various reasons may not want to be touched…!" Tommy was firm in his word

"Quite right…!" Geoffrey affirmed
"But how does it work Tom…?" Fred pushed

"We are used as a conduit, a medium, a vessel… to allow the energy to flow through us…" He paused…. "Like a medium on the rostrum. They receive messages from spirit and pass them on to the individual…
We allow Spirit Healing energy to flow through us, to the recipient.

"Wow…!" Chloe exclaimed…
"Yea Chloe… wow… I still have a lot to learn…"
Tommy smiled

# Chapter 73

Two days later….

"Geoffrey, can you bring the milk in please….?" Joan asked
"Of course, dearest…" Geoffrey replied

Geoffrey went to the front door and opened it…

He went straight to the lounge… and picked up the phone…

"Thomas, you need to go to your front door, before Martha…!" Geoffrey cleared his throat… "Be prepared and watch out for Martha…!" He paused…. "We will convene at midday… here…"

"Ok… will do…!" Tommy was on alert…

"Fredrick, you need to go to your front door, before Chloe…!" Geoffrey cleared his throat… "Be prepared and watch out for Chloe…!" He paused… "We will convene at midday… here…"

"Ok… I'm on it…!" Fred was aware of Geoffrey's tone…

"Joan… will you join me in the lounge please…?" Geoffrey stated
"Ok Geoffrey… is everything ok… where's the milk…?" Joan queried
"I have the milk, bring the coffees with you…" Geoffrey countered

"Joan please sit down… I found this leaning on the door…." Geoffrey showed her…
Joan screeched… "No…...! No…!" Why…?"

Geoffrey held her tight…

"The Millers and Jacksons are meeting here at midday…"
Geoffrey told her…
"Them also…?" She sobbed...
"Yes…!" Geoffrey confirmed.

# Chapter 74

"Martha put the kettle on love…" Tommy asked
"Ok, will do…" Martha smiled

He went to the front door… and opened it…
He also went straight into their lounge…

"Martha, can you bring the drinks into the lounge
please…?" Tommy called out
"Ok, love…" Martha answered

Martha came into the lounge, placing their coffees on the
table….

"Geoffrey phoned me…" Tommy paused… "and asked
me to check something out…"
"What…?" She quizzed
"I found this at the front door…!" Tommy showed her…

Martha went into a rage… "These fucking bastards…
how can they do this… putting us through this again…"

"We will sort it…" Tommy held her tight… "we will sort
it…"
"Geoffrey, Joan… Fred, Chloe…?" She asked
"Yes… definitely Geoff and Joan… most likely Fred and
Chloe…" Tommy took a breath… "we are meeting at
Geoffrey's at midday…"

Martha's tears flowed….

# Chapter 75

"Chloe darling..." Fred winked..." make us a cuppa...?"
"Of course, ... You don't have to wink..." Chloe smiled

Fred got up and went straight to the front door... and opened it...
He too went straight into the lounge...

"Where do you want this cuppa...?" Chloe yelled smiling...
"In the lounge darling..." Fred paused... "come into the lounge..."

Sounds like the fly to the web... She giggled...

Fred closed his eyes...
Chloe entered the room and put the drinks down...

"Geoffrey phoned me...." Fred swallowed... "And asked me to do something..."
"Sounds intriguing....!" Chloe smiled
"I found this.... At the front door..." Fred showed her...

"Oh my God... why... No...!" ... Chloe slumped into the settee... and wailed.... "Why....!"

Fred sat next to her and caressed her ....

"Martha... Joan..." She asked...
"Yes..." Fred confirmed... "That's my understanding... we are meeting up at Joan and Geoff's at midday...!"

# Chapter 76

"This is going way too far…" Geoffrey opened
"It's mind games…" Chloe added
"It's emotional abuse…" Martha added
"It's psychological warfare…" Fred stated
"It's mental torture…" Tommy growled
"It's assault and battery…" Joan confirmed

Tommy looked up… "I still don't believe it's the East End mob…"
Fred nodded…. "It's not military…"
Geoffrey pondered… "Is it the establishment… I'm not sure…!"

"Then who…?" Chloe quizzed
"Who would do this…?" Martha asked
"Who would go to these extremes... cost … time…" … Joan mused… "Risk…?"

"Whoever it is… they need to be stopped…!" Tommy said
"Yea... because each time its intensified…!" Fred added
"What's next….?" Questioned Geoffrey

"What does it say on yours…" asked Chloe
"You mean our wreath…!" Martha scowled
"Three wreaths…!" Joan pointed out

"How macabre though, to place a WREATH...! on each door…" Geoffrey was quite demonstrative in his words…

"Ours says… "RIP Louise Joan Geoffrey" … Joan said…
"Ours says… "RIP Sophie Chloe Fred" Fred stated…

"Ours says… "RIP Tommy Martha Tommy" Martha concluded…

"Pretty basic in their mind set…!" …. Geoffrey affirmed
"I'd say, so are their intentions…!" Fred inserted…
"Time for visits…!" Tommy stated.

# Chapter 77

"Hello Tommy lad…" Jack smiled broadly

Jack stood up and held out his hand, Tommy took it and they clasped each other's hands firmly….

"Hello Jack…" Tommy smiled back…
"Good to see you son…!" Jack said
"Good to see you Jack…" Tommy replied
"So, what you doing in this neck of the woods….?" Jack paused… "although, you know you're always welcome…!"

Tommy looked at Jack… his head on a slight tilt… with a wry smile….

"Thanks Jack…"
"So, son… what can I do for ya…"! Jack asked politely….

Tommy smiled at Jack….

"Ok…!" Jack paused…" I know why you're here… and what's been happening…."
"Why doesn't that surprise me…" Tommy paused… "Put a stop to it Jack… if you don't… I will…!"
"Tommy son… the word went out after our last meeting…. It's not our team…!" Jack sat up straight, stern faced
"Then who…?" Tommy looked puzzled
"We don't know… fingers have gone into pies… words have been had… stern words have been had…" Jack stared at Tommy… "No word on the street…!"
"What…!" quizzed Tommy

"Even Boof Boof has put himself about… He's got a raver on… thinking someone's putting it on ya… when he backed off…!". Jack took a mouthful of coffee… "it's a diabolical liberty… as Boof Boof put it…"

"Jack this don't make sense…" Tommy paused…. "If you can't find out…, how do we put a stop to it….?"

"No one understands what you're doing son… a mystery of life…" Jack took another mouthful… "I'll rephrase that… they understand what you're doing…" Jack paused…. "But not who with…!"

"I've found what I've been looking for all my life Jack… and I'm happy…I've found my purpose in life and what I want to do…!" Tommy smiled at Jack…. "And who with….!"

"I'm on your side Tommy…!" Jack paused…" Just not who with….!"

There was silence….

"Jack…" Tommy smiled… "If you don't heal, what hurt you…. You bleed on people who didn't cut you…!"

"Very profound…!" Jack nodded
"We are all doing it for the kids….!" Tommy stated

"I will put the word out… and see what we can uncover…". Jack smiled
"Thanks Jack…" Tommy nodded

Tommy stood up to leave and shook hands with Jack firmly… as he reached the door…. Jack said…...

"Tommy... son...." Jack looked Tommy square on.... And touched his forehead with his index finger....... "Don't come in here, ever, making threats to me...!"

Tommy bowed his head touching his index finger to his forehead.... "Sorry... and... Thanks...!"

# Chapter 78

"Boss....!" The word went up....
"Hello lads...!" Fred acknowledged

They all stood up to attention, but didn't salute......

There was eight of Fred's old regiment... sitting in the
pub they all used to use....

"Drink Boss...?".

"I've already ordered them...." Fred smiled....
"How did you know what we were drinking...?" Asked
one of Fred's unit....
Fred smiled again... "I've been in, did reconnaissance,
scrutinised the situation, adapted, laid a plan and
exercised it..."

"I didn't see you...!"
"Been in...!"
"Scrutinised the situation...!"
"I've had my eyes on the door since we arrived....!"

"No, you didn't... I think you are all getting sloppy....!"
Fred smiled wryly

"He's like a chameleon..."
"Adapt and blend in..."
"The Master of covert...!"
"That's how he survived....!"

"Six pints of Guinness, two bitters..." Fred paused...
"I've ordered 8 Whiskey chasers....!"

"Great to see you... Boss...."!

"How you been…?"
"How's retirement…?"

Fred sat down with his men… and outlined the entire
episodes of the hostilities, of what had been implemented
on them…
There was silence….

"So, who is responsible…?" Fred looked at them
individually…
"No idea…"
"Not heard a word Boss…"
"No directive has been given…"
"Legally or covert…!"

They all shook their heads….

"Come on lads…… someone must know something…?"
Fred took a mouthful of whiskey… "Nothing gets past
you lot…!"
"Apart from you…!"

"Boss I'm not saying there wasn't conversations, that
took place with regards to revenge…. On your behalf…!"
"Comeuppance… Boss…!"
"But you gave us a directive and we honoured that….!"
"Even Tap Tap….?" Fred quizzed

"Ask him…?"
"He's behind you….!"

Fred turned… and there was Tap Tap… finger pointing at
Fred's head…. A cynical smile on his face….

"You gave the order Boss…!"  Tap Tap winked at
Fred… "Didn't agree with it… but you gave the order
and that was enough…. We respected it…."

Fred shook his head… "Then who…?"
"You want us to take care of the oppo…?" Tap Tap
quizzed

Fred looked at Tap Tap…

"I mean, those who are responsible for the
conflict…being inflicted…!" Tap Tap paused… "On
behalf of you all…!"
"Say the word…" they all nodded….

"We don't know who it is…" Fred shook his head….
"Keep your ears to the ground… observe… a little
digging… nose twisting if you have to…" Fred took a
mouthful…. eyes squinting…. "And let me know before
you take any action….!"

# Chapter 79

"Geoffrey O'l boy…. Its jolly good to see you…!"
"Yes, Childs so pleased to receive your call, to get together….!"
"Not before time, what…!"

"Yes, I'm pleased you could all convene at such short notice…!". Geoffrey smiled

"Dam convenient that the Lodge was free of any functions, I'd say…."
"Yes, once your call was received, with pleasure I might add, the invitations went out instantly….!"
"So, everyone's here, that was present at our last little chat…."

"That's was the intention… and what I hoped for…!" Geoffrey cleared his throat… "Although at our last meeting there was guests hiding in the shadows…" He paused… "And of course, our mysterious guest in the chair, the voice with no face…." He cleared his throat again… "I do hope all could attend….!"

Geoffrey looked around the room… shadowy corners… the desk in front of the patio doors… and the high-backed chair facing the garden…...

"Now… now…! Geoffrey, let's not create acrimonies …!"
"I'm sure that's not your intention…!"
"No, to call this extraordinary meeting Childs O'l boy… I'm absolute, there is a positive conclusion…!"
"Yes Geoffrey, one senses that you may have, after careful consideration to the best outcome, to all concerned… come around to the popular decision….!"

There was silence…...

"So, which one of you, was it….?" Geoffrey cleared his throat…. "Or was it a co-operative order given…!"

"What…?"
"Have you lost your mind…?"
"What are you referring to Childs…?"
"In heavens name O'l boy… what are your accusations…!"

Geoffrey ignored their words… and entered every shadowy corner, with purpose, without hesitation…. Looking into the eyes of the shadows that lingered…. He then turned his attention to the high-backed chair… and walked upright around the desk… and stared at the figure in the chair…. Who stared straight back at him…

"One should take care in assuming one can push their luck…. Childs….!" The voice in the chair stated coldly….

"Luck…!" Geoffrey cleared his throat… "I am most definitely not pushing my luck… but now we know, who we are dealing with…!" He mused and smiled…. "You may consider not pushing your luck any further…!"

There was silence….

"Let me tell you a little story… you may find riveting and interesting…!" Geoffrey proceeded to tell them every detail… in chronological… evidential… highlighted… order….

There was silence….

"I might add… my Two dear friends at this very precise moment…" Geoffrey cleared his throat…. "We are in contact by video, satellite link… A little over my head… but amazing what you can find in the stores… when you know where to look…. And…" He paused… "He Who Dares…" He smiled… "Knows where to look…". Geoffrey smiled broadly…. "As I was saying… my Two dearest friends are having the self-same conversations…. With their individual, shall we say ex-comrades in arms…." Geoffrey face was stone… ice in his eyes…. "The World's Finest and Underworld… who you have threatened to terminate… and by chance, now have all your faces….!"

There was silence…...

"You have made a big mistake Geoffrey…!"
"Don't threaten us…!" Geoffrey remonstrated…

"We have nothing to do with what has been happening…!"
"Not one of us… has sanctioned these actions…!"

"Then who…?". Geoffrey demanded…

"We are not involved with your fairy stories or your unfortunate run of misadventure….!" The face in the chair stood up… emotionless... "You have made a catastrophic error of judgement…" and he snarled….

Geoffrey did the circle of the room… pointing his finger at every individual…. And returning to the face in the chair….
"And you should all remember…!" Geoffrey smirked….
"Everyone of your mug shots and recordings of all conversations… are now in the possession of the most dangerous people you would not like to upset….!"

Geoffrey pondered… "I would ascertain, threatening to top these said people is most likely to upset them… they could well be waiting for you outside….!"

They scurried and vacated the room like rats from a sinking ship…. Including the face from the chair… who was no longer looking so smug….

# Chapter 80

"Well, it wasn't anything to do with the East End firm….!" Tommy assured them… "As you well heard…" he paused… "And I wasn't comfortable being wired up…."

"Was that really necessary…" Martha asked

"Yes, it was…!" Geoffrey cleared his throat… "We had to be conclusive and agree…!"

"Was… Boof Boof… in agreement…" Chloe asked tentatively…

"Yes, Chloe… Boof Boof is on our side… He is upset people are doing it to us… that's a good sign…." assured Martha…

"I still feel like a grass… a snitch…" Tommy shook his head… "Fucking wired up with my own people…."

"It was imperative…!" Joan stated… "We needed to have clarity….!"

"Ok, so we all agree the East End firm are not doing it…" Geoffrey stated

"Or do they have any idea where its stemming from….!" Fred injected….

# Chapter 81

"Fred… any reservations…" Geoffrey cleared his throat… "With regard to your boys….?"
"None… I'm sure they have nothing to do with what's happening…!" Fred nodded his head…
"It certainly sounded convincing…" Martha added…
"I do concur…!" Joan assured

"Tommy to put you at ease… it didn't feel right to me either…" Fred paused… "A traitor in the gang…"
"Thanks Fred…" Tommy smiled
"It, again I confirm…" Geoffrey cleared his throat… "It was essential that we all had the chance to listen to what was being said…!"
"I have to say I believe them…" Tommy said….

"Do you think Tap Tap is on our side…?" Chloe quizzed…
"I would swear my profession on that Chloe…!" …. Joan smiled

"So, it's not the finest…!" Geoffrey stated
"And they have no ideas… who…?" Martha looked round the room…

# Chapter 82

"So… Geoffrey….!" Fred smiled… "Where did the video satellite link… contact… come from…?"
"That certainly was a woozy… inspired in fact…".
Tommy smiled

Geoffrey cleared his throat…. "I, unlike you two chaps… only know some of these individuals from the circuit, the Lodge…" Geoffrey paused… "And now I know some very important... influential faces…."

"None the less it was a very bold move Geoffrey…"
Martha smiled at him

"The Two chaps…" Geoffrey pointed at Fred and Tommy… "Have faith and put their lives on the line… earnt respect… within their individual families…" Geoffrey pondered… "With their comrades and firms… They know them… they have trust built in… and they can feel it…"

"Still a gutsy move Geoffrey…!". Chloe exclaimed

"They are faceless people who hide behind closed doors… who now believe they have been exposed…!" Geoffrey mused… "We don't know them... we cannot trust them… we could not trust their word…. They would stab us in the back in a second… more like get someone else to do it….!"

"But video satellite link… contact…!" Stated Chloe
"You had a microphone connected to a transmitter… that's bottle Geoffrey…!" Martha crowed…

"Notwithstanding that… I am so proud of you Geoffrey…!" Joan hugged him…. "So proud my big love…!"

"You got my respect big man…!" Tommy smiled… "Balls of steel…" and touched his index finger to his forehead….
"He Who Dares…!" Fred saluted him… "And you dared… you've got a rod of iron in that backbone… respect…!"

Geoffrey eyes moisten… and he cleared his throat….

"It's not them…!" Geoffrey composed himself… "Emotionless vessels yes… narcissistic gutless back stabbing rats… yes…!" Geoffrey paused… "The way they ran for cover when they thought they were exposed…. No not them…!"

# Chapter 83

"Tommy will you be setting your couch up next to mine....? Tommy's Reiki Master quizzed...

She looked at Martha and winked... "He deserves it....!"

Joan and Chloe hugged Martha.... "You must be so proud...." And they all began to weep....

"It's all right Tom...!" Fred paused once he had all their attention... "I'll be the skivvy in the kitchen...!" and he roared out laughing.... "Go for it bruvver... I'm proud of you...!"
"Quite right Fredrick... I'm the doorman... come bouncer... in mother care... oh oh oh..." Geoffrey laughed... "And concierge... maître d'...!" he paused... "You are the scullery maid... bottle washer and beverage provider...."
"Yea now old magic hands over there, has got promotion....". Fred threw the tea towel over his shoulder

They all laughed...

Tommy set his couch up....

Parents and siblings, came through the door.... More each week were turning up.... in need ....

The counsellors where ready...
The Indian Head and Reflexologist Therapists were ready...

People chatted and shared their bereavements and grief... Tears were shared by all......

"May I have a one to one….?"

"Yes of course…" Martha took the lady by the hand and escorted her to a counsellor…

"Can I speak to one of the counsellors….?"

"That's why they are here…" Chloe smiled "Come with me…."

"Would it be possible to have an Indian Head massage….?"

"Of course, you can…." Joan smiled and pointed out the Therapist…

One of the dads who had been conscious and slightly embarrassed about having a treatment before saw Tommy who he had chatted to on occasion…. "Is Tommy now doing Reiki treatments…?"

"Yes…!" said Martha beaming…

"Mmm ahhh… would it be … mmmm …" The dad was struggling….

"Would you like to speak to Tommy and maybe have a Reiki treatment…?" Martha held her hand out and smiled….

"Yea…!"

Many of the bereaved parents who knew other bereaved parents were recommending the group… a form of self-help aided by professionals…. The word was spreading…. As was their reputation of being available with open doors and open arms and open ears…… to help….

"We may need to get bigger premises if it continues growing…" Joan stated…

"Yes, or do more than one group a week…" Chloe paused "Maybe two….!"

"We may need to look for our own premises…!" Martha winked

"At this rate…" Fred smiled "I'm going to have some help in the kitchen…."

"A jolly successful evening…" … Geoffrey mused… "If that's the correct terminology…"

"Tommy…" Fred smiled… "How many treatments did you do…....?"

Tommy looked at his Reiki Master….

She nodded in approval….

"I did three…" He smiled… "One man, who was nervous to begin with … then alright… and two mums…"

"Well done, Tommy…!" said Chloe… "I want one…."

"Oh yes….!" exclaimed Martha… I'M proud of you…. I'm your wife… when do I have my turn on the couch….?"

"Maybe just a little too much information, shared their Martha…!" Giggled Fred

"Yes, Tommy you must be so pleased, with what you have achieved…?". Joan smiled

"There is no price that compares to the satisfaction Joan…" Tommy paused… "When after the treatment the recipient smiles… says thank you…" Tommy pondered for a moment…. "And tells you they feel relaxed, less stressed and their mind feels clear… even if it's only for a short space of time…. respite…"

There was a short silence of appreciation in those words……

Joan looked at Geoffrey…. "Geoffrey dear… are you Ok…?" Joan looked puzzled…. "Are you not going to take the opportunity to say some kind words to Tommy….?"

Geoffrey's eyes never raised from the ground....
"Mmm... yes... indeed.... word of mouth... reputation...
bigger premises... growing....!" Geoffrey cleared his
throat.... and raised his eyes smiling... "Yes Thomas,
well done indeed and to all our therapists indeed and to
you lovely ladies and Fredrick...!" He pondered... "In
what you have inspired... in what is being achieved....!"

They all looked at him, the Therapists, the Counsellors,
Martha, Chloe, Joan, Fred, and Tommy....
Inquisitively...

"And you Geoff...!" Tommy stated...
Geoffrey smiled... "I am a mere speck of paint on a
canvas... of a bigger picture...."

"No one player is bigger than the Team Geoff..."
Tommy winked
"And you da man with balls of steel..." Fred said with a
wry smile...

*"One for all..."*
*"All for one..."*

They all heard the words....

The Counsellors, the Therapist... all looked around the
hall...

Joan, Chloe, Martha, Fred, Geoffrey, Tommy, all looked
at each other, with a knowing look on their faces...

"There here you know that, don't you..." said one of the
therapists in a soft tone, who was also a medium...

317

# Chapter 84

"Tom who is that sitting on our doorstep....?" Martha said with trepidation in her voice....
"I'd say crumpled up..." Tommy stated
"Who is it Tom...?" Martha quizzed...
I don't know, I can't tell love... wrapped right up with a hood on...". Tommy slowed the vehicle and scrutinised...
"Tommy don't pull onto the driveway...!" Martha said alarmingly....
"Ok ok don't be alarmed..." Tommy said trying to reassure her...
"Don't be alarmed after what's been going on...!" Martha paused ...." And with the wreath...!"

Tommy pulled into the kerb before the driveway...
He looked at the crumpled-up figure...

"I've got to get out...we can't just sit here..." Tommy started to get out the motor...
"Tom... it could be...."
"Shhhh Martha...." Tommy cut her off... and placed his hand on her forearm....

As he started to walk up the pathway the figure started to rise and unfold....
Tommy approached with care but assertively....
As he got closer the figure pulled the hood back revealing his identity....

"Freddie lad...!" Tommy said startled...
"Hello Mr. Jackson..." Freddie said sheepishly
"What's with the cloak and dagger all covered up...?" Tommy quizzed
"Privacy...!" Freddie said...

318

Tommy turned to Martha, who was still sitting in the motor…

"Martha, pull onto the driveway…" He paused…. "It's young Freddie…… it's ok…"

Martha got into the driver's seat …
Tommy opened the front door…

"Come in lad… come in…" Tommy paused… "It's good to see you…!"

They walked into the kitchen and Martha was right behind them….

"Freddie it's great to see you….!" Martha hugged him…
"I wasn't sure…I didn't think I'd be welcome after my last visit…" Freddie took a breath… "Not after the things I said when I was leaving…."

"Tensions were high…" Martha said sympathetically…
"It was a lot to come to terms with…" Tommy said… "It was for us at the beginning…"
"I'm so sorry… I was so rude and uncaring…" Freddie wiped his eyes… "I wasn't even thinking about what you two… six had been through…" He took a breath… "Please forgive me…"
"We are pleased you have come to see us…" Martha said…
"Would you like a wassa son….?" Tommy winked
"That would be nice…" Freddie smiled… "Thank you…."

"How is the football…?" Tommy enquired….
"Yes, I'm playing, training hard…" Freddie nodded his head almost apologetically… "And made the first team…

I think about Tommy all the time when I'm playing… we should both be out their…"
Martha and Tommy's eyes welled up….
As did Freddie's….

"More importantly… how are you all coping…?" Freddie asked…
"Oh, we're ok…" Tommy smiled…
"Really… it's all over the East End… what's been going on…!" Freddie took a mouthful of his wassa…. "If you know we're to listen…"
"Oh, I see…" Martha said
"No one knows a thing…" Freddie said… "Everyone who's anyone is denying they have anything to do with it… it's like a vail of silence where its coming from…"
"That's what we're getting…" Tommy stated…
"There's some form of evil out their…" Freddie took a mouthful…. "Who for whatever reason, don't want you to succeed…."

There was silence….

"I just want you all to know… it's nothing to do with me…" Freddie stated…

"Thank you, Freddie…!" Martha welled up…
"We appreciate that son…." Tommy choked up…

# Chapter 85

"Chloe I'm popping up the shops…." Fred paused "Do we need anything…?"
"No love, we are ok…" Chloe replied….

Fred grabbed his car keys and left the house….

"Oh my God, what the fuck…!" He exclaimed… "Who has done this….?"

He went back inside…

"Chloe, you need to see this…!" Fred said…

He then went back outside, Chloe following in his footsteps….

Fred phoned Tommy and Geoffrey….

"Oh no…. not again…!" Chloe yelled … "When will it stop…!"

# Chapter 86

"Joan that was Fredrick…" Geoffrey stated…
"Is everything ok…?" Joan answered puzzled

Geoffrey raised his eyebrows…

"He said we need to go outside…!" Geoffrey replied
"Why…?" Joan asked alarmed

Geoffrey looked at Joan and motioned toward the front door…. And started in that direction….
Joan Followed him in expectation… but not of what….

"So, it continues…!" Geoffrey shook his head…
Joan looked on… "Oh no… this has got to stop…"
"Yes love…" Geoffrey stated… "But when…?"
"Before it goes too far…!" Joan exclaimed…
"It's gone far enough…!" Geoffrey quantified…

# Chapter 87

"Tommy your phone's ringing…". Martha called to Tommy… "It's Fred… shall I answer it…?"
"Yes, answer it for me please…." Tommy yelled from upstairs…

"Ok Fred I'll tell Tommy…" Martha replied to Fred's request…

Tommy came down the stairs

"Is everything Ok love…?" Tommy asked
Martha pulled a face… "Fred said we need to go outside…!"

They looked at each other…

"Ok…" Tommy paused… "Why…?"
"He just said we need to come outside…" Martha held her hands out and shrugged her shoulders...

They both started for the front door… and went out…. Standing in their driveway….

"Tommy, look what they have done…" Martha yelled in despair
"Bastards…!" Tommy yelled loud enough for Geoffrey, Fred, Chloe and Joan to hear
Martha looked at Tommy… "What next…?"
"Who is doing this…?" Tommy raged…

# Chapter 88

All Three of the families stood in their own driveway… inspecting the handy work….

Then they congregated each in turn, at their own sites of residence…

"Who has done this…?" begged Chloe…
Joan shook her head… "No one seems to know Chloe…"
"We had a visit from young Freddie…" Martha stated…
"He said there is not a whisper of who is doing this to us…!"

Fred looked at the handy work… "This could only have been done during the night…"
"Yea, whilst we all slept…!" Tommy paused… "They must have been very quiet, experienced no doubt…
"Why do you say, they, Thomas…?" Geoffrey probed
"Three different homes, far enough apart in distance… too risky for one person…in not being seen or heard…"
Tommy concluded
"Yea fair point of fact…" Fred inputted… "More than one person… Two, Three and possibly a driver for a quick escape…"

"A planned conspiracy from start to finish…" Joan stated
"Whatever the end is…!". Chloe added
"This is evil, as young Freddie said…" Martha paused…
"They… are intent in stopping us…."

"So, Thomas what do you think they used… to create this damage…?" asked Geoffrey…
"Brake fluid…!" Tommy pondered… "They have poured brake fluid over our vehicles… which has stripped the paint work back to the metal…"

"Plus, the damage it's done to all the rubber seals… window screen, side windows, back window…" added Fred…

"And possible electrics…" Tommy nodded…

"I'd say Two tins on each motor…." Fred perused the damage

"Hence possibly Three individuals…?" Geoffrey concurred

"Yes…!" Fred paused… "At the same time… one hit…"

"Why, why would they want to stop us from trying to do good…?" Chloe paused… "After what we have all gone through…"

"And come out the other side…" Joan paused…

"Indeed… why…?"

"Because they are evil…" Martha paused… "And are intent on not allowing good from devastation… to prevail…"

"Good cannot be seen to be victorious…!" Geoffrey stated

"Do you think more visits are worth it…?" Tommy asked

"No, this is not the people we know… it's not our people…!" Fred shook his head…

"Then what…!" quizzed Joan

"Then we will pursue a different course of action…!" Geoffrey stated

"We had better inform the insurance companies….!" Tommy said

"And the police…!" Geoffrey paused… "The police will now have to be officially informed…!"

"Criminal Damage…" Joan added.

# Chapter 89

"Geoffrey...!" Tommy queried... "Did you speak with that detective in the squad...?"
"Yea Geoff what was the outcome of that...?" Fred quizzed...

Martha, Chloe, Joan, Fred and Tommy all looked at Geoffrey with anticipation....

"Yes, I did..." Geoffrey cleared his throat...
"Unofficially... off the record... I informed him of all the misdemeanours we are encountering...!"

Silence that lasted for ever...

"Geoffrey please dearest..." Joan held out her hands...
"What was the outcome of his covert investigations...?"
"He is still digging..." Geoffrey's voice was flat...
"And what has he dug up so far...?" Joan cross examined....

Silence....

Geoffrey looked up.... He cleared his throat... "As of yesterday, when I spoke with him last.... There is no evidence, no connections, no collusions..." Geoffrey paused... "Nothing... he can find nothing, no traces...what soever... blind allies...!"

"That's impossible...!" Tommy argued...
"He's in the squad...!" Fred maintained...

"Whoever it is..." Geoffrey mused... "They do not exist...!"

# Chapter 90

They all convened to Martha's kitchen and sat in silence after informing the police and insurance companies......

"I am so stressed..." said Chloe... "Can we have a drink...!"
"No Chloe..." said Fred caringly... We need to keep a clear head..."
"Anxiety levels are at a peak... Joan added
"Tommy why don't you give the girls a Reiki treatment..." suggested Martha...
"That is all I can offer... at this time..." Tommy said...
"And of course, you are all welcome..."

They sat in silence...

Geoffrey broke the ice... "I'd like to take you up on that offer...!"
"I'll go next Tom..." Fred nodded his head... "Unless the ladies would like to go first..."

Tommy gave them a treatment one by one....
They all sat in the lounge whilst Tommy worked on them.... soaking up the calming energy....

Serene....

"What's those noises from upstairs..." Martha looked at the door...
"They're coming down the stairs...!" Tommy looked over toward the door...
"I can smell Louise's perfume..." Joan's eyes wept
"Sophie's as well.... Chloe's eyes welled up... I can smell it...

"Tommy… I can smell Tommy…!" Martha's eyes moistened up…

"My darling daughter…" Geoffrey choked…
"Sophie…" Fred wept…
"It's Tommy's aftershave…" Tommy eyes flooded…

They all sat staring at the door… in supreme tranquillity….

The door opened…
Their children appeared one by one holding hands….
Smiling at them…
They sat in awe at what they were witnessing….
Tears flowing down their faces….

*"Don't be scared…".* They heard young Tommy's words…
*"We have come to see you…"* Louise's words could be heard
*"To give you strength…"* Sophie's words were heard
*"We love you all…"*
*"Unconditional love…",*

Their parents were all crying in seeing their beloved children… in perfect form…

"Oh, our darling Louise…" Joan and Geoffrey hugged so tightly…
"Sophie, our wonderful baby… Chloe and Fred embraced tightly…
"Tommy, my Tommy…" Martha and Tommy said in unison… cuddling each other…
"We miss you… so much…"
"We love you… so much…."
*"Don't give up…"*
*"Don't give in…"*

*"Please keep going on…"*
*"Love will win…".*
*"We love you…".*
*"We are always with you…."*

Were the words they heard from their children….

# Chapter 91

"So, we continue…!" Fred stated commandingly

"Yes, we do…!" Confirmed Martha…

"Absolutely…" Joan added…

"I'm not giving up…" Tommy said stubbornly

"Yes…!" Geoffrey affirmed… "We must…!"

"And when will it stop…?" Chloe questioned…

There was silence….

"Sadly, in every aspect of life there is a battle for supremacy….!" Geoffrey broke the silence… "Those that must be in charge…"

"The concept has been going on for centuries…" Joan added

"Control… power and control… created by man…" Fred stated… "Wars… famine… austerity… for money…. and they are willing to send people to die for their own end…"

"Good against bad… right against wrong… evil against love… pitting people against each other…" Martha said sadly…

"Nations against each other… religion against each other…" Tommy quantified…… "You also have those who cling to the coat tails of those who have the power and money…" He paused… "Hoping for some beneficial drippings, parasites who will do the dirty deeds, sneaky people who crave power…. who desire the limelight, who don't have it within… hopeful of some recognition…!"

"They cannot allow good, love, compassion to prevail…" Chloe pondered… "That's evil…cruel…!"

There was a serenity in the room….

"They do not see it has evil…" Geoffrey cleared his throat… "They see it as their right… to rule…!"
"Narcissistic individuals, unseen faces…" Joan stated…
"Who must control… who must have power…!"
"Do you believe this is who we are up against…?" Martha quizzed…
"Who do you think has the power to arrange these acts without being seen…!" Fred stated
"Hiding behind this vail of invisibility, immunity… silence…!" Chloe specified
"No one knows who's doing it…where it's coming from…" Tommy thought… "Not the establishment… Not the police… not the underworld… not the military… who have all delved deeply…!"

Silence as they took it in… the severity of their plight….

"We continue….!" Tommy said firmly
"We carry on…!" Fred stated sternly
"We have no option…!" Martha affirmed…
"We have an option…" Joan mused… "It depends if you want this evil to succeed…"
"How do we stop it…? Chole queried...
Geoffrey cleared his throat…. "I have an idea that's been whirling around in my mind…."

 They all stared at Geoffrey….

# Chapter 92

"I've been giving this a great deal of consideration since our last conversation, why us…?" questioned Chloe.

"Why not us…!" Geoffrey cleared his throat… "Because they believe they can…!" He paused… "They have the divine right…!"
"But why us…?" Chloe mused… "We're only small fry…!"
"The pebble in the pond syndrome, the ripple effect…!" Geoffrey cleared his throat…. "They are frightened of it spreading…!"

"Of what spreading….?" Chloe queried…
"Goodness…" Geoffrey smiled…. "Love….!"
"But we are mere minnows…." Chloe declared
Geoffrey pondered…. "From tiny seeds… so bushes grow and bloom…. And beautiful roses flower, roses blossom…!" He took a breath… "From tiny acorns, so mighty oak trees grow, with roots and branches that reach far and wide…"
"So, you are saying they stop us…" Chloe thought…
"destroy what we are doing now…!" She swallowed…
"Because we are a threat…!"
"They crush the seed before life has growth…!" Geoffrey professed…
"How do you mean branches go far and wide…?" Chloe asked

There was a moment of silence…

"If we are able…" Geoffrey paused… "If we have it within us, to come together and form an alliance of love and friendship to help others…" Geoffrey cleared his throat… "After the trauma of devastation and loss, individually and as a collective. That we have incurred and create a love and a bond to help others..." He paused... "Then others may follow...!"

Silence....

"You're saying other people in similar situations can forgive...!" Chloe looked to the heavens, her eyes moist from emotion... "Release can relinquish their anger, hurt, resentment and revenge..."
"Yes, if we can show it's possible..." Geoffrey cleared his throat... "Lead by example... Then why can't others...!"

They all looked at each other in silence....

"For oaks to take root and grow, branches to go far and wide...!" Chloe probed... "Are you saying we need to expand, grow bigger...?"
"I have a plan...!" Geoffrey divulged...
"Is this the idea that's whirling around in your mind...?" Chloe questioned
"No...!" Geoffrey cleared his throat... "That's a totally different plan....!"
"Which one do we implement first...?" Chloe quizzed

"We will purchase a premise...!" Geoffrey pondered... "That will meet our requirement's... and service our needs..." Geoffrey cleared his throat... "We will create a retreat... A residential retreat... Offering Complementary Therapies....!"

"And what about what we have grown here...!" interrogated Chloe

"We continue dear Chloe..." Geoffrey recognised her concerns... "We transfer the group to our new premises… once or twice a week if necessary…as needs must…!"

"And what if people can't travel to our new premises…!" Chloe quizzed again…
"Then we do…!" Geoffrey paused… "We will continue to operate from the church hall… until the time comes when we find others who will continue the work, we have started…."

"They are attacking us for what we are doing in a small hall…" Chloe swallowed hard… "Because they see us has a threat…!"
"Exactly…!" Geoffrey confirmed…

"Then on a grander scale, logically…" Chloe stated… "We would be a greater threat…therefore the attacks would continue, on a grander scale….!"

They had all sat back in awe of the depth of conversational intercourse between Chloe and Geoffrey…
Now… They all looked at Geoffrey…

"That's plan B…!" Geoffrey stated as a matter of fact….
"You have really thought this through…?" Chloe grilled
"Yes, absolutely…!" Geoffrey declared… "I've prepared a business plan…!" Geoffrey cleared his throat… "And may I add… the talent we have on hand, we are more than capable of succeeding….!"

Silence….
They all sat viewing Geoffrey in admiration and anticipation….
Silence prevailed….

Chloe broke the silence….

"We now know what plan A is…!". Chloe smiled wryly… "What's plan B…?"

"In good time… in good time…!" Geoffrey cleared his throat and took a deep breath, pondering… "Let it ferment… then when all the fragments come together…as a whole… I'll reveal it to you all…" He paused… "Then we can implement it… and hatch it…!"

"Geoffrey…!" they all exclaimed in unity…

# Chapter 93

"Thomas my dear friend….?" Geoffrey smiled at Tommy
"Oh, my my…!" Tommy smiled… "My dear friend…!
Mmm… come on what do you want me to do…what am
I letting myself in for…"
"Thomas…!" Geoffrey smiled… "Ye of little faith…."
"Be careful Tom…!" Fred roared… "The wig is after
borrowing some money to buy the retreat….!"

They all giggled….

"Heathens…!" Geoffrey cleared his throat… "I surround
myself with heathens…!"
He started to laugh

"Come on commander in chief… what is it you
want….?" Tommy laughed…
"The strategist is plotting…!" Fred giggled…

They all giggled…. But all respected Geoffrey's mind of
thought…

"May I experience some Spiritual Healing please…?"
Geoffrey declared

Serenity returned to the room….

"Yes Geoff…" Tommy smiled… "Of course, you can…"
"That's different to the Reiki…?" Geoffrey paused… "Is
it not, if my understanding is correct…"
"Yes, the true essence of Reiki is recognised as an
ancient science…" Tommy smiled… "Where has with
Spiritual Healing… I'm used has a conduit, that allows
spiritual energy, healing energy to flow through me…"

"Yes, jolly good… I would very much wish to experience that then…!" Geoffrey smiled… "Ye of little faith…!"

Tommy smiled back at his friend….

There was a supreme silence in the room….

"Me too…!" declared Fred…
"So, will I…" Joan smiled
"Yes please…" Chloe chimed in
"In for a penny…" Martha added… "In for a pound…!"

"It will be my pleasure… Tommy smiled… "I'll go and set up my therapy couch….

One by one they experienced Spiritual Healing….

And the footsteps where heard….

As were voices….

*"Don't give up…"*
*"Don't give in…"*
*"Please keep going on…"*
*"Love will win…".*
*"We love you…".*
*"We are always with you …."*

# Chapter 94

"Tommy someone's at the front door.... knocking ...."
Martha shouted from upstairs....

Tommy opened the door....

"Hello Tommy son....!"
"Hello Jack..." Tommy was shocked...
"Can I come in...?" Jack queried
"Yes of course you're always welcome..." Tommy was
visually surprised... "It's just that you're not one for
home visits..."
"I thought I'd come and see ya...." Jack walked in...
"Come into the kitchen, I'll do you a wassa..." Tommy
led the way...

"Take a seat Martha will be down in a bit...." Tommy
poured Jack a large scotch... topped up with coffee...

Martha walked into the kitchen...

"Hello Jack...!" Martha was shocked... "And to what do
we have the pleasure... I mean you know you're
welcome anytime..."
"Thanks Martha..." Jack touched his forehead with his
finger... "Cheers...!"

"So, how's things...?" Jack asked
"You know..." Martha smiled... "So,so..."
"Well, I do know...!" Jack took a mouthful... "So...
so... is not how I'd describe events..." Jack paused... "A
bad accident with brake fluid I understand... in fact three
bad accidents....!"

"I take it you've heard of our last encounter…?" Tommy asked Jack as he poured Martha a wassa… topping up Jacks and his own….

"Tommy lad… I've heard…!" Jack paused… He took a mouthful, then stroked his chin… "It's a bad business… we don't know who are the culprits and that's bad business, encroaching on my turf…"
Jack swallowed the last of his wassa… offering the cup up to Tommy… "And putting the frighteners on one of my own… It's like sticking nails into my eyes….!" Jack paused…. "I'm quite offended…" Jack screwed his face up… "I feel quite nauseous when I think about it…"

There was a silence…

"We are none too pleased Jack…!" Martha said firmly…
"I'm sure you're not my dear…" Jack nodded at Martha and Tommy

They sat in silence… gradually finishing off the bottle of whisky… without coffee…

"A lot of the team think you have lost the plot Tommy…!" Jack paused… "Respect ya… but think you've lost it…!"
"I haven't lost the plot Jack…" Tommy smiled…" I respect the team…" he paused…. "I've found what I've been looking for all my life… and we have plans…"
"That's what I said…" Jack took a swig…. "Tommy knows what he's doing…"

"We are still digging Martha… we haven't given up….!" Jack smiled at Martha….
"Thanks Jack…" Martha hugged him…
"Thanks Jack…" Tommy held his hand tight….

"We think a little show of strength is in order…" Jack took a mouthful… "Just to let whoever they are… know… you're not on your own…!" Jack paused… "You have back up…!"

"Jack…?" Tommy quizzed

"Don't be alarmed if you see cars with…. my people scouring your manor… during the day…during the night… You may even see familiar faces walking your streets…." Jack smiled….

"It's time for me to go…"

They walked Jack to the door…His Bentley was waiting outside….

"Thanks again Jack…" Martha hugged him…

"You'll have people talking Martha…!" Jack smiled…

"Thanks Jack…" Tommy and Jack exchanged handshakes….

"Tommy lad… if he who dares should get his boys to show face…" Jack paused… "Make sure they are aware they are on the same side…. We don't want friendly fire taking out our own…"

Jack touched his forehead with his finger…

Tommy touched his forehead with his finger….

# Chapter 95

Tommy phoned Fred and Geoffrey immediately...
Inviting them over....

"And so that was how the conversation went... and
ended..." Tommy explained to Joan, Chloe, Fred and
Geoffrey...

"We never knew Jack was coming..." Martha
pondered... "He has never visited us before...!"

"It's heart-warming, to know they might not approve or
understand..." Joan mused... "What we are about... but
they are on our side...!"
"Absolutely..." Geoffrey concurred... "I think a visit to
the lodge is in order..."
"I must say I feel more secure..." Chloe smiled...
"I'll take a trip to see my lads..." Fred endorsed
"Yes, good idea..." Tommy stated... "We don't want to
be caught up in the middle of a friendly fire war...".
"They need to know who's who..." Geoffrey stated
"For their sake..." Fred paused.... "As well has ours...!"

# Chapter 96

"Childs Ol'boy... Good to see you at the lodge..."
"Geoffrey... good to see you..."
"Hope all's well...."

You could hear the trepidation in their voices when Geoffrey walked in....

Geoffrey monitored the room.... Then saw the face he was looking for... the man behind the desk....

"I would like to have a word with you...!" Geoffrey was polite but firm...
"Childs... what can I do for you... I believe we concluded our business the last time you were here... in your covert operation...!"

"Indeed... all nicely tucked away for safe keeping...!"
Geoffrey smiled broadly
"What do you want...?"

"We have found ourselves at the end of another mishap...!" Geoffrey was firmer...
"Yes, we heard... and I can assure you it's none of our doing...!"
"Oh yes, I believe that...!" Geoffrey smiled wryly...
"Then what do you want...?"

"I want a presence, to be widely seen... in and around where we live.... and you are in a position to make that happen..." Geoffrey's face turned stern... his eyes cold...
"A presence you say..."
"Yes, a dominant presence... to ward off undesirables...." Geoffrey pondered.... "I might add we

have our own presence in place… underworld and military…!" He paused… "So, don't go treading on the wrong toes… You, particularly, don't want to get involved in crossfire…!"

"Oh, Childs what a waste of talent… You certainly have learned how to play the game…"

There was a moment…

"I'm a quick learner…!" Geoffrey smiled wryly… "And I'm playing for the right side…The winning side…!"

There was a palpable tension in the air.

Geoffrey looked back as he approached the door, and in an exaggerated cockney accent with the menace of he who dares…

Geoffrey said "As my dearest two friends would say, don't piss up our backs and tell us it's raining outside." He winked as he left the room leaving nothing but silence behind.

# Chapter 97

"Hello boss, we have been expecting you....!"

Fred had entered the pub his comrades frequented....
He scrutinised the area as trained... and saw his team
nicely tucked away in a safe position...
He also saw Tap Tap in a chair facing the fire... a mirror
above the fire giving Tap Tap a view of the bar area and
his comrades....
Fred had seen tap taps reflection in the mirror...

"Hello lads..." Fred smiled... "Tap Tap come and join us
if you please..."
"Yes boss..." Tap Tap joined his comrades in arms...

A round of drink was brought to the table...

"So, you have been expecting me..." Fred smiled
"Yes boss, we heard... brake fluid...!"
"A bit amateurish, but it does the job...!"
"Blowing the cars up would have sent a real message..."
"They don't want to draw too much attention to
themselves..." Fred pondered... "They need to remain
faceless... Psychological warfare..."

"More terrorisation then...?"
"Yes...!" Fred answered bluntly...

"We have been digging, but we can only go so far...!"
"Our hands are tired boss..."
"Until you give us the order...!"

"I'm not your Commanding Officer any more lads..."
Fred stated

They all looked at Fred and smiled wryly…

"Say the word boss…"!
"I don't want my friends touched…!" Fred ordered…
It's not them…!"

There was silence…

"Boss we don't understand your reasoning…!"
"But your reasoning is good enough for us…!"

"Thank you…" Fred touched his forehead with the back
of his arm… as a symbol of saluting them…
They returned the action….

"What can we do…?"

Fred explained the meeting between Tommy and Jack,
Geoffrey and the Lodge…
And what was being put forward… offered…
manipulated…

"Consider it done…!" The soldier touched his forehead
with the back of his hand, his troop followed suit.
Fred responded likewise…

"You better sort out a meeting...!"
"Or a password…!"
"So, we know who's who …!"
"We don't want to be taking out the wrong people…"
Tap Tap smiled, menacingly…
"Yes, we do…" Fred paused… "No…! We don't…! Fred
said sternly… glancing at Tap Tap.

# Chapter 98

"Are we all up for the group tonight…?" Martha asked… Knowing the answer…

"Oh Yes…!" Joan exclaimed

"Certainly am…!" Fred endorsed

"Me too…!" Chloe paused… "I really cherish those evenings…"

"I can't wait to get to their…" Tommy smiled… "To give Reiki or Spiritual healing…!"

"Now that brings me to a point of view, I would like to share…" Geoffrey announced…

They all looked at Geoffrey….

"Firstly, he wants us to open a retreat..." Fred smiled broadly… "Now the world…!"

"A global enterprise of retreats…". Martha mused…touching her index finger to her chin…

"And why not…!" Joan injected…

"Pebble in the pond…" Chloe gleamed

"I was kidding…. Fred laughed…

"Why not…?" Tommy paused… "What do you want to share Geoff…?"

They all looked at Geoffrey…

"You are not far off the Pebble in the pond concept…". Geoffrey cleared his throat…. "After experiencing both Reiki and Spiritual Healing…" Geoffrey paused…

"Joanie and I have discussed such…

Joan dived in… "Geoffrey, get to the point…"

Geoffrey cleared his throat… "Ok dearest… We would both like to learn and follow in your footsteps…

If you don't mind asking your Spiritual Teacher and Reiki Master… to take us under their wings…?"

"You wouldn't Adam and Eve it...!" Fred burst out, taking off Tommy's cockney accent... "Chloe and I were going to ask the same question...!"

Tommy looked at Martha... "This is absolutely incredible... Martha and I have been discussing this very subject and Martha also wants to learn....!"
"We also said wouldn't it be great if you all decided to learn..." Martha's eyes welled up.... "And you have thrown your hats into the ring... and beaten us to it....!"

"I would be honoured to introduce you to Charlie..." Tommy's eyes moistened... "And you can ask him... Also, you can ask my Master yourselves, with my blessing .... Tonight...!"


*"Unconditional love..."*
*"Help them...".*
*"Help others..."*

Their voices sang out....

"I guess that's confirmation..." Geoffrey concurred...

They all roared out "YES...!"

And hugged each other....

# Chapter 99

That evening, at their group meeting they each individually approached Tommy's Reiki Master...

"Would you please teach me Reiki... as you did Tommy...?" Martha asked
"Would you please teach me Reiki...?" Joan asked
"I would love to learn Reiki... would you please teach me...?" Chloe asked
"After experiencing Reiki... and how it made me feel... I would like to help others..." Fred paused... "Please teach me...?"
"I would be honoured..." Geoffrey cleared his throat...
"If like Thomas, you would teach me Reiki...?"


Their Reiki Master acknowledged them with Gassho....

"It would be my pleasure "Grasshoppers...!"


The evening continued with more and more people attending, receiving help and helping each other....

# Chapter 100

"I have been looking at various possibilities for our retreat…" Geoffrey cleared his throat… "I do believe I have found the premises that is right for us, as we will be right for it…!".

They had all bought into Geoffrey's idea and the concept of their retreat….
Giving him cart Blanche to proceed and put together a business plan…

They all nodded…

"Ok…!" Martha enthused
"Where...?" Chloe sounded excited…
"You say it's suitable…?" Joan inserted
"How many rooms…?" Fred enquired
"How much is it….?" Tommy quizzed

"Now now…!" Geoffrey cleared his throat…. "Settle down…!" He giggled….
They all giggled….

"All your questions will be answered….in good time…" Geoffrey cleared his throat…. "As you put me in charge of the project... Project manager no less…!" Geoffrey smiled amusingly… "I have taken the progressive steps and viewed the premises…"

They all waited with baited breath…

"I have organised a viewing for your perusal…." Geoffrey concluded…. "I believe you will find the premises delightful and appropriate…"

"Wow…!" Tommy gasped… "No grass growing under your stewardship…!"
"When Geoffrey…!" Fred probed
"Yes, when we inspecting it…?" Joan asked…
"Yes, when…?" Chloe enquired
"When…?" Martha pulled a face at him… "Geoffrey Childs… When… You tease…!"

They all laughed….
Geoffrey loved it…

"Instead of breakfast at Martha's Bistro Kitchen…" Geoffrey cogitated… and nodded at Martha… "I knew we would all be free Wednesday morning…" Geoffrey cleared his throat… "So, Wednesday morning at 10am…"
"Where is it …?" questioned Joan…

"Suffolk dearest…" Geoffrey answered
"How are we getting there...?" questioned Chloe
"We taking two or three motors…?" queried Martha

"I've organised the hiring of an 8-seater mini bus…" Geoffrey cleared his throat… "I considered Fredrick as the driver…" Geoffrey smiled… "Taking his troop on a sortie…"! Geoffrey paused… "We just need your license details…"

Fred smiled and nodded without hesitation… "My pleasure Project Manager…!"

"So, that's plan A… in progress and taking shape…"
Tommy hesitated… "What is plan B….?"

# Chapter 101

"Thomas…!" Geoffrey gained Tommy's attention…"

The gang all looked on….

"If I'm not mistaken…" Geoffrey cleared his throat…
"Tonight is your Spiritual healing teaching, is it not…?"
"Yes Geoffrey…" Tommy smiled… "As you well know
you conniving devil…!"
"That's rather inapt…" Geoffrey roared… "Taken in
good spirit though…!"

They all laughed… which pleased Geoffrey immensely…

"Would it be appropriate if we accompanied you…?"
Geoffrey paused…. "To meet your Spiritual healing
teacher…?"
"Geoffrey… your such an impatient… Devil…!" Joan
giggled… "It would be respectful and polite,
accordingly… For Tommy to ask if it's Ok for us to
attend…"

"My, apologies Thomas…" Geoffrey nodded….

"Thank you, Joan…" Tommy chuckled… "No apology
required my dear friend…"

Geoffrey smiled and his eyes moistened… He thought…
*"My dear friend"* It warmed him…

"I have already asked Charlie…" Tommy glanced at all
of them… "He knows our history..." His eyes welled…
"And he is more than pleased for all of you to attend and
start your probation and training…!"

A chant went up…

"Yes….!"

# Chapter 102

"Geoffrey dearest…" Joan took another peek through the bedroom curtains… "I'm not being paranoid, but there is a lot of unusual activity outside…"

Geoffrey took a gander through the slight gap…

"Discreet activity but not withstanding that… activity none the less…!" Joan concluded
"I concur my dear…" Geoffrey cleared his throat…
"Is that good or should we be alarmed…" Joan questioned… "And be prepared to defend ourselves…!"
"It's been occurring all day dearest…" Geoffrey smiled

"Fred, I think you need to take a reconnaissance and observe the movement taking place…!" Chloe had been watching for some time…
"Yes, Chloe I've been monitoring these manoeuvres for the past three days and nights…." Fred said calmly, so to comfort and not alarm her…
"Are they friend or foe…?" Chloe queried evenly
"Some are military covert style…" Fred paused and rubbed his chin…. "Some are blatant, in yours face… not hidden…!" He mused… "but they are out there…

"Martha…" Tommy bade her attention…
"Yes Tom…" Martha knew the tone of Tommy's voice…
"Just to mark your card…" Tommy smiled at her…" We have had visitors over the past few days and nights…"
"I know Tom… I've been watching you…!" Martha smiled back at him… "Watching them…"
Tommy winked at Martha… "You are one of a kind…one in a million…"

"There's a cricket bat by the front door…" Martha winked back… "And a pick handle by the back door…!"


Geoffrey made a conference call to Fred and Tommy….

"Are you aware of the activity in our vicinity…?" Geoffrey stated calmly
"Yer…! It's been going on for a few days and nights" … Tommy specified
"Three days and nights…!" quantified Fred
"Should we make ourselves present and be seen to be seen…?" Geoffrey quizzed...
"Yer,..! Let them know we know…!" Tommy state firmly…

"Fred… Fred…!" Geoffrey probed… What do you think…?"
"Fred…! Tommy called…
"It's ok… I'm here… I'm observing…" Fred paused…
"Some of their manoeuvres are military… covert, but military… some are not…!" Fred mused… "They could be your mob Tommy… or yours Geoff…!"

"So, do we show ourselves Fredrick…" Geoffrey asked
"Fred… Do we make a show of strength…?" Tommy paused… "It's your call… It's your expertise…?"

There was silence….

"No pressure there then…!" Fred half giggled… "They haven't hit us in three days or nights…. Stand down…"

354

# Chapter 103

Fred and Chloe pulled up in the mini bus he had acquired earlier…

The rest all piled out of their individual homes….

Like a kid's day outing….

"All aboard…" Chloe roared
"The magical mystery tour…" Martha sang…
"My word… It's so exciting…" Joan glowed
"To pastures new…!" Tommy crooned
"To new adventures…!" Geoffrey chaunted
"Tickets please…!" Fred exclaimed

They all sat their… And the mini bus never moved….

"Fred…!" Tommy queried
"I'm waiting for the post code from the navigator…"
Fred struggled to keep a straight face… "To put into the Satnav…!"

They all roared…

"Oh dear… Oh dear…!" Geoffrey flustered… "So sorry my dear's…"

The bus pulled off with them all chastising Geoffrey…
Geoffrey lapped it up…

"To great expectation…!" Joan said…
"With fewer bumps along the way…!" Chloe added
"May all the bumps belong to the camels…" Martha stated

"To the camels…!" They roared…

# Chapter 104

"Guys and girls, I don't want to be alarmist…!" Fred checked his rear-view mirror… "We have had two cars following us for the past five miles…" Fred paused… "More or less since we left home…" He checked again… "I have taken evasive action in changing lanes… twice around a roundabout…" He paused… "They are still with us…They are good, but so am I…!"

"I thought it was your crap sense of direction…" Tommy winked

"Do we pull over, do we confront them…!" Martha demanded…
"One may be the bad guys…" Joan took a look through the back window… "One maybe the good guys…"
"You won't see them Joan…They are three cars behind now…!" Fred said calmly…
"I knew there was a reason for you driving…!" Geoffrey smiled
"If anything is going to happen…!" Fred frowned… "It will happen when we arrive at our destination…!"
"I'm glad I brought my first aid kit…." Chloe smiled

"This is like walking on cracked ice…!" Martha growled
"Never knowing what's going to happen…!" Joan nodded
"Or when…!" Chloe added

"Fuck this for a game of soldiers…!" Tommy roared…
"Pull over Fred… next services…Lets have it out…!"

"No Tommy…!" Geoffrey stated calmly… "What happens will happen… I'm confident it won't…!"

Geoffrey paused…. "Fortunately, I have a contingency plan…!"

"Is that plan B by any coincidence…?". Joan enquired…

"Not exactly… I have arranged for a couple of reliable discreet journalists…" Geoffrey cleared his throat… "Newspaper men I trust, that we will give interviews and take pictures too… should we be in agreement to purchase this property…."

Silence….

"And if we don't decide to buy…?" Tommy questioned for all of them…

"This is risky mate…!". Fred glanced at Geoffrey…

"You're playing it close to the chest Geoffrey…!" Joan mused… "Dearest…!"

"This is likening to Russian roulette…" Martha raised her eyebrows... "Bad night in Canning Town…!"

"This is playing with our lives…" Chloe swallowed hard… "If these are the bad guys…"

"They won't hit us if there are photographers present…" Geoffrey stated calmly… "They couldn't take the chance…."

Silence……

"Be assured though…" Geoffrey paused…. "Plan B comes into operation…" Geoffrey cleared his throat… "Today, if we decide to buy or not…. This stops….!"

# Chapter 105

They drove on in silence….

"Satnav is saying we are 5 minutes away…". Fred broke the silence….
"It's semi remote…" Joan said…
"Yes, semi remote and peaceful…" Geoffrey cleared his throat… "But on the edge of civilisation…"
"Yes, its peaceful and calming…" Martha smiled
"Ideal place for a retreat…" Tommy paused… "Peaceful, calming, quiet and semi remote…"
"Quiet and remote enough to get hit…" Chloe said with a wry smile…

They all looked at Chloe….

"Woops… Just saying…" Chloe's expression never changed
"Before you ask...!" Fred pre-emptied their thoughts…
"They have been with us all the way…" He paused and viewed his rear-view mirror… "Estimate 200 yards back… always maintaining a discreet distance…!"

The atmosphere in the mini bus changed… pensive, agitation…

"It's saying we are here…" Fred slowed

As did the cars tailing them…
There was a gap 20 feet wide sitting back from the edges and the trees…on the opposite side of the road

"Is that the driveway in…?" Asked Fred
"Yes…" Stated Geoffrey

Fred pulled on the steering wheel... They approached even slower...

Stop...! Chloe exclaimed... "Should we go in..." she paused "Its isolated..."
"Ideal place for an assault..." Fred murmured

"Fred..." Martha protested...
"Sorry... it slipped out from experience..." Fred had pulled to a stop at the entrance
"Do we proceed...?" Joan quizzed

Silence....

"Where are they Fred...?" Tommy asked calmly
"Just back up the road..." Fred took another look...
"They have stopped...!"

They all looked at each other... five minutes past...

"Not a vehicle has gone past us..." Joan stated...
"It's like cat and mouse..." Martha fumed
"They could have taken us out by now..." Tommy stated firmly....
"Agreed...!" Fred stated
"That's true..." Chloe agreed
"I concur..." Geoffrey nodded

"So, we go for it...?" Fred questioned.

# Chapter 106

Fred put the mini bus into gear and slowly proceeded, constantly checking his rea view mirror…

"There they are…!" Fred stated
"Are they following us up the drive…?" Asked Geoffrey…
"No, it appears the two cars have manoeuvred into a dove tail…rear ends…" Fred stopped the bus… and viewed again… "Blocking the entrance….!"

"Pursuer's…?" Joan asked
"Or Rescuer's….? Martha countered…
"So, what now…?" Quizzed Chloe

In an instant Tommy was out of the bus….

"Tommy, stop…!" Yelled Martha….

Geoffrey was out Next…

"Geoffrey… wait…!" Bellowed Joan

Fred followed suit…

"Fred No…!" Chloe screeched…

The three of them strode towards the two vehicles…
As they got nearer four doors of each car opened….

Bodies started to grow out of the vehicles, until there were eight… mean looking… large men, standing erect with their hands inside their Crombie overcoats…

"Is there a problem Tom…?" Asked one of the chaps…

"You Ok Captain…?" Asked one of the other chaps…

"What the fuck…Boof Boof…!" Tommy smiled, more in relief… "What are you four doing tailing us…?"
"Jack gave orders to look after you lot….?" Boof Boof smiled

"Tap Tap… Sargent…!" Fred looked up to the heavens with a wry smile… "Corporal… Corporal…! What the…"
Fred touched his forehead with the back of his hand… they responded immediately….
"Just keeping an eye on things boss…" Tap Tap smiled as did his comrades…

"How may I enquire…" Geoffrey cleared his throat…
"Did you come together in tailing us…

"We worked it out…" Tap Tap nodded and smiled at Boof Boof and the others… "We had the same interests…!"
"Once we worked it out…." Boof Boof touched his forehead with his finger… "It was easy…Common ground…!" And he winked…

"Most unlikely correlation…" Geoffrey smiled gratefully…. "Most welcome…Most welcome indeed…!"

# Chapter 107

"Oh Geoffrey…" sighed Chloe… "This is an amazing building…"
"So suitable to our needs…" Martha added
"It fits our requirements like a glove…" Joan glowed
"Spectacular mate…" Fred nodded
"You certainly did your homework here Geoffrey…" Tommy smiled broadly… "Can we afford it…?"
"Yes, I did my due-diligence…" Geoffrey cleared his throat…" I perused many possibilities…"

They all looked at Geoffrey….

Once again, he cleared his throat…. "Yes, we can afford it…" He mused…" I also did a business plan… costings and such… Its viable…"

They all looked at Geoffrey… smiling, beaming, grinning….

"Shall we provisionally say it's a go…" Geoffrey queried

"Provisionally…! … Dam yes…!" Martha yelled
"Are we all in accord…?" Geoffrey smiled
"Yes….!" They yelled in unity.

# Chapter 108

"Now is the time to execute plan B…!" Geoffrey cleared his throat… "If we all concur and are all in alliance…"

They all looked in abeyance…

"I give you fair warning…" Geoffrey cleared his throat… "It may churn up memories emotions and tenderness…" Geoffrey pondered… "But I believe it is imperative we do this…!"

"Divulge the details of plan B Geoffrey dearest…". Joan quizzed

Geoffrey cleared his throat…. "The last thing these enigmatic collaborations, individuals, undertaking their destructive murky work…." Geoffrey paused…. "Court, is …Exposure…!"

They all studied Geoffrey in admiration…

"We will make a public announcement via the media…" Geoffrey pointed to the newspaper reporters and photographers…. "The newspapers, the TV and radio will pick it up… I have contacts…" Geoffrey pondered for a moment… "What we are doing… Why we are doing it… What we aim to achieve…Our sole purpose… Our objective…!" Geoffrey became emotional… "Most importantly, what drives us on…! What inspired us…!" Geoffrey wiped his eyes… "We will give candid brutal interviews…" Geoffrey choked… "How after experiencing, witnessing… the harrowing macabre devastation…" Geoffrey held his forehead in his palm…. "We as a collaboration of individuals…" Geoffrey nodded at his audience modestly, emotionally… "Came together despite many dramas and traumas... blame and counter blame...". Geoffrey had tears rolling down his cheeks... "We united in love.... For a belief far greater than grief... and revenge... to leave a legacy of love... The Gift of Love...!"

They all had tears rolling down their cheeks....

Geoffrey composed himself... And cleared his throat.... "We will also tell them what we have endured since beginning our quest... The hostilities... The threats... The psychological warfare..." Geoffrey paused.... "The public attention may well persuade them to leave us be..." He looked at the group.... "No one in their right minds, in their positions... would want to be in the public view.... Under scrutiny...!"

They hugged as a collective....

"We will do it...". They agreed
"Warts and all...." They agreed

"Forgiveness means, our pain is not the final word on the matter...!" Fred stated sombrely "For all to bear witness...!"

They all hugged and wept....

# Chapter 109

They all composed themselves….

Geoffrey summoned the newspaper reporters….

They sat in the lounge and told their collective story, individually reiterating the events …

The history of their early years… their education… their work… their dreams and aspirations…
For a better life….

"We moved to where we live now…" Martha paused…
"We believed at the time it was for the best…"
"We honestly did…" Tommy nodding in agreement with his wife… "For a better opportunity…"
"We thought we were making the right move…." Fred stated...
"In hindsight would we have moved there…" Chloe quizzed
"No, none of us would…" Joan wiped her eyes… "If we are being totally honest…"
"No, not knowing what was going to transpire…"
Geoffrey's eyes moistened…

There was a deathly silence….

"We all formed such an alliance…" Geoffrey smiled remembering good old times… "A bond of acquaintance…"
"Do you remember when we went to Portugal on our holidays…" Joan asked….
*"Always look on the bright side of life…"* Tommy sang the words quietly...

*"Always look on the bright side of life…"* They all joined in as a chorus…

Silence… Their heads dropped….

"In a blink of an eye…" Chloe said in a whisper….
"Time flew by…!"
"Memories…" Martha murmured… "Such beautiful memories…"
"Do you remember going to watch Tommy play football…?" Joan asked
"Do you recall the surprise party's….?" Fred wiped his eyes
"We were so proud of them…" Geoffrey smiled
"Sophie representing England…" Joan nodded
"Louise going to University…!" Chloe nodded
"Tommy signing professional…!" Tommy wiped his eyes
"And representing England…" Martha said proudly wiping her eyes

Silence….
The reporters wrote down everything, all the stories in detail… in depth….

"The years rolled by…!" Martha said
"And then the inevitable happened…". Tommy smiled wryly
"Yes… Love…" Joan smiled
"Ah love….!" Geoffrey cleared his throat and wiped his eyes…
"It wouldn't have happened…" Joan stated… "If we hadn't moved there…"
"No, it would not have…" Martha quipped
"Or would it…?" Geoffrey asked
"Destiny…!". Joan asked
"As in meant to be…!" Tommy countered

"As in meant to be…!". Geoffrey cleared his throat…
"Look at us now…!".
Silence….

"Destiny… Meant to be… mmmm…" Chloe mentioned
"It would not have happened…" Fred paused… "If we
had not…! All moved there…."
"No, it would not have…." Chloe wiped her eyes… "If
we all… had not moved there…."
"What was meant to be…?" Fred quizzed…
"Resentment…?" Chloe stated
"Jealousy…?" Fred raised his eyebrows
"Hatred…?" Chloe specified
"Destiny…" Martha nodded wiping her eyes…
"Meant to be…" Joan smiled caringly…

"You really believe what took place…." Fred choked….
"Was meant to be…" He paused…" It was
predestined…. made to occur…?"
"You honestly believe that what we all
shared…witnessed…" Chloe shuddered…
"Experienced…
and where we are now…! was destined…?"
"The total concept and outcome… Here now… the
present… was preordained…" Fred held his chin in his
hand and looked upward….

"We will never know…"! Smiled Geoffrey
"But we have overcome…!" Smiled Joan
"And we are here now… in the present…!" Martha
patted her chest
"Yes…. Don't you…?" Tommy probed... with a smile on
his face

"In all honesty…" Chloe pondered… "I can now, see a purpose in what happened… there is closure and a new beginning…" tears rolled down her face…

"There is nothing we can do about the past…! The future… Who knows…!" Fred wiped his moistened eyes…. "The present is a gift…that keeps on living…!" He paused… "So, let's live it…!"

The rest of the story unfolded…
The reporters couldn't believe their ears…

"After all what has taken place…" The reporter quizzed…. "You believe there was a greater good…?" The other reporter jumped in…. "This greater good was fated…preordained…?"

"You are getting warts and all…". Tommy said firmly "Everything straight from the horse's mouths…". Fred wiped his eyes…
"Make of it what you will…" Geoffrey cleared his throat… "You just write the facts, as you have been, being given… in honesty…" Geoffrey mused… "Let the people decide…!"
"And we will hold you to account….!" Joan voiced in her legal tone…

The reporters nodded … in abeyance… Knowing of Joan's reputation….

"Maybe, there is a greater knowing… that we are not connected to…" Tommy paused… "Maybe…We have forgotten how to connect to it…!"

There was silence….

Tommy broke the silence…. "It is not only releasing what has damaged us…" He paused… "It is relinquishing ownership of it…!"


The reporters looked at them…...
"May I ask a question…" the reporter delved….
"Yes…" Joan answered
"Ask away…" Chloe added
"Feel free…" Martha studied him

"Do you intend to carry on… with your dream, your idealistic project…" He paused… "Despite the past… and the present hostilities…You have all endured…?" "Psychological emotional warfare…" The second reporter stated… shaking his head… "A rollercoaster from the beginning to now…!" He smiled… "We appreciate you are here sharing these incredible events…" He paused… "Forgive me for asking…. do you have the strength and passion to continue…?" He took a deep breath… "Do you intend to fight on…? And fulfil your desired beautiful… dream…!"

# Chapter 110

"You have had the interview..." Geoffrey cleared his throat...smiled and nodded... "Now we as a solidarity consolidation... Wish to make a joint statement..."

"Psychological Emotional Warfare.... Mind Games...!
The perpetrators of such...
Play these games to inflict...
Demolition, Destroying and Corroding... in others...
Their Self Worth...!
To chip away at their...
Self-Belief...
Self Confidence...
Self Esteem...
Self-Liking...
Self-Loving...
Worthiness of one's Self Being..."

Geoffrey cleared his throat....

"To Grip and to Crush... with their upper hands...!
To impose their Power and Control...!
Over others...
In Fearful... Bullying... Controlling... Intimidating...
Narcissistic actions....!
As they themselves need the Power and to Control...
So, to exist.... to survive...!
For they have nothing within...
Except...
Resentment and Hatred...!
Self-Loathing...!
As they have...
No inner liking...!
No inner growth...!
No inner self love...!

Emotionless Vessels…!
They are parasites who take….
Without return…."

"To answer your question… Yes…! We have the strength and passion to continue… We intend to carry on… We have a desire to fulfil our beautiful dream…!" Geoffrey cleared his throat…. "Inspired by beautiful people…" Geoffrey choked back the tears… "Who we love…!"

Tears rolled down his face…
Tears rolled down everyone's face…

Tommy spoke "True Love will always win…" … His voice cracked…. "Love over powers everything…"

*"We Love You All…"*

The words were heard…

Even the reporters looked around the room…

# Chapter 111

"Taking into account all that you have shared with us…" The reporter paused… "It must have been incredibly hard to come back together… to forgive and regroup, as it appears… as one…!"

They all looked at each other…

"Considering the pain, the damage, of what you witnessed…" The reporter wiped his eyes… "The aftermath… And then the hostilities you have encountered…" He paused… "To be here now… How…!"

Tommy broke the silence… "To know who you truly are, is that you find inner peace and love… and to connect to who you truly are…." He pondered… "To become the person, you are meant to be…!" Tommy closed his eyes... and smiled… then opened them again… "Allowing you to give without agenda… Unconditional love…" He looked at his wife and friends… then back at the reporters… "The ripple effect that emanates, giving and receiving love...!"

They headed home after one more look around the property… Taking notes… Determined to buy it…

Fred pulled out of the driveway… Their escort right behind them….

"We will wait and see what transpires from the press release…" Geoffrey smiled wryly
"And your statement…!" Chloe added
"That was some statement…!" Joan raised her eyebrows

"Will ripple some feathers...!" Martha stated
"Will piss some people off...!" Fred nodded his head
"But it might just do the job..."! Tommy smiled

*"Stay strong, we are with you...!"*

They all smiled....

# Chapter 112

"Fred darling…" Chloe opened up… "I've been thinking deeply with regard to some of the things said today….!"
"Ok and what conclusion, if any have you arrived at…?" Fred smiled caringly

"Why in the world that we live in, does negativity try to rule…?"
"Does it…?" Fred probed

Chloe continued…. "We see… lies deceit and trouble making… Using of and manipulations… Controlling, control, and abuse...
Interrogation, intimidation… Mind games, emotional games… Psychological blackmail… Emotional blackmail… Bullying and negativity…" Chloe pondered… "Evil exists in life… Motives an agenda…" Chloe mused ... "They are in regular use… and a common denominator…!" Chloe squinted her eyes for a second or two… "And they know…" She pointed her index finger upward making a point… "Who they are…!" Chloe closed her eyes tears cascading down her checks… "Why…! we ask…!"

Fred studied his wife closely… with compassion… then took her in his arms….

"It cannot prevail… The truth will always win...!" Fred gently eased her back from him, one hand on her shoulder, the other holding her face… He smiled… "Positivity…! Truth honesty… Integrity ethics… Morals… Principles… and… Standards…!" Fred deliberated… "Transparency kindness… Care… Consideration….!" Fred reflected… "Magnanimous… Happiness… Peace… Contentment… The true essence

of… Love… Love will always win…!"    Fred winked at
his wife… "Love over powers… Everything…! …. It's
eternal… Love just keeps on giving and growing…"

Chloe smiled… "I love you Fred….!"
Fred smiled… "I love you Chloe…!"

*"We love you…!"*

They comprised passionately…...

# Chapter 113

"Tommy with all that has happened to us… Chloe, Fred, Joan and Geoffrey…" Martha took a moment… "And it's been hell, traumatic… spiteful…!" Martha's eyes moistened… "Why are we here…?"

Tommy held his chin in his fingers… and looked at Martha pensively

"What are we here to learn…?" She questioned
Tommy was thoughtful… "Perhaps we don't give ourselves enough credit…" Tommy paused… "Perhaps we are here to teach…!"

"Wow that's deep…" Martha hesitated… "Here to teach…?"
"Yes… Look what's happened in our lives…" Tommy stopped… "Look how our lives have changed… Look how we have changed as people…"

They sat in silence…

"But that's happened through circumstances…" Martha stated
"The fundamental concept of our soul's journey…" Tommy looked at Martha contemplatively… "Is to reconnect to the true essence of who we are and our being…"
"You are not a stupid man…" Martha smiled… "But where do you get this from…?"

Tommy raised his eyebrows… And looked up…

"I have no idea…!" Tommy shook his head… "It just comes into my mind… To be honest it shocks me at times…!"
"Carry on… Tommy its deep, but interesting…!" Martha encouraged him…

Tommy closed his eyes… smiled then opened them…

"To re-enhance our spiritual correlation… Hence our spirituality grows. To be true to ourselves and treat others as we wish to be treated...!". Tommy smiled reflectively… "Truth, honesty, transparency. Caring kindness and consideration… Magnanimity, empathy, understanding…" He took a breath… "Moral's principles, integrity, ethics, standards and respect…" He smiled at Martha… "Love… Consistently and persistently…"

"I love you Tommy Jackson…!" Tears rolled down Martha's cheeks. she didn't wipe them away…

"We need to learn to like ourselves… We must learn to love ourselves… Without arrogance…" Tommy paused… "For without this how can we love others…!"

Martha was entranced by his every word….

"Then the pebble in the pond concept will take effect and the ripples will flow…" Tommy took a breath…
"If this connects to one person and helps them to change their perception and change themselves within… In turn they teach others and the ripple becomes a domino effect… And peace will prevail….!"

"Love is the greatest power… Peace will prevail…."
Martha embraced her Tommy…

*"We love you...!"*

# Chapter 114

"Geoffrey...!" Joan looked at him adoringly... "This has been a harrowing, emotional, painful and traumatic journey... At times I'm sure we all wanted to give up...!" "Yes dearest...!" Geoffrey listened intently

"To bury our heads in the sand... to hide away... To fill our lives with hatred and revenge...!" Joan paused... "Regrets... anger... resentment...rejection... This would have eaten us up from within...!" Joan composed herself... "And we would have emanated this to others...!" Joan wiped her eyes... "We could have become bitter and twisted and transmitted those emotions on to others..." Joan's tears cascaded down her face and she allowed this emotional release to continue... "In turn fuelling their mental and emotional negativity... empowering their sorrow, pain and emptiness... sanctioning their anger and self-loathing to grow..."

"Yes Joanie..." Geoffrey cleared his throat...

"When all they wanted was someone to care... to give them consideration and help, someone to hear them...!" Joan swallowed hard... "To give them love...!"

"Yes, my love...!" Geoffrey cleared his throat... His eyes welled up as he heard his wife's sentiments....

"Through all of our upheaval... Grief... Pain... Sorrow... Resentment... Anger... Revenge... Hatred... we have found the way forward to release and relinquish these feelings... Emotions... from within..." Joan spoke softly... Haven't we Geoffrey...?"

"I truly believe so… My dearest love…" Geoffrey's voice choked

"We have found peace and love from the most horrific journey and unusual source…!" Joan smiled wryly at Geoffrey… "Martha, Chloe, Fred, and Tommy….

"Yes Joanie…" Geoffrey was crying openly…
"We have found a bond of kindship…!". Joan looked at her beloved husband… "We do all love each other…Don't we Geoffrey…!"

 Geoffrey cleared his throat… "Anyone can say they care…. Anyone can say they love you…! Geoffrey wiped his eyes… "But the truth is, in how they show it… and how they treat you….!"

Silence….

Geoffrey cleared his throat... and smiled broadly… "Yes Joanie... We do all love each other… deeply…!"

They caressed each other…...

*"We love you…!"*

# Chapter 115

They all met in Martha's kitchen for breakfast....
And shared their conversations....

"We all have a wassa..." Tommy held his mug high...
"Here's to friendship....!"
"To friendship...!" They all cheered
"Do you all believe we came together for a reason...?"
Joan questioned
"Through all the adversity...!" Chloe added
"We are still here...!" Fred stated
"One would believe..." Geoffrey cleared his throat...
"There must be a fundamental concept, more than a
reason..."
"Considering what we have all gone through...." Martha
wiped her eyes... "There must be something more...!"

They sat in silence pondering... deeply....

Tommy spoke quietly... slowly... almost as though he
was relaying... as a translator would....

"People come into your life for a reason, a season, or for
a lifetime...
When you know which one it is, you will know what to
do for that person... Tommy paused...
When someone is in your life for a reason, it is usually to
meet a need you have expressed...
They have come to assist you through a difficulty, to
provide you with guidance and support...

"How do you mean...?" Asked Chloe...

"To aid you…emotionally, mentally, physically…
Spiritually…
They may seem like a godsend and they are…" Tommy
paused…
"They are there for a reason… You need them to be…
Then, without any wrongdoing on your part or at an
inconvenient time, this person will say… Do something
to bring the relationship to an end…"

"Why…?" Questioned Joan

"Sometimes they die…" Tommy mused… And wiped his
eyes… "Sometimes they act up…! And force you to take
a stand…!"

"That's not fair…!"   Martha wiped her eyes…

"What we must realise is that our need has been met, our
desire fulfilled, their work is done…!" Tommy nodded…

"What…!" Quizzed Fred…

"The prayer you sent up has been answered and now it is
time to move on, some people come into your life for a
season…! … Because your turn has come, to share, grow,
learn…" Tommy pondered…
"They bring you an experience of peace or make you
laugh….
They may teach you something you have never done…
They usually give you an unbelievable amount of joy…
Believe it… It is real… But only for a season…"

"Oh my, that is so sad yet joyous…!" Geoffrey cleared
his throat… and wiped his eyes…

"Lifetime relationships teach you, lifetime lessons, things
you must build upon in order to have, solid mental and

emotional foundations…!" Tommy considered for a moment…

"Your job is to accept the lesson, love the person and put what you have learned to use in all other relationships, and areas of your life…"

They all sat in silence… watching waiting for Tommy to continue….

"It is said that love is blind…" Tommy smiled… "But friendship is clairvoyant…" Tommy paused and wiped his eyes….
"Thank you for being a part of my life…! … Whether you were, a reason, a season, or a lifetime…!"

They were all crying, wiping their eyes… and crying more….

"Angels exist… Only sometimes they haven't got wings… and we call them friends…!" Tommy wiped his eyes… "You all are one of them….!"

"As we are you Thomas…!" Geoffrey cleared his throat… wiping his eyes…
"We are more than friends we love each other…!" Martha wept and smiled…
"Yes, we do…!" They all exclaimed

*"One for all…! … All for one…!"*
*"Unconditional love…!"*

They all heard the words…

"One for all…! … All for one…!" They yelled as they hugged each other, as a group… tears where abundant…

# Chapter 116

They sat in the garden at Tommy and Martha's

"Tommy you're very quiet…?" Fred queried
Tommy looked up…. "I want to share something with you…" he smiled
"That sounds ominous…!" Joan smiled

"I had a conversation with a bloke and his wife at spiritual church…" Tommy started…. "We got talking about healing and I told him what we were involved in…". Tommy paused… "He asked me what I knew about Shamanism…"
"Shamanism…?" Chloe quizzed….
"Yes… I said I knew nothing of Shamanism…". Tommy continued
"What is Shamanism…?" Fred asked….

They all looked at Tommy….

"Well, it turns out that he was a medium… still is a medium, but was drawn into Shamanism…." Tommy mused for a second… "Now he is a Shaman teacher, and his wife…is the High Priestess…. So, I asked him to explain to me…."
"Sounds very interesting…" Martha was all ears…
"Well yes, it is… We all got into Spiritual Healing…". Tommy took a breath… "We all got into Reiki… and what he has told me, I believe this is a pathway I want to explore… and learn…" Tommy smiled… "Let me tell you what he said… Then you can decide if it's up your street….!"

The was silence…

Tommy started to transmit what he had been taught….

"Shamanism started or originated around the Palaeolithic period which was way before any organised religion, which Shamanism is not. Shamanic stuff is very common among tribal people like artic people aborigines' African groups and more.
When native Americans are called Shamans, it is not true, they are medicine people, but do similar work all based on healing and divination. All these have kept up the work to date.
It was said that the Tungus people of Siberia were the most well-known. The word Shamanism comes from Tungus northern Asia.
All this goes back 30,000 years plus and said possibly 100,000 years. Shamanic practice involves drum and rattle as the basic and most important tools, as well as animal spirits as guides and helpers' stones and almost anything in nature."

Tommy paused... then continued

"The drum being the important journey tool, as certain beats, around 160 beats per minute takes the Shaman into altered states, bit like trance. But that Shaman will journey into different realms while in a trance like state, to gain information and knowledge.
Especially where healing and soul retrieval is concerned to bring back missing or fragments of lost soul energy and return it to the person asking for retrieval, not like the postman though, a ceremony would be performed on the person.
Also, the rattle which can be used to journey to and to heal and bring comfort, remember when a new born babies were given a rattle. Now they are given an iPad.
All elements, earth, air, fire and water are worked with as we are made up of all these elements.

Takes an awful long time to master even a few things correctly as it's a way of life.

It's said that you have to be born into Shamanism, but this modern time so many doing it, or think they are, a big difference as messing with people's lives is serious business!

This Shaman told me... They had been working Shamanic stuff, now for 40 years plus and learning every day new stuff.

Working with spirit guides also and the ability to journey to the 3 worlds, lower, middle and upper, lower is where I gain knowledge… middle is this world and upper is the higher being.

So, to become a practitioner this ability to journey and connect with spirits, not always nice ones, as sometimes these nasties have to be confronted and worked with, so you have to be strong and at the same time an impartial observer.

Shape-shifting is part to becoming an animal, not literally, but its qualities and power. The Shaman walks the grey path not white or black, in between so he she, Shamanka… may see both sides of everything…"

There was silence in the room, whilst they all took in what Tommy had relayed to them…...

"It comes in three's…" Geoffrey cleared his throat…
"Reiki, Spiritual healing… Now Shamanism….!"
"That's life…. Coincidence… Synchronicity…. Take notice…!" Joan added
"I'm fascinated…" Chloe glowed… "Truly fascinated…!"
"Me too… intrigued…!" Fred had listened intently….
"I'd like to explore…!" Martha nodded smiling

Geoffrey cleared his throat.... "We understand there is a
difference between Reiki and Spiritual Healing..." He
paused.... "One being an ancient science... The other,
we, being used as a conduit to allow Spiritual healing
energy to flow through... from what we have been
taught...!"

"Is there a conflict...?" Joan questioned... "Should we
investigate Shamanism and learn...!"

"If we follow the true essence of our teachings..."
Tommy smiled wryly.... "No, there is no conflict...!" He
paused... "They are three different modalities... As long
as they are given in love... That's all that matters...
Names...some believe, are only labels...!"

There was contemplation in the room... in their minds....

"It's a pathway I'd like to follow...!" Chloe looked
happy....

They all nodded in support....

"So, we follow this pathway as well...In the same true
essence..." Geoffrey cleared his throat.... "As we have
Reiki and Spiritual healing...!"

"That is your freewill...!" Tommy smiled ironically...
"But yes, I believe we are on the journey....!"

They all smiled....

"By the way, out of interest, what's the name of that
bloke you got taking to, and his wife....?" Joan
quizzed....

"Les and Jackie...." Tommy smiled.... "I felt like I'd
known them forever....!"

# Chapter 117

Geoffrey cleared his throat... "The papers have been very kind and spot on, precise in their wording...!"
"Yes, indeed they have...!" Joan added...
"That may have something to do with the vailed threat you threw at them Joan...!" Martha smiled

They all smiled...

"She frightened me..." Chloe laughed out loud

They all laughed...

"There's been a lot of positive response...!" Fred stated
"Yes. invites to do radio interviews..." Tommy paused...
"And TV appearances..."
"Best brush up..." Martha smiled amusingly... "And get our whistle and flutes dry cleaned..."
"Can I wear a dress...!" Chloe mocked...
"You wear what you like...!" Fred raised his eyebrows

They all nodded...

"For the children...!" Geoffrey choked
"For all the children...!" Joan hugged Geoffrey....

"Do you think..." Chloe hesitated... "Do you think, they will leave us alone now...!"

There was a stunned silence...

They all looked at Chloe....

"Does the Pope kiss tarmac...? Tommy smiled at Chloe... "Do bears..." He took a breath...

"Yes Tommy, we are quite aware of what bears do in the woods…!" Joan cut in, closing her eyes, shaking her head… with a massive smile on her face…

"They shite don't they…!" Geoffrey had missed the beginning of the conversation, composing himself…

They all roared with laughter….

"Yes, Chloe I do believe we will be left alone…!"
Tommy assured Chloe
"They won't want the unfriendly flak Chloe…" Fred took her in his powerful arms…

Geoffrey had quickly caught up…. "Chloe dearest… People in high places… The Establishment…" Geoffrey cleared his throat… "Military… Gangland… Do not want to be exposed to the limelight…" He paused… "As I don't consider these blighters will…!" Geoffrey nodded… "Too much digging will go on, if we were to encounter further hostilities…" He pondered… "And we would make it public…!"

"We have created a ring of security…!" Fred stood firm
"With help from our acquaintances!" Tommy smiled wryly at Geoffrey… "Our comrades…!" He touched his forehead with his index finger…to Fred…. He paused… He smiled….  "And friends….!" He nodded…

"Valued comrades valued friends…" Geoffrey cleared his throat… "We have put in place, a barricade of fire…To protect us!" He smiled ironically… "With an added security to keep the shielding fires fuelled and burning…!".
"How so…?" Quizzed Joan…
"How intriguing…!" Chloe looked on intently

"We have received offers from four major publishers...!" Geoffrey cleared his throat... "To write a book...!"

"A book, A book of fiction... A joint autobiography...?" Martha probed... "Or a book of the history... of our coming together, and our kids' story....?"

"The truth... Nothing but the truth...!" Geoffrey mused for a second.... "A book of our lives, our move, our children's lives...!" Geoffrey cleared his throat... "And the demise..." He wiped his eyes...He contemplated... "Revenge... Releasing... Relinquishing..." He swallowed hard... "That cleared the way... in propelling us forward.... That allowed us...! Brought us...!" Geoffrey paused... "Back together... on our children's journey...!" He smiled... "On our journey...!"


*"We Love you...!"*
*"We are with you...!"*

They heard the words....

# Chapter 118

"That sounds like confirmation to me...?". Geoffrey stated
"Sounds very much like it....!" Chloe smiled

There was an eerie silence...

"We will survive and flourish, for the sake of the living species ......!" Tommy spoke up... "The pebble in the pond syndrome causing a ripple of positivity...!" Tommy pondered.... "It will flow strongly...freely... creating a domino effect, for the sake of humanity...!"

They all looked at Tommy...... Waiting....

"People are locked into the cell of their situation....!" Tommy continued... "The situation is in your mind...." He paused... "We were locked into the cell of our situation... The situation was in our minds...." He mused.... "We broke free...!"

"Do you believe people are frightened to break free...?" Quizzed Joan
"Absolutely...!" Geoffrey cut in... He cleared his throat... "The majority of people believe they are free..." He paused... "But they delude themselves...and survive in the safety net....!"

They all looked at Joan and Geoffrey....

"But it's not their fault....!" Stated Chloe... "If they are unaware, they are in a safety net....?"
"No, it's not...!" Fred stated... "That's why it's wrong to condemn them...!" He paused... "Firstly they have to recognise where they are. Take responsibility... and act

accordingly…" Fred contemplated…. "When they have found inner growth….!"

They all looked at Chloe and Fred…

"Aren't those in the safety net… Being aware or unaware, frightened of coming out of the safety net…!" Martha deliberated… "It's a massive brave step… a new world…!" She took a deep breath…. "They know where they are, it is not healthy… but they need the security… of that net….!" A tear dropped onto Martha's cheek… "They need the co-dependency…" Martha wiped her eye's… "It's how they have been systematically programmed… From childhood… adolescence, adulthood…...!"

They all looked at Martha….

They all had tears flowing… some could resonate… some had compassion…

"Like the butterflies in the box…. Of safety… asking those on the outside of the box…" Tommy reflected… "Why do you fly outside the box…? Those butterflies on the outside say…I fly outside the box because I can…!" Tommy smiled… "But we know the box. We are safe inside the box…! They say." Tommy stroked his chin… contemplating… "That, my friend, is why I leave it…" Tommy grinned… "For you may be safe… But I am free…!"

They all look at Tommy…

"And those that escape the safety box…" Tommy held his hands out… "They are free…!" He nodded his head… "We are free…!" Tommy smiled…

*"We are all free...!"*
*"We love you all...!"*

# Chapter 119

"Talking of being free…!" Geoffrey cleared his throat…

Everyone looked at him…

"A publisher has offered us a deal…...!" Geoffrey said nonchalantly
"A deal…?" Chloe quizzed
"Indeed, a deal…!" Geoffrey looked unmoved...

"A good deal…?" Queried Martha...
"A very good deal…!" Geoffrey nodded
"How good a deal…?" Martha explored

"A splendidly good deal…!" Geoffrey looked up at the sky
"How splendidly good…?" Crossed Joan
"A very, splendidly good deal…! Geoffrey smiled

"An, exceptional deal…?" Fred interrogated
"Oh Yes… An exceptional deal…!" Geoffrey smiled drolly
"How exceptional is this deal…?" Fred raised his voice….

They were all getting tetchy with Geoffrey's indifferent manner

"Oh, splendidly exceptional…?" Geoffrey smirked…
"How, splendidly exceptional…?" Tommy grilled
"Oh... So… So… Exceptionally splendid…!" Geoffrey simpered

"Geoffrey….!" They all shouted….

"What…!" Geoffrey looked so innocent

They all leered at Geoffrey… menacingly

"One would be inclined to say….!" Geoffrey laughed out loud… "You really are spoiling a chap's fun…"

They all laughed…

"An offer as been made…!". Geoffrey exaggerated clearing his throat… "They want to make an offer…" Geoffrey smiled sardonically… "You can't refuse…!" putting on a mafia toned voice….

"You have been mixing with too many gangsters…!" Martha smiled sarcastically…

"It's an amazing offer… An upfront payment…!" Geoffrey composed himself and was serious… "Enough to clear the mortgage on the retreat… and a working capital…" Geoffrey smiled… "Plus very generous royalties…!".

There was a dumbfounded silence…

"I have the contract; you can all scrutinise it..." Geoffrey placed it on the table… "A trusted associate, I trust, as fine toothed combed it…" Geoffrey cleared his throat…. "It's kosha… water tight… to protect us… in our desired journey…!"

# Chapter 120

"Great news…" Geoffrey was beaming… He cleared his throat…. "May I say I have the pleasure in announcing…" Geoffrey paused…. "I have just received confirmation that the publishers absolutely love it…!" Geoffrey smiled… "They even have an ISBN number… 9781784653590…!"

"Love it…!" Chloe chorused … "I mean they love it… even the gory bits…!"

"Wow…!" Fred stroked his chin…" Warts and all…. I've got to admit there were times in writing, dictating…". Fred closed his eyes… Bit his lip… "It was dammed hard…!"

"Yes, Fred it was exceptionally difficult…" Joan considered her words…. "In recalling and reintegrating the memories… the events… onto paper…"

"It certainly was… it was macabre at times…" Martha swallowed hard… "Having to relive those days…Those horrific events…".

"It was a bitter pill to swallow…" Tommy closed his eyes…. "Then to regurgitate it all up…!"

"Yes, I agree…. I concur with all the sentiments…" Geoffrey breathed deeply…. "Anguish… Pain… Vengeance…!"

Silence became them….

"It was a story that needed to be told…!" Chloe claimed… "And we, all together, told the whole account…!"

"We did… And in doing so…" Joan announced… "Showed we could find solace in sorrow….!"

"We showed we had a common comfort, companionship from…" Fred hesitated…. wiping his eyes… "Carnage and cruelty…!"

"Love friendship family…!" Martha looked at each person individually… "As grown from…" Martha's voice was strong… "Devastation…Mayhem… Violence…!"

"Yet there were some magical times…!" Tommy emphasised… "We must remember those… Love… Laughter… Fun…!"

"My dears…!" Geoffrey choked…. Holding back the tears…. "That is what they upheld the most…The sincerity, the raw pain… The guts…" Geoffrey cleared his throat… "The pure candidness of what was shared and the depth of feeling released…!"

They sat in silence… acknowledging their joint inner growth….

"The book has been proof read… punctuation done… now waiting to go to press…." Geoffrey cleared his throat… "Alas there is one stumbling block…"

"Indeed…!" Joan queried… "What may that be…?"

"The title…" Geoffrey smiled

"The title…!" Joan echoed…

"Yes, we have not agreed a title…!" Geoffrey shared
"What shall we call it…?" Fred scratched his head…
"An appropriate name…!" Joan accentuated
"Let's think, what the story was about…?" Geoffrey quizzed
"About our children…!" Tommy stated
"About us…" Chloe added
"About us coming together…!" Martha concluded

"What is the common denominator…?" Geoffrey explored
"They all had a gift…!" Joan elaborated
"Love…!" Chloe wiped her eyes
"The Gift of love…!" Tommy accentuated
"They were nick named the three musketeers...!" Martha supplemented
"A French association…!". Fred connected

**"Le Cadeau De L'amour"** … Joan smiled… "I did French at university… translated from "The Gift of Love…!"

"Agreed…?" Asked Chloe…
"Oh yes…!" They exclaimed

"They also want a synopsis…" Geoffrey added

"Any pearls of wisdom…?" Martha looked at Tommy…

They all looked at Tommy….

Tommy closed his eyes…

**"Le Cadeau De L'amour"** …. Tommy smiled…
"A Labyrinth of an intertwining journey of… Kindness and Understanding… Emotional Growth and Loyalty….

Laughter and Humour… Romance Love and Affection… Tears of Joy…" Tommy waited… "Paralleled Existences…. Tommy waited… "Tears of Sorrow… Jealousy and Deceit…Intrigue and Mystery… Encompassing a Thrilling Twist… Spiritual…. The Gift of Love…"

There was a spooky sensation all around…

"So… **Le Cadeau De L'amour**… Now as an ISBN… 9781784653590…!" Fred concluded

They all bellowed…" YES….!"

*"Yes…!"*

# Chapter 121

"Guys, Guys, Guys…!" Geoffrey paused to get his breath…

They all looked on with baited breath… and looks of concern...

"And you gloriously lovely ladies…" Geoffrey breathed easier…

The edginess, concern, atmosphere lightened….

"What's wrong Geoffrey dearest…?" Joan exclaimed

"Nothing wrong Joanie…" Geoffrey smiled... "Solely excited with oodles of stupendous news…"

"Share then...". Tommy was smiling
"Geoff…" Fred looked on; eyebrows raised… "And...?"
"Stop teasing…!" Chloe exclaimed

"Ladies, Gents…" Geoffrey was lapping it up….

"Geoffrey Childs…!" Joan gave him the index finger…
"Do you want me to take you in hand…!"

Geoffrey blushed… "Oh I declare…!"

There were all round giggles…

Joanie blushed… "You're terrible…" she giggled …

"It's quite wonderful…" Geoffrey smiled wryly

"Child's spill the beans... or I'll take you in hand…!" Martha squinted at Geoffrey

"Yes quite…!" Geoffrey nodded... smiling… loving it… "Time to elaborate…"

All five of them... were looking at Geoffrey

"A second edition print-run has been put into production…" Geoffrey gleamed… a smile as wide as the Grand Canyon…. "Under the Title of…." Geoffrey paused… **"The Gift of Love"** … with its own unique ISBN 9798477697854"

There was stunned silence….

"What about the first edition… **"Le Cadeau De L'amour"** cross examined Joan

"As it was put in the advertising blurb…" Geoffrey cleared his throat….
"Congratulations to everybody who purchased the first run, you are now the proud owners of a collectors edition, never to be reprinted. Make sure you keep it safe…!"

Silence, you could hear a pin drop….

"Can the first addition still be obtained Geoffrey…?" enquired Joan

"Ho yes dearest…" Geoffrey smiled broadly at Joanie, then Chloe, Martha, Fred and Tommy…
"Whilst stocks last…!"

# Chapter 122

"Do you think they will want a sequel...?" Joan quizzed

"That has already been suggested..." Geoffrey stated

"About...?" Chloe asked

"About our journey...!" Martha answered

"To the present...!" Fred smiled

"What will we call that one...?" Tommy smiled quizzically

They all looked at Tommy...

"Without you... We wouldn't be on this journey..." Martha enthused

They all agreed...

"The East End Healer...!"

*"YES...!"*

Printed in Great Britain
by Amazon

63138621R00231